I0564061

MINTWOOD PLACE

A NOVEL

BOB GILBERT

CALUMET EDITIONS

Minneapolis

**CALUMET
EDITIONS**

Minneapolis

SECOND EDITION DECEMBER 2022
MINTWOOD PLACE.
Copyright © 2015 by Bob Gilbert.
All rights reserved.

This is a work of fiction. Names, characters, places and incidents either are the product of the author's imagination or are used fictitiously.

10 9 8 7 6 5 4 3 2

ISBN: 978-1-960250-14-8

To Ian Graham Leask, who taught me and so many other writers how to tell their stories

MINTWOOD PLACE

A NOVEL

BOB GILBERT

Chapter 1

I'm hemmed in. Yes, there it is. My life in a nutshell: hemmed in. It came to me while walking down 18th Street. I'm hemmed in.

A strong case can be made that it is the hallmark, the telltale of middle-aged American men at the beginning of this new millennium. At every turn, hemmed in with so much responsibility that oft-times all sense of self disappears and what passes for manhood is a series of pressure-filled obligations that play out with ambiguous results.

I hate being hemmed in. I'm fifty, and I pine for room to move, to break free from my shackles and dash, if only to put some distance between me and my anxiety.

The externalities of being hemmed in include high blood pressure, self-doubt, an ornery disposition, sexual abandon, hemorrhoids, drug use, alcoholism, lapses in moral judgment and a dozen other calamities resulting from the high stress levels circulating through my body and impairing my judgement.

Here's some of what I reckon with. Three teenage children: eighteen-year-old twins Rose and Aidan, and Jack, younger by three years. The two Washington, D.C. businesses with twenty-six employees whose livelihood I am responsible for. My ex-wife, Joannie, who lives down the block and earns twice the money I do. There's a series of never-ending bills, which are, thank goodness, current. Washington D.C. sales tax, D.C. property tax, tuition for three at Sidwell Friends—a fancy private school—and a congress of thirty ids that pull my mind in that many different directions in order to satisfy my responsibilities and urges.

To reckon with the predicament of being hemmed in, I seek to master ambiguity, irony, outrage, neurotic plots and the vicissitudes of fortune.

"Hey, gimme a dollar, bitch." I looked up to see the source of this demand and the bicycle tire stuck in my path. A small Black kid not more than eight years old sat on a BMX.

"Gimme a dollar, bitch? Did you really say that?"

"That's right," he answered.

"How's that line working for you?" I asked, while examining his shiny bike and Air Jordon sneakers. His clothes were clean, his haircut recent. I saw the bulge in his pocket and suspected it was a wad of bills. Then I remembered there were only about six one-dollar bills folded in my own.

"Good," he answered.

"Tell you what, I'll give you all the money in the front two pockets of my pants for all the money in the front two pockets of your pants. Even-steven, straight up, don't even count it. You hand yours over to me and I'll hand mine over to you and that's that. What do you say, kid, is it a deal?"

He looked deeply in my eyes and scrunched up his face trying to determine if I was pulling a fast one.

"Fuck you, man." He slipped onto his bike seat and quickly rode off, looking back over his shoulder after two revolutions of the bike peddle to make sure I wasn't chasing him.

I looked at my watch. It was ten minutes to five and I was only a half block away from my restaurant, Harry's Bistro, an Adams-Morgan steakhouse.

As I crossed the street I spied J. Cosmo Della Rocca through the bistro's big picture window. He stood behind the bar looking like a deer caught in the headlights. One glance through the window pane and I saw it plain. He momentarily paused from his chore of slicing lime wheels with a serrated knife on a cutting board and was lost in reverie. That look on his face said it all: "What am I doing here?"

It was his first bar shift in over five years. Perhaps he questioned his ability to maintain that old persona that once made him such a bright young man about town. His bartending gig gave him the opportunity to meet the wide variety of people, big and small, rich and poor, powerful and powerless, populating the nation's capital. It was no stretch either since they all came to him so he could pour them drinks and listen to their stories.

He was a good-looking kid too whose respect for older men came naturally. True, he did have some rage issues typical of young men from the urban part of New Jersey, but they only manifested themselves in his private life. Publicly, on stage, behind the bar, he was a consummate professional.

Certainly he held no power, influence, or name identification like so many of his customers, but what good is being a big shot with power, influence and name identification if nobody recognizes you? Cosmo made it a point to know and recognize everybody, and if he didn't recognize you the first time, he always recognized you the second.

Thus when men came into my restaurant dressed in Brooks Brother's suits throwing money around with their wives or sweethearts beside them throwing their cleavage around—and that's what it was all about, money, power and tits—each was greeted warmly with a firm handshake and the calling out of his name by the kid behind the bar. For Cosmo the tips just flowed and there were many weeks when he made more money than I did.

Looking at him through the window, the tall, New Jersey Italian looked straight out of Gentleman's Quarterly. His starched white shirt was straight from the dry cleaner. He monogrammed his initials in black stitches at the breast pocket. I could see it from across the street. A new haircut, somewhat on the short side, and a clean shave revealed to me that he was taking his comeback seriously. I couldn't see, but I was sure his shoes had a brand new shine.

I was about to enter the restaurant, which I owned since my uncle, Harry Green, died of a heart attack years ago, when I was intercepted by Terry Kennedy, the local beat cop.

Kennedy had been working in the neighborhood for ten years and he considered it his own. He was something of a neighborhood personality too. He stood five-foot-two and was almost as wide. Troublemakers who came to his part of town thought of him as an easy mark, a short, fat, Irish flatfoot with a red face. Even people passing by in cars took notice of his small stature. He was self-conscious of it too and in defense he projected a kind of clownish swagger.

A few years ago Kennedy was making the rounds in the neighborhood and entered my place on a Friday night at closing time. One of my patrons, a drunken bureaucrat I had never seen before, called out, "Hey look, the D.C. cops are hiring midgets."

Kennedy had him face first on the floor and handcuffed in twenty seconds. Were it not for me the guy would have spent the weekend in jail. Though the big mouth got off, I did not. Kennedy issued me a citation for over-serving my customers and not only did I pay a fine, I also paid for the drunk's cab ride home to Chevy Chase. When Kennedy showed up it often cost me money.

"Listen, Joe," Kennedy said to me. "Word on the street is that J. Cosmo is coming back to work for you. I got to tell you I'm a little worried—it could mean trouble."

"He's just filling in tonight. Jocko got the flu."

"Don't blow smoke up my ass. Jocko is going to the National's game."

"Okay, so I'm giving the kid a chance." I said.

"Well, if I stick my head in a few more times a night than usual just know that I'm not looking for underage drinking, I'm looking out for everybody's protection."

"Come in as much as you want. It doesn't bother me. Just get there before ten if you want to eat."

"How's the kid doing?"

"Take a look for yourself."

Kennedy turned around and checked him out through the window. "Nice tie," said the cop. "Nobody ties a double Windsor like J. Cosmo."

"I hear he only likes to be called Cosmo now," I answered. "Not J. Cosmo, not J.C. and certainly not Jiro which actually is his first name. Just Cosmo."

"Cosmo. Like the drink?" asked the cop.

"Maybe. It could also be an indication that he's a little older and wiser than he was the first time he worked here."

"I don't care. I'll call him whatever he wants," Kennedy said. "You know in the old days he once promised to take me out clothes shopping."

"He's always been known for his fine sartorial taste."

"Looks a little gray at the temples. How old is he now?"

"About thirty-three."

"He looks a lot older than when he went to prison," Kennedy said.

"Maybe that's what prison does to you."

"I hope I never find out. Anyway, I'll be around. Let me know if anything suspicious goes on."

I said goodbye and entered the bistro right on time. At the host stand I looked at the computer. I recognized seven names. I saved them the tables where they could see and be seen. That done I walked to the bar to say hello to Cosmo.

He put on a brave face. It was going to be a busy night and he knew that there were times this evening where he would be buried, in the weeds, treed, up a tree and the other dozen euphemisms restaurant folk use to convey the fact that they are stressing out from the restaurant's frenetic pace.

But in the old days that's why he made big money. It took courage to realize that your blood pressure was going to soar, that the demands put on you were going to be unrealistic and you were going to have to work your way out of it. And when those times arrived Cosmo was my go-to-guy.

He was fast at mixing cocktails, charming customers and making it all look easy. Rarely did he lose his smile or composure. He was the master of the twenty-second exchange. A quick anecdote, a quote, a comment about who had been in and what had been said or a joke stolen from the likes of old school comedians like Henny Youngman.

That was part of his skill behind the bar. He could deliver drinks like a machine and still make time to acknowledge a regular with real heart.

My business suffered plenty following his arrest and during his trial. He was not only tried in the courts, but in the newspapers as well. Since he was my employee and the crime happened in front of my place, we took a big hit.

I could have abandoned him and saved myself. But I stood beside him, hired his lawyer and helped orchestrate his defense.

When he began serving his prison sentence I drove to Hagerstown, Maryland to visit him. I'd bring him an armload of books, usually ones that I knew and had read. Since I also own "Tomes Greatest Hits," a used bookstore in Adams-Morgan, I was also able to find the rare tomes he requested. We'd sit in a room and discuss them. And since he had plenty of time on his hands I even got him to begin keeping a journal and I think that helped him heal.

I made his rehabilitation my responsibility. I wasn't Italian, or Catholic, or a blood relation but we did share something in common. We both were raised in New Jersey, that valley situated between two mountains of conceit, New York City and Philadelphia, and shared some of the cultural lower middle class ethnic scars one obtains when growing up in that state which we called, "The Big Onion." But more than that I always looked at him as my third son.

"You ready?" I asked.

"I think I can do this," he said softly.

"You think? What do you mean, you think? It's a three-count pour. What's so hard about that, Cosmo? Either you're going to do it or you're not going to do it. Don't think. It will only slow you down."

He straightened up his posture.

"Aidan will be the bar back tonight. And don't ignore the waiters at the service bar or we'll both hear about it when the shift ends."

"I got it."

"Here's one more thing. I invited Reverend Battle in for dinner tonight. If you're going to work in this neighborhood again you're going to have to square things with him. Forget what he said at your trial. Shake his hand and show respect or this is not going to work."

"Tonight? Why tonight. Don't I have enough to worry about?"

"Did you turn into a little bitch in prison? Do your job and don't break my balls. Let's find out what you're made of tonight, then we'll talk about tomorrow night."

The bistro was still empty. The wait staff finished their side work. Stella Diaz, my Cuban-American hostess arrived, turned on the lights, unlocked the coatroom and made ready for the evening. The two of us manned the door five nights a week. She was also my assistant manager.

She was the first person customers saw coming in the front door and their initial gaze was always returned with a warm smile framed in Stella's big lips.

She never provoked a sense of lust, leastways not with me. Her breasts were too small for that. But she had the effect of centering you the moment her eyes met yours. You'd find yourself emotionally present. And lucky me, when people experienced their sudden awakening, it was in the middle entrance of my little salon. She loved her job and as a result people loved her. And I could rely on her good energy to keep me upbeat even on nights when I was not as emotionally present as I should be.

Back in the office I put on my jacket and tie. I also pulled a snub nose .38 out of my locked top drawer and put it in my pocket. Sometimes the neighborhood wasn't safe. I never stood at the front door unarmed. I carried it to protect not only my customers but my employees as well. I had a permit and the proper training too. Four times a year, Kennedy and me went out to the shooting range in Virginia and blew off a hundred rounds each.

But as I discovered, shooting an assailant doesn't end your trouble, it only initiates it. And those troubles can linger on interminably. In the old days Cosmo was packing too. But now, out on parole, that was illegal.

A lot of politicos come through my door and we were never without a camera. Pictures going back to the 1960s, when my Uncle Harry opened the place, were all over the walls.

On my way through the dining room I noticed one of my favorite photos. I stopped and stared at it. It featured me, Cosmo and the late

U.S. Senator, John Glenn. All of us were laughing and if I remember correctly, it was because just before the shutter snapped Cosmo asked Senator Glenn why Ohio was known as "the mother of mediocre presidents."

When I returned to the bar a man and a woman were sitting in front of Cosmo, drinking wine. They had never seen him before, knew nothing of his past. They were involved in an intimate conversation. Smiles were everywhere. I saw it as a sign that he was getting comfortable back behind the bar.

When a group of my regulars came in at 6:45, including several past employees who had worked with Cosmo back in the day, he actually looked excited at the idea that the life he once knew and loved might still be available.

I had Aidan, my oldest son, a high school senior, help Cosmo pour drinks even though he was underage. I commissioned Mario the busboy to take responsibility for Aidan's bar-back duties so that Cosmo would have the time to accept the good wishes of those welcoming him back.

At seven o'clock, a tall, silver-haired gentleman arrived at the door and announced himself. "Senator James Copley, table for two."

Stella and I recognized him immediately as the senior Senator from Indiana. But there was nothing on the books to indicate that the reservation had been made.

"Sorry, Senator. You are not listed on the books," Stella said. "Did your office make the reservation?"

"No, I am meeting a lobbyist from the American Medical Association."

"Oh, sure. Here it is. It's under Joannie's name. You're a bit early and we don't like to seat incomplete parties. Perhaps you can have a drink at the bar until she arrives."

"She's a little short for you, isn't she?" I muttered with my head down.

Copley didn't seem sure I was speaking to him. He let the remark pass. Stella kicked my ankle and I shut up. Copley found a place at the bar.

Then Dave Paulus came in. He was a gossip columnist/neighborhood reporter from the Washington Post. He was a short, stubby New Yorker with thick black glasses and thick black hair. That wise guy always had a good quip but most often it came at somebody else's expense.

He had been on the beat longer than Kennedy the cop and not much went on that he didn't know about. He wrote a twice-weekly column called "On Capitol Streets" in which he mimicked the form of the New Yorker Magazine's, "Talk of the Town" in that he wrote his first person plural accounts of local drama with the pronoun, "we." It read like a collective adventure.

"I heard Cosmo's back." said Paulus.

"Come on, Dave. Give the kid a break. It's his first day back. It's bad enough that we're going to be busy tonight, but I also invited Reverend Battle in to shake hands. One confrontation at a time."

"Battle was the one who told me to come. He said he thought it might make an interesting column."

"Battle is coming, isn't he?"

"All I know is that Battle promised me a good story. So if you don't mind, I'll just sit at the bar and observe the night's activity."

I could just imagine what he had planned for his newspaper column...

"Last night, we walked into Harry's Bistro to discover that J. Cosmo Della Rocca, convicted shooter of Gaston Thomas and Dominique Matthews, was back behind the bar after serving a five-year sentence for manslaughter. It was originally thought to be self-defense since the assailants attempted to rob Della Rocca at gunpoint before he shot and killed Thomas during an exchange of gunfire. But when the un-armed second assailant ran from the scene, Della Rocca chased him down the block and shot him in the back. The city attorney's office turned it into a hate crime. Especially when Della Rocca was over-heard at the scene to say, 'There was no way I was going to be looking over my shoulder for the rest of my life, waiting for that nigger to come back and kill me.'"

Nigger. That is the word that incensed the public. I was there at the scene when he uttered it. The word he actually used was jig.

But I suppose nigger made better copy than one of its euphemisms. Regardless, Paulus was made for mischief and his column portrayed Della Rocca as a racist.

What did people expect? Cosmo just had a gunfight on 18th Street and killed two men who if given their druthers might have killed him first. It was 2 a.m. and he had just left the building. He had a pocket full of cash and he'd been drinking.

"Stella," I whispered, "take Mr. Paulus to table twelve and have Sasha keep a close eye on him. Cut him off after his fourth drink."

Paulus had a way of playing you, just when you thought you were playing him. During the trial, Reverend Battle—the local Baptist minister and community leader—and I played a rhetorical chess game in the press using Paulus as our mouthpiece. When a medical examiner admitted to me that the suspects were high on crack at the time of their death, it found its way into Paulus's column.

When Battle discovered that Della Rocca was the great-nephew of the late Newark Italian Gumba, Anthony Imperiale, who organized armed vigilante squads to protect Italian neighborhoods from roving mobs of Black rioters in the 1960s with the help of the Mafia, and was later elected to the U.S. Congress on the strength of that event, it made it into Paulus's column as proof of Cosmo's bigoted family background.

I bloodied Battle's side and he bloodied mine and as a result I lost a considerable amount of restaurant business and Battle lost face because he appeared more interested in defending his people than the law.

The only one who benefited was Paulus who was at no loss for copy. That he seemed to now be salivating, was not only from the rib-eye steak cooked medium well that he usually ordered, but also from the idea that the vicarious battle between James Battle and Joe Green might re-ignite.

Joannie, my ex-wife, entered next. Before the divorce we spent sixteen years together. Today, we both owned homes on opposite ends of Mintwood Place, a one-block street in the Adams Morgan neighborhood. The kids shuttled back and forth and back and forth from her home to mine in the course of their week and often grew weary of it.

Soon after the divorce she landed a job with a big six-figure salary, let her blonde hair grow long, lost thirty pounds and spent seven thousand dollars on a boob job.

"You're late," I said.

"My meeting went longer than I expected."

"Senator Copley is in the bar waiting for you."

"This should be interesting," she said.

"Business or pleasure?"

"Strictly business."

"Monkey business?"

"No," she barked.

"Good. I don't like it when you bring your swells into my place."

"Relax, he's twenty years older than I am. Besides, my personal life is no longer your concern. We're divorced."

"I haven't forgotten."

"How big are the lobsters tonight?" she asked.

"Two pounds to six."

"Good. Save me a big one and we'll want it taken out of its shell at the table. Ask Tony to wait on us."

"Who's paying, you or him?"

"You owe me $575 for Rose's wisdom teeth. So I guess you are. And tell Aidan that I want him home right after work. No hanging around here playing cards or drinking with the fellas till dawn like he did last weekend."

She walked away without any fireworks between us and such restraint from us both was the kind of progress our therapist would be proud of.

But after a few steps I called to her.

"Joannie. Cosmo is behind the bar. It would be nice if you went over and said hello."

She turned. "Taking him back is a little risky, isn't it, Joe? It took you two years to bounce back last time he worked here."

"I've never been much of a businessman."

"Alright. I'll go say hi."

Harry's Bistro was set with white linen and crystal goblets. Its location, far from Capitol Hill, made it safe for meetings that were supposed to stay off the radar screen. It had a long-standing reputation for conspicuous consumption, deal making, political intrigue and gossip.

As the Bistro's master of ceremonies, I diligently committed myself to reinforcing the perception that my place was a cultural clearinghouse where big shots could be recognized by other big shots, new friends were made and old alliances maintained. That perception was more important than the cuisine.

Poet Johann Wolfgang Von Goethe's last words were, "more light." Light's okay, but in these times, it was conversation, and its attendant oratory, more than light, which seemed necessary in the nation's capital. More conversation, those would be my parting words.

There were no televisions in the Bistro. The blab of talking heads and commercials on electronic media were not only bad for digestion but were also a detriment to conversation. I didn't play music either. Since it was conversation I was selling over fine wine, dry-aged steaks, seafood, brandy and port, it was one of my pet peeves that nothing should compete with the discourse.

I did my homework too. I read *The Washington Post*, *The Washington Times*, and *The New York Times* front to back, in addition to the glossy city magazines, the alternative weeklies and the community newspapers in order to keep abreast of who was doing what in the city.

Sometimes I googled the names on the reservation list. If they were important it was good to know that before they arrived.

When James Britton, Undersecretary of State for African Affairs, walked through my door at 7:30, I recognized him from a Washingtonian Magazine feature story.

Britton was a fifty-year-old African-American who formerly ran a non-profit in Africa. Tall in stature, his care-worn face, close-cropped beard and bald head reminded me of an old Talmudic scholar.

"Good evening," I said, but a look at his gray suit distracted me and I just blurted it out. "Oh, you have a son in harm's way."

I should have shown more sensitivity because it caught Britton off guard. He inhaled deeply, grimaced, threw back his shoulders and asked, "What did you say?"

"Your pin," I answered, pointing to the tiny badge attached to his lapel. It was no more than a half-inch wide. A red border surrounded the blue star with white background. I'd seen it before. American parents with kids fighting in the Middle East wear it. "Is your son in Afghanistan?"

"Yes."

"Regular army or National Guard?"

"National Guard," he said, raising his eyebrows. "He's married with four kids."

"Kind of makes you religious, doesn't it?"

"I suppose it does."

"You're James Britton from the State Department, aren't you?"

"Yes," he said and with that he extended his hand in friendship. "Are you the proprietor?"

"Yes. I'm Joe Green. Welcome. Is this your first time here?"

"Yes," he said, and then grinned. "But my father used to tell stories about the 1960s when he played high stakes poker in your backroom with big shots. One night he walked out of here with three thousand dollars. The next day he paid cash for a 1971 Chevy station wagon with that imitation wood grain siding and vowed never to gamble again. He told that story till the day he died."

"When my Uncle Harry owned the place it was more of a card room and a brothel than a restaurant. Would you like a little tour?"

"Yes, I'd like that," he said.

The photographs hanging on the walls were arranged by political party. The right side of the dining room featured Republicans leaders, the left side, Democrats. It wasn't always that way. I used to mix them. But separating the luminaries by political parties mirrored the current political climate. The painting of the nude Black woman over table 31 momentarily hijacked Britton's attention.

"That's the house Goddess," I said. "Her name is Minnie."

"I'd like to meet her in heaven."

Ironically, Britton favored the GOP. We paid special attention to the photographs taken here of Everett McKinley Dirkson, Gerald Ford, Barry Goldwater, and former presidential candidate, Wendell Wilkie, as an old man.

The private dining room, which we called the Potomac Room, was the best part of the tour. Framed portraits of George Washington and Thomas Jefferson hung on the wall. I once had Abraham Lincoln too, but that offended my Southern clientele who decried Lincoln and the "War of Northern Aggression," so I took it down.

I hang it back up for Illinois delegations and other Yankees. The room had deep pile carpeting, a large round table that sat fifteen and comfortable leather arm chairs.

It offered a special four-course menu, access to the captain's list with all my rare vintages, and was checked out by a private security firm to make sure it wasn't bugged.

"This is the room where your father won his station wagon," I told Britton.

Because I asked, Britton told me about his new state department job, which focused on conflict resolution between contending political bands.

"That should keep you busy."

"We'll see," he answered. "I've only been at the job for four months. I still have a lot to learn."

So I led him into the kitchen and introduced him to James and Bindy, my two Nigerian cooks. He shook their hands and greeted them in their native language.

Seven years ago the three of them lived in Abuja, its capitol. When they fell into a deep conversation that excluded me, I took a few steps towards the dishwasher area to watch the plates coming back from the dining room.

I did it periodically to see what people ate and what they left un-eaten. No one seemed to like the beet salad that came with the crab cakes and I made a mental note of that.

A few minutes later, when Britton finished his conversation, I escorted him back into the dining room. "Bindy called you a great Nigerian patriot," said Britton. "Why is that?"

"Nothing much really; earlier this year I closed my restaurant and had a fundraiser for the opposition leader, Mr. Kenessee. Bindy acted as a host and he's been my guy ever since."

On the way to his table he stopped at a 1969 photo of Willie Mays.

"You know," he said, "before my family moved to D.C. we lived in San Francisco. I used to sit out in the Candlestick Park center field bleachers with my dad just to watch Willie run down fly balls."

"He was a big personality," I said. "That's my uncle standing next to him."

"Who's the Black woman standing with them?"

"That's Minnie."

"Is she the same woman in the painting?"

"Yes."

"Your uncle had good taste in women."

When we arrived at the table his friends were waiting. I pulled out his chair and before he sat down he shook my hand once more. I started to walk away but then remembered one more thing.

"I almost forgot. What's your son's name?"

"His name is Andrew. Thanks for asking."

When I returned to the host stand Stella was waiting. "How'd that go?" she asked.

"Think I might have made a new friend."

We got a push around 8:15. Six parties showed up without reservations and that made it a lucrative night. Joannie and Copley rang up a $300 check. From what she told me they had come to an understanding. I picked up the tab. She left the tip.

Cosmo was doing great. He wore a big smile and his tip jar was full. The only one disappointed was Dave Paulus. Reverend Battle never showed so he lost the best part of his story. He wasn't bored though. He loved to drink and had the gift of gab.

At 10 p.m., four young African-American men marched past Stella at the host stand. All of them were over six feet tall and dressed in black three-piece suits. My first impression was that they were Black Muslims. But their baseball caps were turned aside, suggesting a gang affiliation, but which one was beyond me. One had balanced a boom box on his shoulder that was blasting an angry rap song that immediately got everyone's attention. I couldn't decipher the lyrics except for the word "motherfucker," which made up the better part of the chorus. The small crowd parted as they marched to the bar.

I waved my hand and Aidan came over.

"You know any of those kids?" I asked.

"They're not from the neighborhood," he said.

"Run down to the coffee shop and see if Kennedy's there. Get him here fast. There's going to be trouble."

My boy bolted out the door. The boom box and one other kid went straight to the bar while two others faced the crowd and watched their backs. When I made my way to back up Cosmo the two kids facing the crowd blocked my path.

"Stay out of this, Joe. That's Tyrone Thomas, Gaston's brother. He got something to say."

"How do you know my name?"

"Now don't go reaching for your piece because we're carrying too and somebody might get hurt."

"Listen fucker, this is my place and nobody tells me what to do here."

"Stand back and be cool," he answered with both hands up. "Let First Amendment Rights be observed."

"Hey you," one called to Cosmo. "Get your white honky ass over here." He turned to his partner. "Shut that boom box off. I want everyone to hear this."

Stunned, Cosmo walked over, slow and stiff. As he came into range the big Black kid grabbed a glass filled with red wine and threw it at him. It hit him in the sternum, staining his pressed white shirt and splashing up into his eyes.

"My name is Tyrone Thomas. I know who you are, motherfucker. I know where you work and where you live. You killed Gaston and he was my brother. Your chicken shit prison sentence might square you with the law but it doesn't square you with me. If you were smart you'd get out of here tonight and never come back. Otherwise, your life won't be worth shit. Got it?"

The words were delivered with a practiced eloquence. Cosmo stood speechless waiting to see what came next.

With the warning delivered, the boom box came back on and the sound of the angry Black voices filled the silence of the restaurant.

At the front door, Aidan rushed in with Kennedy the cop behind him. There was a standoff.

"Back off, Shorty. No laws were broken here," Tyrone barked at Kennedy.

They brushed by the diminutive cop and walked out into the street.

"Jesus, Kennedy. You let him get away," I said. "What good are you?"

"Hey, ease up Joe. I didn't want to embarrass him."

"Embarrass him?"

"The kid was crying like a baby," Kennedy said.

"Is that true, Aidan?"

"That's what I saw."

"Sorry to have disturbed you folks," I called out to the bar crowd. "In my day we called that Guerilla Theater."

A few people laughed, but most seemed embarrassed to be a part of it all. It took several moments before the silence was relieved with chatter.

"Aidan, get behind the bar and relieve Cosmo."

Cosmo grabbed a bar towel and excused himself. He went to the employee bathroom and cleaned himself up. I followed him inside.

"You okay?"

"I'm fine," he answered.

"Listen, kid, it was bound to happen sooner or later. Let's just be glad it's over and done with."

"Joe, you don't owe me anything. Maybe coming back here isn't such a good idea."

"You know that's not true. I owe you everything. It could have just as easily been me doing that jail time were it not for you covering my ass."

"Stop," Cosmo said, glaring. "We agreed never to speak of it again."

"You're right."

Then there was a pause. Cosmo stared into space.

"Why did you come back?" I asked. "You have enough money to do and go wherever you want. Why did you come back?"

"I have to find out something."

"What is it?"

He grew very still as if he were trying to center his mind in order to reveal a long kept secret. As a result I grew still too and waited for him to speak. But seconds passed and none of it passed his lips. Finally he spoke.

"Not just yet, Joe. It's tricky."

"You did a great job tonight. The job is yours as long as you want it."

"Are you sure?"

"Yes."

"Thanks."

"Alright. Clean up. Get back out there fast. I don't want people losing faith in my restaurant, or in you."

"What about my shirt?"

"Wear it like a badge."

When I returned to the front door Paulus was walking out. He stopped. "Well, I guess I got my story after all."

"I would have preferred that Battle show up instead."

"That kid with the boom box was his son, Chris."

"It was?"

"Don't be naïve. You've been in this town long enough to know everything that happens here is on purpose."

"You write this fair and square."

"Whatever happened to freedom of the press, Green? You got played. Deal with it. Besides, it's not about you. It's about Cosmo."

Chapter 2

Later that night, with guests departed and doors locked, I herded the front house staff and the back house staff into the bar to toast Cosmo's return. It was a group of eighteen. My waiters and waitresses were evenly mixed between African-American, white and Moroccan. The bus-boys and dishwashers were Mexican, the cooks, led by Shameem, my Pakistani chef, were from El Salvador, but there were also Africans like James and Bindy. We even had a Chinese girl in the kitchen named Yu Chin who made pastries. For many of these immigrants restaurants were their first jobs.

I took pride in the fact that my staff was black, white, brown and yellow. The multi-culturalism of globalization worked better here in the bistro than in the rest of the world. It was Protestant, Catholic, Muslim, Jewish and Buddhist. Skin color, God and language were transcended. When the voice of nationalism, fundamentalism, or Old World prejudice echoed off the bistro's wall it sounded stupid. We were there to earn a living. That took precedence over all else.

I opened three bottles of the Perrier Jouet Champagne. My female employees liked the painted bottles, which they took home to use as flower vases and candleholders.

I poured champagne for everyone in the room and then climbed onto the bar. Standing tall, I raised my glass.

"Ladies and gentlemen, the reason we succeed here is because we are a family. True, it's sometimes a dysfunctional family, but family nonetheless. Tonight, I'd like us to all raise a glass to celebrate the return of our very own Cosmo Della Rocca. The law took him from our midst several years ago. But he has paid his debt to society and I'm asking everyone to welcome him back into our fold and help him remake his life."

I raised my glass and Shameem called out, "Welcome back."

"To Cosmo," I said—and with that my crew tipped their glasses in his direction and sipped the bubbly wine.

"Speech, speech," someone yelled out.

Put on the spot, Cosmo blushed. He bought a few seconds by tilting the glass up to his lips. Then I reached down my hand down to him. Using a bar stool as a step, he jumped up onto the bar beside me. He held his champagne in his right hand and with his left hand self-consciously covered the wine stain on his white shirt.

"Friends, not a day went by that I didn't miss this place," Cosmo said. "I know the bad press hurt you all financially and the many bad things said about me probably made you embarrassed to even know me, so this support means a lot. I'll try not to let you down again."

At the end of his speech, Cosmo choked up. The crowd might have clapped, but they were holding champagne flutes. After a few seconds more with their eyes upon him, he gracefully jumped to the floor as if he were stepping off a curb.

When I hesitated a moment, deciding the best way to descend, Stella, standing beneath me, looked up with her big brown eyes and held up her hand to help my balance. Grasping it, I stepped onto a bar stool seat and then to the floor.

"Thanks, Honey," I said.

I put down my glass, walked to Cosmo and gave him a hug. With that cue, a line of his co-workers formed to congratulate him.

"Too bad Dave Paulus is gone," I said to Stella and Aidan, standing next to me. "He should see this."

With the salutation offered, the staff went back to finish their side work. After collecting the credit card receipts and paying the servers their tips, I went to the walk-in cooler with a white dinner plate. I piled a handful of romaine, a few carrot sticks and a few berries. Then I unlocked the door at the back of the restaurant and climbed the stairs to the second floor apartment.

Years ago, Harry used this space as a brothel. Powerful men, old political names from the 1960s and 1970s, fucked up here. A good meal followed by good sex kept Harry's business brisk.

That small apartment space was now my sanctum sanctorum. It had a living room, a small bedroom and bathroom with a shower. There was a television, a stereo system, a desk facing the door, a couch perfect for sleeping, lots of bookshelves and a Lazy-boy recliner. The carpet was gray and the walls raspberry.

A sliding glass door at the back led to a metal porch big enough for two chairs overlooking the alley. In the distance, a red blinking light atop the Washington Monument and jets cruising to and from Reagan National Airport were visible.

After a hectic shift, a quick trip to my apartment always chilled me out. It took less than an hour. When I came back downstairs to put the bistro to bed, the jacket and tie were gone, my jaw was unclenched and I usually wore a smile.

My employees speculated about what I did up here. Rumors had me snorting lines of cocaine, sipping from a crack pipe, pounding downs shots of rotgut whiskey, reading from the Bible, smoking pot, or watching M.A.S.H. reruns.

While I wasn't opposed to any of those nostrums it was "the pen" that calmed my stress. The pen consisted of railroad ties in a rectangular shape that acted like a fence around a packed down dirt floor. The pen had green plants and an arched piece of tree bark to make it seem like the outdoors. It was right in the living room. Inside those wooden barriers lived four Russian tortoises named after dead Jewish relatives—Ruthie, Rebecca, Louis and Sidney.

Their shells weren't enough to make them feel safe or warm, so I provided electric blankets, which they hid beneath. I used the old kind you can buy at the Salvation Army because the newer high tech blankets shut off automatically after twelve hours. Beneath the heating blankets the reptiles stayed toasty even in the winter.

There were three families in my life—my tortoise family, which was peaceful; my restaurant family, which was dynamic; and my own family with Joannie and the kids, which was in chaos.

Of the three families, the tortoises were the easiest to deal with. They had no anger issues and never complained. The highlight of their day consisted of basking in the sunlight shining through the sliding glass door. Being among them was soothing because they were slow and seemed to specialize in meditation.

I pulled a small camping chair next to the railroad ties so I could get closer to them. The fresh romaine crunched as I tore it with my hands and piled it on the plate beside the carrots and the berries, hoping the sound might induce one to emerge from beneath the blanket.

Suddenly, there was movement and after about three minutes, Ruthie's gray head popped out from beneath the blanket. She seemed in no hurry to come out into the open.

Ruthie was the largest of the four. I've had her for fourteen years. She was as wide as two palms placed side by side and almost twice the size of the males. Her shell was blonde and black. She had the most wonderful personality too, not only with me, but also with her fellow tortoises. She was the tortoise pen matriarch.

"Yo, Ruthie. How's it going, girl? Come on out and have a snack," I whispered so as not to startle her.

Have you ever had a staring contest with a Russian tortoise? Sure, you can cheat if you want. Make a sudden move and they'll dart back into to their shell. But eye-to-eye—they rarely blinked—their deadpan faces, and their slow clumsy gait promoted a soothing calm.

From experience I've found that Russian tortoises make better pets than their American counterparts, the American Box Turtle. The Russians are vegetarians and a hardier breed. Books claim they can live seventy-five years if cared for properly.

But when they died on you, and I've had several die on me, death comes slowly. They get so still, like a statue of Buddha. They will not walk. They will not eat or drink. They do not open their eyes. They linger in limbo for weeks. And it's painstaking to watch since neither antibiotics nor vitamins can stem the tide.

Now it might seem silly that a restaurateur like myself should take such recourse to soothe his stress. But ask anyone working in the restaurant business and they call it "blood money." It takes a certain bearing to stay at it, and succeed.

I've seen too many of my competitors fall apart from the pressure of paying the bills, dealing with wayward employees, fickle customers, crooked purveyors, venal health inspectors and the like. And it can be dangerous to your health too.

There you are, all hemmed in from the demands put upon you while at your disposal is as much food, wine and booze as you want. Not to mention the bad influence of wayward men and women trying to ingratiate themselves into your life because you own a bar.

I watched Charlotte Opitz go from a shapely, blonde beauty to a fat, falling down drunk in three years. She couldn't take the pressure of owning Fiddlers Restaurant.

Chef Joe Bigante got so stressed at Casa Di Firenza one night that he took a carving knife in a fit of anger and stabbed one of his waiters. After many months of litigation they finally settled the lawsuit. The waiter landed the restaurant and Bigante landed in rehab.

So if you think tending tortoises is ridiculous, picture how ridiculous Bigante looked arriving at a Minnesota alcohol rehabilitation clinic in the middle of January.

I'll take the tortoises, thank you. That reptile family helped me chill out without resorting to excessive self-medication, which before my divorce from Joannie, was an issue.

The most difficult family was my own. Since the divorce an intense rivalry existed between me and Joannie. There was no stopping it, no way of avoiding it, no bailing out or backing down because we had three children caught in the crossfire and neither of us trusted the family values of the other.

The kids kept to a schedule, sometimes at my house, sometimes at Joannie's. But now they were teenagers and thanks to cell phones, public transportation and the Internet, they were pulling away from their parents.

Aidan gravitated to me. In part it was because he liked working at the bistro. At the end of every shift he had a pocket full of cash just like his wealthy classmates at Sidwell Friends. The older waitresses treated him like a young darling. They gave him dating tips and reminded him about the importance of foreplay. To many of the bistro men he was a surrogate son.

His fraternal twin, Rose, also a high school senior, emulated her mother. They had the same pretty Irish face, same curly hair and the same fiery temperament. Rose was the better student of the two and the attention she paid to her responsibilities was impressive.

Our Jack was a high school freshman. Following behind dynamic and competitive twins, he watched their drama and decided he didn't want to play. I never saw him angry and only once in the past five years did I even see him cry.

Someone was climbing the stairs. Aidan came through the door.

"Hey Dad, I'm taking off," he said. "Do you mind if I sleep at your house tonight?"

"I think your mom wants you home tonight."

"Dad, there's a party tonight. It's going to be crazy. Amanda Swanson is going to be there and I just got to tap that."

"Amanda?"

"She's in my English class and she's hot for me," he said.

"What about your curfew?"

"Dad, come on. Mom's a crazy bitch these days. What's the difference whether I get home at one or three in the morning? All the cool kids hang out late and that's when the fun starts. Besides even if I do get home on time mom will be asleep. I'll knock on her bedroom door, tell her I'm home and then I'll just climb out my bedroom window anyway. But that could put me an extra hour behind. If I tell her I'm staying with you I can get my fill of fun and still get home early."

"Don't make me lie for you," I said. "Sneak out the window."

"Yeah, but if Rose hears me she'll tell Mom and then I'll get busted and me and Rose will fight all week."

"I'm not sure I can stand that."

"Me neither."

"Are they doing liquor inventory downstairs for the weekend?"

"Cosmo already started it."

"Okay, call your mom and tell her it's Cosmo's first night back and you're staying to help. But that means you be home no later than two. I'll cover your ass until then, but after that you're on your own."

"That works for me."

"Hey, how much did you make tonight?"

"A hundred."

"Not bad," I said. "How do you think Cosmo did?

"How do *you* think he did?" said Aidan.

"Did I miss something?"

"He got that restaurant spin look on his face once or twice, you know when you get so busy that you don't know what to do next."

"I didn't see that. Is it something I should be concerned about?"

"I don't know. After all, it was only his first night," he said.

"Do you like having him back?"

"Cosmo was cool when we were kids. But he's not the same guy."

"For now, give him the benefit of the doubt."

"He's waiting for you at the bar. You should go down and have a drink with him."

"Has Stella left yet?"

"No, she's still at the bar."

"I think I'll wait."

"Dad, that girl's a doll."

"I know," I said. "I think I'll wait."

"You're making a big mistake."

"Listen, I'm calling your cell phone at two. And if you don't answer I'm calling your mom's house."

He gave me a big shit-eating grin because he knew I was bluffing. I watched him turn and walk down the stairs.

"Hey," I called. He stopped. "Come back here."

He walked back up the creaking stairs and poked his head through the doorway.

"Do you have a condom?"

"No."

"There's one in the bathroom, bottom drawer," I said. "Go get it. Just in case."

He ran down the stairs a minute later.

Ruthie crawled out from beneath the blanket and ambled her way to the food. When I returned to the chair beside the pen she was munching a carrot stick. She stopped and looked me in the eye.

"Ruthie, do me a favor," I called. "Send Cosmo some of your good karma, will you?"

When I walked downstairs to the bar it was empty except for Cosmo and two of my dishwashers enjoying their post-shift drink. I hung back and waited for them to finish.

Here is a part of the story I haven't mentioned. Cosmo was someone Joannie brought into our lives. She hired him to be her nanny after we separated. Cosmo was attending the University of Maryland, but dropped out. He was looking for a place to stay in the city when he saw Joannie's ad on Craigslist offering free rent in exchange for child care.

Those two clicked immediately. With me gone, Joannie was happy to have Cosmo be the man of the house.

Of course I resented him. He was Joannie's stooge. But I couldn't hold the grudge. And it wasn't only because he was a Jersey boy, it was also because he loved my kids and they loved him in return at a time when they'd lost confidence in their parents.

When the kids were old enough to fend for themselves, I kept Cosmo in our lives by hiring him at the bistro. He started off as a host, then a bar back and finally bartender. He was a natural. Later he became my accomplice when we went into our shadowy, political back channel, public relations business. Before Cosmo's trouble, George W. Bush hammered away at the "axis of evil." Agents from those isolated nations, Iran, North Korea and Venezuela were my best customers.

The busboys finished their beers and it was just Cosmo and I. I could tell he'd had a few drinks. His demeanor had changed from an hour ago when he made his speech to the staff. He was mulling over the night's events.

"Well, you made it through your first night. How are you feeling?" I asked.

"I have this incredible urge to beat the shit out of a helpless old lady and get thrown back in jail."

"That's not funny."

"I know."

"This is where you belong."

"Here? I'm not sure, Joe. Who are these people? Where are all the normal people that used to flock here?"

"You've been away a long time. Things have changed."

"I don't even recognize America anymore. People are so jacked up on caffeine and their own egos that nobody seems real to me."

"Welcome to my world."

"Joe, what's with the menu? This lady sits down at the bar tonight and asks me about the kepis menu on the sirloin steak."

"It's a sweet soy sauce. I had a restaurant consultant brought in to redesign the menu. It might seem bourgeois to a Jersey boy but people are buying it and that's all I care about."

"Joe, you always considered yourself a red diaper baby, you know, the son of socialist Jews. But you've changed. Is that why you've lost the old crowd?"

"Maybe, but I've changed my opinion about some things too. I used to believe in socialism. Now I believe in the velocity of money. The faster it travels in and out of your hands the more socialist it becomes because everyone gets a share. Besides this place is not about the kepis menu or the pictures on the wall. It's about concourse and conversation."

"Oh yeah? Well, I listened in on a lot of dumb conversation to-night. There were these two, short-haired stiffs at the bar. They were laughing loudly about nothing. Then they debated about how many millions they were going to need before they felt comfortable enough to retire."

"I know. A lot of them are dopes. But since they started coming in here I'm paying my bills on time and can spend money on the kids. And you know that's important to me."

"Joe, you've never been able to compete financially with Joannie. Why is it suddenly an issue?"

"Male ego, I guess. Plus Rose and Aidan are going to college in the fall and that's expensive. I need to come up with my share of the tuition soon."

"Aidan has fifteen pairs of sneakers. Are those the values you're trying to instill in him?"

"He's a teenager," I said "That's what he's into."

"That boy is wild and you should keep a tighter rein on him. You treat him more like a frat brother than a son."

"After the divorce, after you went away, he was all I had."

"Aidan's probably the easy one," Cosmo said. "At least he listens to you."

"For now."

"Rose and Joannie are fighting because Rose wants a tattoo. Joannie's against it. Jack says they never stop yelling at each other and it goes on for hours."

"I know," I said.

"And Jack is fourteen going on twenty-one. I stopped by Joannie's house to say hello right before I came to work tonight. When I walked into Jack's bedroom I found him with his lips pressed against the lips of a tenth grade girl named Olivia. I thought that was cool until he pulled away and she exhaled a lungful of pot smoke."

"Did they have clothes on?"

"Yes."

"Did Joannie find out?"

"No, she was at work and then came right here for dinner. By the time she gets home all traces of it will probably be gone."

"Do the kids still trust you?"

"Yeah, they complain about you and complain about their mom."

"Good, at least that's the same."

"You know about the G-Spot, don't you?"

I could tell he disapproved. Yes, I knew about the G-Spot. It stood for Green or garage or ghetto or perhaps it really referred to that source of female sexual gratification. I'm not sure what Rose and Aidan had in mind when they named it.

It began one day when Rose came to me and asked, "Dad you're not using the garage, mind if me and friends hang out there once in a while?"

"Sure, go ahead."

The next day she showed up with a gang of five and cleared out all clutter. Then they brought in a long table, chairs of assorted sizes and shapes, a couch and a lamp. They blackened the windows with spray paint so people walking in the alley couldn't see in. The G-Spot was born.

Rose brought in her friends and Aidan brought in his. It became the preferred hangout for kids from three different area high schools. Whenever you went in you'd see Aidan or Rose sitting in the chair at the head of the table holding court. My only rule was no television, no music, just talk.

Teenagers need a space of their own and it was a good clubhouse. However, I was not prepared for the pot smoking and drinking that went on inside. I stifled many anxiety attacks on nights when returning late from work I'd find thirty teenagers congregated together inside my garage. My response to these meetings was ritual. I repeated it until it became a cliché.

I'd slam the door open for effect with narrow eyes. An angry grimace, dimly seen in the single lamp light, was on my face. The silence was immediate. New comers froze thinking they were busted. I created the tension and made it last, staring into each and every face intending to intimidate. Finally, I'd bark, "Bad kids. Don't scare the neighbors!"

I knew they were going to smoke and drink anyway and I figured it would be best if they did it in a safe place, which unfortunately, was on my property. So I turned a blind eye.

Besides, I tried to play by the rules of middle class morality and I failed. The divorce, which followed, embittered me so that bourgeois pretension was bullshit, a fucking hypocrisy, something I despised even though my livelihood depended on it. I suppose we men all get hemmed in like that but do it in the name of family. Civilization depends upon it.

But I was more than happy to let those kids rebel against it. And while most of their friend's parents knew about the G-spot, all of them were perfectly content to say nothing. Fortunately, it was still a secret to the cops.

"I know about the G-Spot, Cosmo. How did you find out?"

"I had a beer with Aidan and his buddies in it last night."

"As long as the neighbors don't complain I'm fine with it."

"Aren't you worried even a little?"

"Reckless abandon is the hallmark of youth."

"They're teenagers."

"Let them sow their wild oats now while they're minors and can't be held responsible. Relax, they're not going to crash and burn."

"Sounds risky," Cosmo said.

"You know what I've always told them."

"Yeah, yeah, yeah, 'the only good is virtue and the only virtue is self- control.' Epictetus got it, not sure your children do."

"For now, I'm going to let them have their way. Keep an eye on them for me."

"After all that's happened to me, I'm not sure that I'm a good role model for any of them," Cosmo said.

"Would you rather they get their values from the two stiffs sitting at a bar discussing how many million they'll need to retire?"

"No."

"Good, I need you and they need you and Joannie needs you too, even though she's too stubborn to admit it."

"She barely speaks to me."

"You alienated her and a lot of her friends," I said.

"You know, the whole concept of family scares the shit out of me. If your family isn't the death of me, Gaston Thomas's family proba- bly will be."

He said it as a joke but I couldn't help but feel that his troubles were, in part, a direct result of getting emotionally mixed up with the Green family drama.

"I'll try to smooth things with Reverend Battle so everyone be- haves," I said. "But Dave Paulus told me the kid with the boom box was Battle's son. I don't know what that was all about."

"I do."

"What?"

"Something you aren't going to like, Joe."

"Tell me."

"Next week Battle is going to announce his candidacy for the D.C. City Council."

"He's becoming a politician?"

"Yes."

"Oh fuck. Tonight's incident might just be the first of several others," I said.

"That's what I am afraid of too," he said. "I appreciate you letting me come back. But if you change your mind I'll understand."

"Let's just see how it all plays out," I said.

"I'm not sure how well I can shoulder the stress."

"You got to go slow with these changes, Cosmo. To think that you can just get on with your life as if these past five years never happened is unreasonable. You need to process all this and wait for life to happen to you again."

He paused for a moment, looking out the window, considering my words. Then he remembered himself and turned back to me. "Hey, I almost forgot. I'm a bartender. Want a drink?"

"Give me a Johnny Walker Red and water. Make one for yourself."

Chapter 3

I once read a book written by a sommelier whose intent was to teach his readers to become wine connoisseurs. In the first chapter he wrote something I've never forgotten. He said, "A waiter is an introvert temporarily posing as an extrovert in a restaurant dining room."

That line was just an aside in a long narrative but it struck me. I think it applies to most individuals working in the restaurant business regardless of what role they play in its operation. Our job description compels us to be emotionally present, hospitable, gracious and extroverted. But that's not really who we are. We're mostly introverts and I'm no exception.

So during the daylight hours I lead a counter-life to the one I've been detailing at the bistro. I own Tomes Greatest Hits. It's a used bookstore located at the corner of Mintwood Place and Columbia Road, a half block from my row house and a fifteen-minute walk to the bistro.

Within those bookstore walls are thousands of old, inanimate objects that stand up on shelves like tombstones. They're a testament to the work of old, mostly dead scholars.

Selling used books in a digital age might seem like a fool's errand. But people still care about the written word in D.C. and I consider this stewardship a civic duty.

The bookstore has a big picture window with the store's name written with in green block letters. Inside it's big, floor-to-ceiling bookshelves lining the outer walls and mazes and alcoves in the middle, housing specific topics. A large wooden desk at the door serves as a counter and iTunes deep house music stations like Ibiza Sonica and Dogglounge play on the store's stereo at a soft volume. I like it way better than classical music and feel that its tribal drumbeat betters the concentration of a reader in the hunt.

The best part is that I own the building which not only houses the bookstore, but also a small carry-out deli next door, called, "The Regent." It pays enough rent to supplement the modest income the bookstore brings in.

Restaurant and bookstore; it's a good balance. At the bistro's podium I live as master of ceremonies, host, maître d', waiter, psycho-pomp, butler, oracle of informed opinion, valet and extrovert all rolled into one.

But here at the bookstore podium it's different. I do not engage people since book buying is intimate and requires concentration. Here I am a quiet introvert. And so in scheduling my own shifts, I like to have a morning shift following a busy night at the bistro.

Were I a Buddhist I might refer to this double life as the yin and yang of my existence. If it were a coin, it would be the heads and tails of my workday. Hegel might have understood it in terms of dialectical materialism: the tension between the thesis and the antithesis, which streamlines into a synthesis.

That dialectic stuff sounds more complicated than it actually is. I could explain it, but nobody reads Hegel anymore, so why bother? Four books by that German philosopher have sat unsold on my shelves for the past three years.

My favorite clientele are mostly older white folk, college professors from local universities and erudite lawyers. They're old school like me, and love to discuss what they're reading. I see a lot of young nerds too. Young hipsters don't read old books anymore. They find their well-lit tablets and Kindles more compelling.

Over the years I've become a historiographer in that I understand the etymology of books and authors within most genres. Show me four biographies on Ronald Reagan and I'll tell you which one was written by the conspiracy theorist, which one by the New Deal liberal, which one by the American patriot and which one by the economist.

That's important because currently, in D.C., point-of-view is everything. Republicans and Democrats are hemmed in. The customers who come into my store want to make sure the authors they're reading support the worldview of their political party. They'd rather die than be caught reading someone from the other side of the ideological spectrum who might intellectually taint them. It's just the lay of the land these days. I can address those questions about an author's politics when customers stand at my desk with books in their hands and money in their wallets.

Of late, a growing amount of business is done from my on-line catalogue, which specializes in first edition European literature before the Holocaust.

Reading time during the slow hours of a bookstore shift is a luxury. It's certainly beyond most Washington bureaucrats whose big jobs keep them overworked, overstressed and unable to enjoy such time and ease. Then again, I am often interrupted.

Friends know where they can find me. Each morning I make a big pot of coffee and see who might drop by. It also affords Joannie, who also lives down the block, the opportunity to come in and talk about the kids.

I sit at the front desk four days a week. Rose and Jack fill in at night. Cosmo committed to three shifts here too. Of us all, he has the most enthusiasm for the bookstore.

Cosmo lined his jail cell with bookshelves. He measured the passing of time not by the number of days but by the number of books.

How many wayward men have gone to jail, spent their time studying books and molted into someone new? Nelson Mandela comes to mind. Unfortunately, that's Adolph Hitler's story too.

I started Cosmo on a diet of biographies. The stories of Martin Luther King, Abraham Lincoln and Ho Chi Min inspired him.

A few months later he was telling me what to bring. He read each book with a pen, a notebook and a dictionary, looking up any word he came across that he could not explain off the top of his head. He was inspired in this practice by a book called "Language and Responsibility." Its author, linguist Noam Chomsky, claimed that language and thought are synonymous. By expanding his vocabulary Cosmo meant to get smarter and compete in the world he was taken away from.

In prison he earned the reputation of a learned man. His scholarship was contagious. Soon, I was bringing books not only for him, but for his friends as well, including his cell mate, a rather daffy young Egyptian named Ali Bin Hassan, who was one of the first men convicted under the Patriot Act.

Ali started off his prison sentence in league with other Muslim convicts. But sharing a prison cell with Cosmo had an effect on him. He developed a taste for books about Marxism. Despite its alleged Godlessness, which flew in the face of Islam, Bin Hassan felt it offered a way to liberate the Arab masses weighed down by the yoke of Arab oil sheiks and the ghost of Muhammad.

He morphed out of that when he started reading books by Tom Friedman and Fareed Zakaria. These men understood globalization and it opened Ali's eyes to better possibilities. Ali was fascinated with me, a Jew, the first Jew he'd ever met, and often referred to me as "Rabbi."

Following his parole, Cosmo continued his existence as an eremite scholar, who collected money behind the desk of Tomes Greatest Hits while lost in the literary dream. In his free time he sat in seat 190 at the Library of Congress where, inspired by its august space, he read some more.

"I've found my calling," he told me. "I want to be the world's smartest American."

"That's going to be difficult to prove or measure, don't you think?"

"That's the beauty of it."

"A man of letters," I said. "It's an old fashioned ideal in a world dominated by video."

Cosmo smiled. "That makes me a revolutionary."

My first customer of the day was Sally Jones. She walked through my door carrying a large brown paper bag. She had been in two times before and I'd learned her name from the Visa card she'd handed me.

I remember the first time she came in. She was wandering around the store and landed in front of the ancient history section. I walked by. She startled when she saw me. I excused myself and passed. Then she found her way to the romance novel section and after two minutes bought three and walked out the door.

Sally was straight out of the Ozarks and spoke with a soft southern accent. She came to Washington to serve in her country's giant bureaucracy and to escape her small town Missouri upbringing. She had a rich creamy complexion, was a little thick in the middle, a little big on top and definitely built for pleasure.

She wore thin, retro looking, dark framed eyeglasses whose style was big in the 1950s. She had big hair too, jet black, which I do not think she colored. Her finest feature was her mouth: perfect thick lips covering straight white teeth. She was a flirt too and if I was to guess I'd say hovering around forty years old.

Now it is true that I took a special delight in trying to keep my book stock as highbrow as possible but I was reminded of what a snooty pretension that was when I looked into the bag she had placed on the counter.

"I'd like to sell these books," she said.

It was filled with Harlequin Romances whose covers featured beautiful busty babes and shirtless guys with big muscles.

It was from this lovely stream of lonely-hearts that I found the majority of my dates. It was easy too because they knew where to find me.

From experience I decided that the bistro was the bistro and the bookstore was the bookstore and never the twain shall meet. That was especially true with women.

I remember a young attorney named Jennifer I met at the bistro. She was a hot blonde with bangs that hid her forehead. One night she was the only one left at last call. She made a pass at me. Being newly divorced and flattered by her attention, I brought her upstairs.

The problem was she was also a drunk who came back the next night and the night after that, expecting the red carpet. She was also a gossip. After a rather ugly scene in the bar, I kicked her out.

Romance readers make better dates. Many of them didn't even know I had a restaurant and I liked it that way.

"No work today?"

"Committee deadlines ended last night," Sally said. "We were working at the Capitol until three. The boss gave us the day off."

"Let's see what you have here," I said, emptying her bag.

"How are the kids?"

"They're good."

"I walked by the store the other afternoon and saw your boy sitting behind the counter. God, he's getting tall."

"That's Jack. He's catching up to his brother."

"You're looking a little thin, Joe. Have you been eating? I once had this boyfriend that got so caught up in books that he'd forget to eat."

"I'm okay."

"How about if I go next door and get us a couple of scrambled egg sandwiches while you figure out how much you're are going to give me for these books."

"Are you looking for cash or do you want to take it out in trade?" She winked.

"I'll pour the coffee. You get the sandwiches."

Sally and I ate breakfast seated at the front door. Business was slow in the morning so I had time to talk and we killed a half an hour of my shift. I ended up giving her ten dollars for her paperbacks. She bought four more from the shelves at two bucks apiece, traded the sandwich for three cups of coffee with cream and sugar and promised to cook me dinner one night.

Later that afternoon, a short Black man with pink lips entered the bookstore. He was about five-foot-five and weighed a buck fifty. I should have suspected that he would come here instead of the bistro. It was Reverend James Battle.

"Reverend," I said. "What brings you to this side of the neighborhood?"

"I'm looking for a book—*Parting of the Water*. It's about Martin Luther King and the Civil Rights movement."

"I'm surprised you haven't read it already."

"I have. The copy I own is all beat up and doesn't have a dust jacket and I'd like a newer edition."

"I have it right here." I walked a few short steps from the door and there it was on a nearby shelf. I pulled the book down and handed it to him.

"I heard you're running for city council," I said.

"Did you hear that in your bar?"

"I did."

"They gossip like women at your place." he said. "It's true. I'm having a press conference next week to make it official. And know this, Joe Green, part of my platform is going to be fighting the gentrification of my ward and the displacement of Black folk who have lived there for generations."

"What does that have to do with me?"

"The people who inhabit your restaurant are the very carpetbaggers I'll be campaigning against. And make no mistake, I'll also be taking aim at Cosmo Della Rocca."

"Do you really have to go there?"

"Absolutely."

"No Christian charity or judge not lest ye be judged?"

"No one shoots a Black man in the back and lives to brag about it. Not in my political ward."

"It isn't your ward."

"Politics being what it is, it will be come November."

"I saw an example of your politics last night when your crew entered my dining room."

"You were intimidated, weren't you?"

"Do you know that I almost pulled my piece?" I said.

"Wouldn't that have been apropos, a white guy pulling a gun on unarmed Black men?"

"You risked that to make a point?"

"Give yourself some credit. I knew you wouldn't pull it out. If you had, you'd be done in this neighborhood forever."

"Don't let the glasses fool you," I said. "Cosmo is no one to fuck with. I'm holding you responsible if something happens to him or Tyrone Thomas."

He leaned in on me. "We'll just have to wait and see."

"You didn't come here for a book. What do you really want?"

"To tell you this. I want your boy Cosmo out of my neighborhood."

"Go fuck yourself." I said.

"You fuck yourself."

Both of us startled when we realized Jack was at the door. He looked taller because he was standing on his skateboard. The leash of his Golden Retriever, named Shortstop, was in his hand. When we turned our attention, the dog's tail began beating against the front door, propped open to take full advantage of the beautiful spring day.

Jack's Washington Nationals baseball cap was turned backwards on his head. He had a brown paper bag in his hand from the drug store around the corner. If my guess was correct it was filled with Red Hots, a Coke and pretzels.

"Hey, Jack, how's your day?"

"Am I interrupting something, Dad?"

"Say hello to Reverend Battle. He runs the Baptist church on Mount Pleasant Street."

Jack stuck out his hand. Battle shook it and gave him a smile.

"Did Shortstop pull you all the way here?" I asked.

"Yeah, she's really fast," Jack said.

"She looks thirsty. Take her in the back and get her a drink. I'll be with you in a minute."

There was an uneasy timeout as my boy and his dog walked for water. Once out of earshot, Battle continued.

"I don't want to embarrass you in front of your son so I'll be brief. Get rid of Della Rocca or I'll make it a campaign issue. I'll have a steady stream of picketers outside your store that will scare your clientele. I'll make it my mission after I get elected to punish you with health inspectors and the licensing bureau. I'll ruin Cosmo and I'll ruin you."

"That's ten dollars for the book," I said.

"I don't think I want the book after all." He gave it back.

"Don't let the door hit you in the ass on the way out."

"Think it over, Joe. Della Rocca's gotta' go." He strolled out the door where he was met by three suited members of his crew. The four of them made their way down the street.

"Is he going to hurt Cosmo?" Jack asked.

"Were you eavesdropping?"

"Sort of."

"Don't be doing that."

"But is he going to hurt Cosmo?"

"He might try. But not yet."

"It's 3:30, Dad. Go home, take your nap. You got to be dressed and at the Bistro by five."

"Thanks, kid. Call if you need me."

"Can you take Shortstop with you? I don't want her running out the door while I'm watching the store."

"Do you have homework to do?"

"A little."

"Get it done."

"Come on Shortstop," I said, grabbing the dog's leash. "We both need a nap."

Cosmo's second shift at the bistro was like a day at the circus. Everything was going swimmingly. Stella was delightful at the door too. She glowed as bright as the noon sun. Everybody wanted to be near her. After they ate and paid their tabs, they congregated with her at the door before leaving.

Lawrence Grimaldi, ex-Mafia attorney turned K Street big shot and my rival for her attention, came in for dinner with three of his colleagues. Like me, and Cosmo, Grimaldi's family was originally from Jersey. At American University we actually played together on an intramural football team called, "Never Again In Newark." He was a big fan not only of Cosmo, but also of Stella.

He stood very close to Stella and was chatting her up at the host stand to impress his friends. Noticing my eyes upon the two of them, Stella accidentally dropped her glasses, which she always removed during conversation. When she knelt down to pick them up, she turned her head to me with a smirk suggesting, "Can you believe this guy?"

I was really busy at the time so I didn't have more than a few seconds to dwell on it, but it was one of the highlights of my night.

"What's new with Grimaldi?" I asked her later on.

"He wants me to quit this job so he can set me up in my own apartment. I can finish graduate school without the distraction of work."

"Did he tell you that you'd have to be his mistress?"

"Of course. How naïve do you think I am?"

"Didn't he make that proposition once before?"

"Several times," she said. "He's a lobbyist. He makes a living being persistent."

"So what did you say?"

"I said, you have to ask my master."

"I wondered why he called me 'Master Green' on his way out the door. Do you make a habit of that?"

"Yes," she said, "It protects me from mashers. It's either that or wear a wedding ring."

"Clever." I said.

The well-oiled human machinery that constituted my staff fed a hundred people. The food came out on time, the check average ran above average of a typical night and we sold a lot of desserts, always a harbinger of happy guests.

Other telltale signs prevailed. When Tony Colazzo, my hotshot gay Italian waiter, walked by I asked, "How's it going tonight?"

His answer validated the night's success when he announced he was making "stripper money."

With his tight pants, strong chin, dark brown eyes, shaved head and thin lips, which easily broke into a smile when uttering words in his Bronx accent, he could be, on his good days, the most charming man I ever met.

And when I asked him what kind of night he had and he answered, I was happy because it meant it was a good night.

"Stripper money," was an expression he coined and we all borrowed. His boyfriend, Troy, was once a male stripper at the Zebra Club on 17th Street and that phrase indicated that his customers were more than happy to give twenty percent tips and more for the opportunity to sit in his section.

Tony's success in part was due to Stella's growing expertise at the door. She's good at gauging the temperament of customers and assigning them tables in stations where they might feel comfortable with their servers. Each member of my wait staff has their own wheelhouse.

Tony does best with young, high roller attorneys with big egos. He knows the captain's list and sells rare vintages of wine with confidence. When he wheels out a four-pound lobster appetizer on the cart his deft hands can filet it tableside in two minutes. Guys looking to spend that kind of money go to Tony. He makes sure they get their money's worth.

Mary Costigan does best with the political old guard. She's about fifty-two and her rock hard Boston Irish demeanor wins over politicos who look upon her as somebody's sister from the old neighborhood.

For sightseers from the South, Kathy Thorndyke, a thirty-nine-year-old married mother of three from New Orleans, radiates Southern hospitality.

Sascha Berlovitz, my French-born Jewish waiter, whose Warsaw born grandparents somehow survived the Holocaust, can speak Polish, Russian, Yiddish, French and German. Lifting the language barrier from European customers makes him valuable even though his A.D.D. is sometimes a problem because he makes mistakes ringing in orders on the computer. Last night, after a French party of five left him a ten percent tip on a four hundred dollar bill, he stormed out of the dining room and into the kitchen where he threw a temper tantrum and screamed, "Fucking Euro-trash!"

Abdel and Reda worked tonight. They're Moroccans who despite their Muslim religion seem to like my Jewish clientele best. According to Abdel, the King of Morocco won't let anybody but the Jews handle his finances and as a result Jewish Moroccans are held in high esteem, he said.

Cosmo seemed more in the flow of things and the evening just flew by. I didn't mention Battle's visit to the bookstore. But it was only a matter of time until he found out through Jack or Joannie or by some second- or third-hand account.

What to do about Battle? I needed an action plan. That night after we closed and everyone had gone, I had a long staring session upstairs with Louis, the ranking stud in my tortoise pen. Twenty minutes eye to eye with him wasn't enough. I walked downstairs and behind the bar, grabbed a glass and filled it with ice. I walked along the long row of bottles deciding what to drink.

I stopped when I came to the bottle of Johnny Walker Black. I poured myself a healthy dose and drank it fast. That wasn't going to be enough so I grabbed the bottle and went back upstairs. On the back deck, overlooking the alley, I drank under a star lit sky. I crashed around 2:30.

My cell phone woke me. It was Joannie.

"Where are you? I've been calling you all morning."

It took me several seconds to remember. "I slept at the bistro last night."

"Did you see this morning's Post?"

"No."

"Dave Paulus wrote a piece about Cosmo and the Black kids who came into the bistro Thursday night."

"Are you're kidding?"

"No, I'm not kidding," Joannie said. "Go outside and pick up the paper."

Chapter 4

Following Joannie's call I slipped on my shoes and walked down-stairs to the street for a copy of the Washington Post. Dave Paulus, the story's author, was sometimes a sloppy drunk. Since I was an eyewitness I was curious to know if he was a sloppy storyteller too.

My cell phone rang. It was Rose.

"Daddy! You and Cosmo are in the newspaper. Have you seen it?"

"No, not yet."

"Oh my God, you guys come off like a bunch of bad asses."

"Honey, that's not exactly what I aspire to."

"Why is it always about you? Think about my reputation. Do you know how many obnoxious brats I have to put up with at Sidwell Friends?"

"Is that a rhetorical question, or do you really want me to guess?" I asked.

Rose started mimicking her classmates. "My daddy is the Maharajah of Punjab. My daddy is the U.S. Ambassador to France, my daddy runs the Ford Foundation. When I get to school on Monday I'm going to brag that compared to my daddy, their daddies are just a bunch of wimps."

"Rose, settle down."

"I'm sorry, it's time for a little pay back. All those prissy little bitches make me sick."

"Where are you?"

"Right where I'm supposed to be. Me and Louisa are getting ready to go inside the Daughters Of the American Revolution Hall for their used book sale."

"You're going to let the Arab spend my money on books?"

"Daddy, her family is from Lebanon. They're not Arab, they're Phoenician."

"Oh, baloney. I asked a guy from the Jordanian embassy about the part of the Lebanon Louisa's people come from. He said the tribes who live in those hills are definitely Arab. She's just trying to pass."

"These days can you blame her?"

"I suppose not."

"Well, it is what it is," said Rose.

"Is there a big crowd out front?"

"Yeah, the line is all the way down the block. But we're numbers nine and ten in line. We should get a crack at some of their best books."

"You know the drill. When those doors open, something resembling the Oklahoma Land Rush is going to happen. Make sure you coach Louisa on how to act."

"I have six banana boxes," Rose said, "and Jack is supposed to stop by with two duffle bags. He's late."

"Remember, you go for the literature section. The stacks are a little slim at the bookstore right now. Look for literary criticisms with obscure titles. Most of them will be somebody's doctoral thesis. Make sure they're well written. Let the Arab pick the history books."

"Quit calling her the Arab," Rose scolded. "You know you like her."

"You're right."

"She just got a new tattoo on her hip. It's written in Arabic."

"What's it say?"

"God Bless."

"God bless what?" I asked.

"Just God bless. It's religious. You got a problem with that?"

"I only have a problem if you want one too."

"Well, I'm eighteen and I do want one."

"Great, why don't you just get 'born to lose' tattooed on your forehead?"

"You're mean and I'm hanging up."

"Come to my house for brunch tomorrow morning. Bring Louisa."

"Trying to get off cheap, huh? Won't even spring for dinner?"

"I've got a date tomorrow night."

"With who?"

"Nobody you know," I said.

"Let me guess, some overused bar whore?"

"Rose, what happened to my sweet little girl?"

"I started hanging out with Louisa and became sophisticated."

"Honey, I've got to go."

"I just talked to Mom," Rose said. "Her phone has been ringing off the hook with people commenting on the newspaper story."

"Really? What are they saying?"

"I'm not sure. But you better prepare for a big night at the bistro. You could get clobbered."

"I hadn't thought of that. What are you and Louisa doing tonight?"

"We're double dating. Two boys from Georgetown University."

"College boys? You're still in high school."

"We told them we're freshman at American University."

"Forget it. You're not going."

"You can't stop me, I'm eighteen."

"Wanna bet? One call to your mom, you'll be grounded all weekend."

"Daddy."

"Besides, I'm going to need the two of you to work the door with Stella tonight."

"No way."

"Listen, you owe me for that new cell phone and a dozen other minor expenses which when added up become major expenses. Dress up and be there at six. Make sure Louisa hides her tattoo."

"Daddy, I'm already working for you today."

"Listen, this fall you'll be away at college and you'll pine for the days when you bonded with your father at the bistro."

There was a long silence at the other end of the phone.

"Come on, Rose. I need you tonight. Cosmo's going to be in the spotlight and I know he'll do a lot better if you're there for moral support."

There was still no response. I could tell she was pouting.

"Okay, listen. I'll make you a deal," I said. "Have the boyfriends pick you up at 9:15. I'll interview them, check their IDs and remind them what's going to happen if they lay a hand on my daughter. We'll make a big fuss over you and Louisa, spring for appetizers and you'll be still be out the door early enough to enjoy your dates."

"Promise me that you won't tell them we're in high school."

"No promises."

"Oh, come on. We met them at a museum for Christ's sake. It's not like their crack heads. If you tell them we're in high school they might back off and we'll have to do something really naughty to keep them interested."

"Is Louisa this honest with her father?"

"Hold on, I'll ask." Rose put her hand over the phone and mumbled something to her sidekick.

"No," she said.

"Then take a lesson," I shouted, "and be at the bistro at six."

I continued down the streets to the Better Bean Coffee Shop to grab the Post and a cup of hot bitter black liquid. Kennedy the cop was there.

"Woo, did you see that piece in the Post?" he asked. "You can't pay enough money for that kind of advertising."

"I haven't seen it yet."

"Yeah, well it might be great for you, but it could suck for me because now there's a public spectacle on my beat. If you think Battle was mad about Cosmo being back yesterday, wait until he sees the article."

"Really?" I asked sheepishly.

"Really," repeated the cop.

I looked at the newspaper rack. It was empty.

"Hey Kennedy, what are you doing tonight?"

"I thought I'd hang out at home, rent a movie and drink a few beers, why?"

"I'll pay you twenty bucks an hour to hang out at my place in uniform. I'll feed you dinner and put in a good word with Anya Tomarovich, the salad girl from Bulgaria."

"The one with the big knockers?"

"That's her. Let me tell you something. She's a lot more fun than the porno movie you're going to watch. Besides her work visa runs out in ten months and she's looking for an American guy to latch onto."

"I don't want to get married, Joe."

"She doesn't have to know that. Besides she's an inch shorter than you and she hasn't been laid in six months."

"How do you know?" Kennedy asked.

"Gossip travels fast in a restaurant."

"Can I get the steak without the black beans and soy sauce?"

"Sure, for you, I'll smother it in baked potatoes."

"It's a deal. What time should I be there?"

"Six o'clock and try not to be late."

My cell phone rang again. "Hold on Kennedy," I said.

It was Stella.

"Did you read the paper?"

"No, not yet but I've heard about it. What do you think?"

"The computer is pinging with reservations from Open Table. I think it's going to be a mob scene tonight," Stella said. "Half of them want a table in the bar. Cha-ching. I think you're about to hit the cash register."

"Rose and Louisa are going to work the door with you tonight while I float around the bistro troubleshooting. See if we can get a few others to come and help."

"Okay," said Stella. "See you at five"

I hung up.

"Hey, Joe, is Cosmo freaking out about the article?" Kennedy asked. "Suddenly, he's the spotlight kid. Hope he doesn't crack under the pressure."

"He probably hasn't seen it yet." I answered. "I can't have him coming in and getting cold-cocked by all this. I better go see him."

"That's what I'd do if I were you," Kennedy said. "But don't worry about me, I'll be there at six."

I hoofed it up the bluff to Cosmo's building, which was about a mile and a half away. It was a seven-story apartment of red brick across from Malcolm X Park at the corner of Chapin Street and 15th. In the 1970s and 1980s the corner was an open-air drug market where I used to pull up in my car and buy nickel bags from Black kids. But that was ancient history. The block is now gentrified.

When I made it to the front door a young man was walking out the security door and I was able to enter unannounced. Since I helped Cosmo move in, I knew which door was his.

After four raps with my fist, Cosmo's voice invited me to enter. I turned the doorknob and walked in. I found him sitting in an armchair looking out the big picture window. The morning sun was shining on his face and the cool breeze fanned the drapes.

I was taken by the Spartan nature of his apartment. The freshly painted walls were a bright white but had nothing on them. Aside from the chair there was a bed, a desk and a chest of drawers. What really surprised me was the absence of electronic media. There was no television, no stereo or computer. There wasn't even a boom box in his efficiency apartment.

"Don't you lock your door?"

"I'm never sitting behind locked doors again," Cosmo said.

One thing I did notice was a stack of books piled vertically on the floor beside the desk. I knew they came from my store and he hadn't paid for them. We glanced at them at the same time and he realized that he'd been busted. He raised his eyebrows in apology, but I let it pass because that's not why I came.

"Is everything all right, Joe?"

"Did you see the paper today?"

"No. What did it say?"

"To tell you the truth, I haven't seen it either."

"Then what's the problem?"

"You went to journalism school. Do you remember what an emerging issue is?"

"Sure. What emerging issue are you referring to?"

"You. You're an emerging issue."

"If you haven't read the newspaper how do you know?"

"Joannie, Rose, Kennedy and Stella all told me about it and that's all within the past thirty minutes."

He was startled that his personal life was now a public event. But since he hadn't seen the story, he stared at me for a moment, then looked down at the worn carpet in front of his chair.

"It was Dave Paulus's story," I said.

"Look, if you came here to fire me, it's okay. I understand."

"No, you don't get it. I came to tell you that we're going to be busy tonight and it's all about you."

"What exactly did Paulus write?"

"Not really sure. All I know is that we're already booked for to-night and its only 10:30 in the morning. I think you're the reason they're going to be lining up at the door."

He listened carefully.

"Cosmo, I remember a time when you were king. You had a full bar every night and were so charming that you made more money for me than tap beer. You can have that back if you still want it."

"Okay."

"I'm not convinced," I said sternly.

"Why not?"

"For one, look at this place. It's like a jail cell. You're a free man and you don't even know it."

"Let me get this straight. You're worried about me because I'm not into conspicuous consumption? When did being bourgeois start conferring manhood? I don't need all the bells and whistles you guys surround yourself with. I don't have to stay wired to all the ridiculous media you all gorge yourself on. I don't need a phone, the Internet, DVDs, a TV. I got a life. Why is that so hard to understand?"

"Because it's a solitary life and you're now a public commodity in a town that values such things."

"Why did you come here, Joe?"

"Because you don't have a phone and I didn't want you walking into a shit storm."

"What's the worst that can happen?"

"You tell me."

"People are going to wait an extra five minutes to get drunk. Believe me, your insurance agent will be happy."

"Battle came to see me."

"He wants me gone, doesn't he?"

"Yes."

"When were you going to tell me?"

"I'm telling you now."

"Did he threaten your business?"

"Yes."

"Did he say he was going to get me?"

"Yes."

"What did you say?"

"I said don't let the door hit you in the ass on the way out."

Cosmo smiled. I walked over to the books piled on the floor. They were of a new age genre called channeled works, which were written by psychics who dictated information from spirits about what life on earth is really all about. As a businessman, a father of three and a man with terrestrial appetites it never really appealed to me, but they sold pretty well at the bookstore and hooked Cosmo.

"Are these my books?"

"Yes, I'm almost done. I'll bring them back."

"Not sure these books are good for you right now."

"Do you ever wonder why I read them, Joe?"

"Searching for some sense of peace from your past?"

"Not even close."

"What is it then? Tell me because I'm worried that you're losing it."

"Only by Washington, D.C. standards."

"True, but you live in Washington, D.C."

"I don't read them to rebel against my environment."

"Then what is it?" I asked him.

"It's Gaston Thomas and Dominique Matthews, the two guys I shot. I've seen them. At night they hang out in my bathroom. I see them in my dreams and catch quick glances of them following me on the street."

"Do they talk to you?"

"Once," he confessed. "It was Thomas who spoke."

"What did he say?"

"He said he likes me better than Battle."

"You believe them?"

"I do."

"I'll take your word for it."

"Listen, Joe. At work tonight, I'm going to kick ass and take names."

"Hopefully the names of some good looking babes."

"Maybe."

"Listen, kid. I can't fire you now even if I wanted to. It would make me look stupid. We have to weather this storm together and I need to know that you're going to accept the responsibility that's just been foisted upon you."

"You mean because of that newspaper article?"

"Exactly."

"What does one thing have to do with the other?"

It was a fair question. I had no ready response.

"Maybe we should walk downstairs," I said, "pick up the newspaper and find out."

"Maybe we should," Cosmo said.

Chapter 5

Cosmo and I walked out of his apartment building and down 14th Street towards a commercial block looking for a coffee shop and a newspaper. A Starbucks appeared. When I started in the door he balked.

"Is there a problem?"

"I don't drink there. Let's go somewhere else."

I stopped and stared a minute at their green logo and then stared at Cosmo who assumed a rigid pose.

"Okay, you're not going to get an argument from me. I prefer small operators to corporations too. Let's keep walking."

"Good, I hate big business. I hate big government and all of the creeps who maintain it," he said, staring at the cement slabs along the way.

"Back in the day Capitol Hill fat cats considered you their little darling for the respect you showered on them. Why the sudden change of heart?"

"I was a fool."

"How were you a fool?"

"When I first got to prison I bragged about all the big shots I served drinks to. I thought it made me better than the jailbirds surrounding me. Instead it made me sound like a pretentious asshole."

"What tipped you off?"

"A high pitched voice with an Arab accent."

"Ali Bin Hassan?"

"Yeah, Ali. One day he said to me, 'The prestige you pretend by telling everyone here that you know famous men only proves that you yourself are of small account.'"

"Compared to them you are of small account."

"Maybe so, but I don't have to like it. When five years of your life gets taken from you, you look at the establishment differently. The land of the free and the home of the brave is peopled with money grubbing assholes."

"Money might be the root of all evil, but it's also the root of all civilization."

"Yeah, right."

"If you want to espouse your contempt for the establishment I'll be glad to listen. But if you spill that rhetoric on your bar customers I will fire you."

"Don't worry about me, I got a great poker face."

Five minutes later we were at Smith's Java Clutch, which was nothing special, just a quiet neighborhood coffee shop. A local artist had landscapes of Chesapeake Bay on the walls. A small bookcase filled with dog-eared paperbacks was available for customers. On this Saturday morning twenty people sat beside each other. Some listened to headphones. Others stared at computer screens. Some read books, a newspaper or a magazine while sipping hot coffee out of big white mugs while soft folk music filled the room. Nobody talked. It reminded me of the parallel play of toddlers on a playground.

I walked to the counter and ordered two cups of dark roast. Cosmo saw a copy of the *Washington Post* on a table in the far corner of the coffee shop and went for it. Dave Paulus's column was on the front page of the metro section below the fold.

The skinny white girl behind the counter had tattoo sleeves up and down both arms colored with red, purple, green and blue ink. I couldn't help but stare. She wore a tiny white T-shirt that exposed them in their entirety.

When I lifted my eyes to meet hers, I spoke.

"I guess I'm old school. My eighteen-year-old daughter wants a tattoo and I'm against it."

"My dad doesn't like it either," she answered. "In his day only tramps got tattoos. It's much more acceptable today. I wouldn't worry about it."

"Thanks," I said, grabbing the coffees.

Standing straight and stiff beside the table, the newspaper unfolded to its full length in his hands, Cosmo read the review of his first night back at the bistro.

After a minute, the paper jumped out of his hand like a hot plate and hit the table. People around him momentarily lifted their heads and stared. He looked like he wanted to scream. Turning his body, he headed for the door. But after six steps, he stopped, took a deep breath, mumbled a few words to himself, returned to the paper, and finished the story.

We both sat down. He began reading it out loud.

"Let me see that paper," I said, grabbing it from his hands.

The first thing I noticed was the picture, a file photo taken at Cosmo's trial. The young man in the image was no longer the man who sat across from me. His face was fuller, touches of gray hair were at his temples and there were small lines beside his eyes. The boyish good looks faded but were replaced with a maturity I thought more compelling.

The newspaper story described the fright on the faces of my customers at this sudden piece of theater and how Cosmo had faced his accusers. Paulus saw me face off with the two Black kids and even caught some of the back and forth.

But best of all he saw the tears in Tyrone Thomas's eyes after he threatened Cosmo and the look on Kennedy's face after the standoff at the door when the cop decided to let the kid go.

Paulus's narrative showed sympathy for Cosmo and the victim's family as well. A recap of my pissing contest with Battle finished the story with the suggestion that with the Reverend's city council bid, the drama might only have just begun.

When I finished, I took a deep breath, let go of the paper and took a large sip from my coffee. I let the brew swish around in my mouth for a few seconds before swallowing. I put the cup down and only then did I look into Cosmo's eyes. The silence lasted several seconds.

Cosmo grinned. Then we both burst out laughing.

"Holy shit," Cosmo said.

"Holy shit, indeed."

"Is that really what happened?"

"I think so," I said. "But I must admit I was so jacked up on adrenalin that I didn't see all of it."

"Me neither."

"It's a moot point now, don't you think?"

"Why do you say that?" Cosmo asked.

"Because tens of thousands of people have already read it."

"You always say a good story is better than the truth."

"Well, it is a good story," I said.

"I'm feeling a little naked."

When I stared at him and started giggling, he narrowed his eyes.

"What's so funny?"

"Remember the establishment you claim to hate so much?"

"What of it?"

"Even Washingtonians like a bad boy. That newspaper story may very well admit you into the establishment's ranks."

"Or get me shot."

"Or get you shot," I repeated. "But don't worry, kid. You're fast becoming old news. Tomorrow there will be another edition of the Post and some other guy will get his fifteen minutes of fame."

"Okay, but tell me this. If this article were the content of a book, which shelf would you put it on at the book store?"

"Searching for genre?"

"Yes."

I visually put the map of the bookstore in my mind and pretended to walk along the green-carpeted aisles, looking left and looking right at tall stacks of books, trying to imagine where this story might belong.

"It could do well in the urban studies section since it details race relations. It would also fit in the true crime section. Of course, the way Paulus wrote it might be in fiction."

"Fiction?" Cosmo asked. "How about melodrama."

"I was thinking along the lines of epic. I'd put it on the same shelf as Homer's *Odyssey*. It's a story about a man trying to get home."

"You'd put it with Homer? Oh, don't flatter yourself."

"Flatter myself? This isn't my story, Cosmo. It's yours. If anyone's playing Odysseus here, it's you. The best I can claim is Tiresias, the blind prophet trying to help the hero find his way back home."

We both stopped talking and sipped our coffee. Cosmo stared at the newspaper photo. It must have reminded him of the old days because a brief look of melancholy came over him.

"Listen, kid, I've been in this town a long time. Here's one thing I learned. Never believe your press notices. It's the kiss of death."

"Then what's the proper response of an ex-con working behind your bar tonight?"

"You could play dumb. Mouth boring platitudes so that people would be embarrassed for you and immediately drop it."

"And let them think I'm a dumb Wop from Jersey? Not a chance."

"Okay, but be careful," I said.

"Careful of what?"

"Next time you're in the bookstore grab a book on ancient Greek religion. It was based on one fact: the Gods are jealous. They'll be looking down from Mount Olympus at some mortal who's getting all the glory and say, 'Look at that bastard. He thinks he's a God. Let's fuck with him.' And then, suddenly, the guy's life turns to shit."

"Dude, that's just mythology."

"No, it's not and you go fuck yourself. It's still the way of the world."

And then I leaned into him to emphasize my point.

"It happened to Nixon, it happened to LBJ and it happened to Clinton. They thought they were Gods and as a result took liberties they were not entitled to. All of them were hounded out of Washington. Even Reagan, who went out a star, lost his mind to Alzheimer's. So listen to this and listen carefully. You've just had a bout with fame. The Gods are jealous. Don't invoke their wrath. Act unimpressed and stay off their radar screen."

"So you're telling me to dumb down?"

"Yes, that's my advice."

"But the restaurant is going to be busy tonight, right?"

"According to Stella, it's a full house. And though they'll shake my hand at the front door, it's you they're coming to see."

"Well then, I can't let my public down, even if it's only for tonight. I think I'll head home, take a little nap."

Later that afternoon, when I got to the restaurant, Aidan was behind the bar setting up.

"Hey, Dad. Cosmo called. He's running late."

"Is everything okay?"

"I think so. He's said he's on his way."

"So what time did you get home last night?"

"About 1:30."

"Did your mom catch you?"

"No, she was asleep."

"How was the party?"

"It was the bomb."

"Did you spit game at Amanda?"

"Absolutely."

"Good boy."

"So how are you doing with the babes these days, Dad?"

"What kind of question is that to ask your father?"

"It's just a question. You don't have to get all defensive about it."

"When I was your age I'd never have had the guts to ask my dad that kind of question."

"That's because he was married to Grandma."

"Well, mind your own business."

"Dad, I heard it in the kitchen. You got mad skills with women. You know the college level birds and bees talk. I'm just looking for some pointers."

"Not now, later."

I walked to the front door where Rose and Louisa were standing. The two teenage girls were wearing the exact same black dress.

"Let me guess, great minds think alike?"

Rose pointed her finger at me and raised her eyebrows. "Don't you say another word. It's just how we both showed up, we didn't do it on purpose."

"How did the book sale go?"

"I bought about a hundred books," Rose said.

"How much did you spend?"

"About $415."

"That much? I thought you were going to stop at $250."

"Daddy, the stuff was really good. I bought twelve first edition novels. If you put them on your website you'll recoup your money from them alone."

"Where are they now?"

"I took them to the bookstore and put them by the back door."

"Okay, I'll go through them tomorrow."

"When are you going to have time?" asked Rose.

"You're right. I forgot I invited you and Louisa for brunch tomorrow. I'll do it tomorrow night."

"What do you mean tomorrow night?" Louisa asked. "You have a date tomorrow."

I gave her a scowl. "Louisa, I only take that tone from Rose."

"You can't cancel on Sally," Rose said.

"How do you two know about my date?"

"Sally walked by the bookstore and told me."

"It's going to be busy here tomorrow night too," I said. "I need to work."

"Come on, Dad. That's bullshit," said Rose.

The pearls around Rose's neck once belonged to her great grandmother. They hung down askew because the strand was caught on the top button of her dress at the back of her neck. When I stepped beside her and released them with my fingers, they fell and hung straight down.

"Look at you. You can't even accessorize correctly without your father."

"Thank God you're here."

"I never told you Sally's name, honey. How do you know about her?"

"When Louisa and I dropped the books off this afternoon she was there."

"She bought five books," Louisa said.

"She didn't come in for books," Rose said.

"What did she want?"

"She wanted to know if you were the same Joe Green in the newspaper article."

"We never talked about the bistro," I said.

"You came this close to humiliating her," Louisa said.

"How did I do that?"

"She was going to serve spaghetti and meatballs and sangria," said Louisa. "Serving that cuisine to a big operator like you is a paltry dowry."

"What do you mean a paltry dowry?"

"When a prince comes to call, you want to show off like a princess, not like a peasant."

"It's just a date."

"Lucky for you we set her straight," said Rose.

"She's not a stalker is she?"

"No, Daddy," said Rose. "But we got her to change the menu, the music and probably her outfit too."

"We told her to lose the glasses," Louisa added.

"She's feeling a lot better now," said Rose.

"And I suppose I owe you both a thank you?"

"Don't worry, Joe. We got your back," Louisa said.

"And bring a good bottle of California wine," Rose said. "Not that cheap French Beaujolais you like to drink."

"Rose, stop parenting your father."

Stella walked to the host stand. Looking at the clock, she said, "Okay, girls. It's five o'clock and there are people outside. It's time to unlock the doors."

"I'll do it," Louisa said.

"Where's Cosmo?" Stella asked.

"Beats the hell out of me," I said.

Chapter 6

My shoulder rubbed against the white plaster wall as we ascended the narrow, dimly lit staircase to my apartment. Three of us were in a row. Aidan was on the right side, I was on the left side. Cosmo was in the middle.

Together we weighed over five hundred pounds and I worried it was too much for the rickety wooden steps. Any minute, I feared, they might collapse beneath our weight and we'd all be flat on our asses on the basement floor amid broken wood and plaster.

Cosmo was barely conscious. His arms were slung over our shoulders. Aidan and I were carrying him to my living room couch. It was our only option. since he was too drunk to send home.

"Come on, Cosmo." I shook him a little. "Pick up your feet. We're halfway there," I said.

Suddenly, he took a deep breath and started to gag. Aidan, fearful Cosmo was going to vomit again, slipped out from underneath his arm and jumped two steps down. Cosmo's dead weight was too much to shoulder by myself, and we tumbled into the wall where Aidan had previously stood. Were it not for the boy standing behind us and pushing his hands against our backs for support, we'd have tumbled to the bottom.

"God damn it, Aidan."

"Hey, it's bad enough I have to smell that barf breath in my face. There's no way I'm letting Cosmo hurl on my neck."

"Relax. He's already puked up everything in his stomach. This is just dry heaves."

"I'm a sympathetic vomiter, Dad. If I have to smell that stink again I'm going to puke and this time you're cleaning it up."

"Breathe through your mouth."

Cosmo let out another retch. Nothing came up.

"Let's sit him down on the stairs for a second. He needs a rest."

"Why did I have to clean up his puke? Why didn't you ask Fernando, the dishwasher?"

"Because you're the bar back and he puked on the bar."

"If I ever got this shitty you'd kick my ass."

"And you'd deserve it."

"Why is it okay for Cosmo to get drunk and stupid and not me?"

"Because I don't have to answer to his mother."

"Sometimes it seems that like he's more of a son to you than me."

"Quit your bitching. If he's anything, he's the prodigal son."

"The what?"

"You've never heard of the prodigal son? It's in the Bible."

"The Bible? Where would I ever see a Bible? Your fear of Catholicism is as intense as Mom's fear of Judaism. We've hardly ever been to a church or a temple and I'll bet there's not a Bible in either one of your houses."

"One day you might thank us for it."

Cosmo sat down on the stairs with his eyes closed and his mouth open. I put my hand on his shoulder when he started to fall forward. Another dry heave was on the way.

Aidan's cell phone rang. He grabbed it from his pocket and looked at the caller I.D. "Oh, shit. It's Mom. It's 1:15. I'm out past my curfew."

"Tell her you're still working. Don't say anything about Cosmo."

"Hi Mom, I'll be home…"

Cosmo lurched forward in anothbreater retch but this time something shot out of his mouth.

"I got to call you back, Mom." Aidan put the phone in his pocket. "What the fuck, Cosmo? You just barfed on my new kicks."

A collection of white business cards fell out of his breast pocket when he fell forward. I bent down and, picked them up.

"Let's get him upstairs, already," I said.

We laid him down on the couch. I took off his glasses and put them on the coffee table. Aidan went into the bathroom to clean off his shoes. He emerged with a garbage pail and placed it beside Cosmo.

"Glad this night is over," Aidan said.

"Cosmo was good right up until the minute we locked the door," I said. "Let's keep this our little secret."

"Secret?" Aidan stared right at Cosmo, laid out straight on the couch. "Cosmo, you bitch, you're never living this down."

"Want a piece of advice, father to son? Put it in your back pocket. One of these days he's going to get tough on you about the G-Spot or being mean to your mother or for not doing something right behind the bar. That's when you should throw it back in his face. Consider it a trump card."

"Right now I'm so pissed off I want to tell everybody just to humiliate him."

"There's a bottle of beer in the refrigerator. Go get it. I'll split it with you."

"Good. After tonight, I deserve a beer."

Aidan opened the beer and divided the contents into two juice glasses. Then he sat down beside me at the kitchen table.

"Did you make good money tonight?" I asked.

"Oh, yeah. You saw how crazy it was at the bar. But Cosmo was so busy being Cosmo that I had to work extra hard just to keep up."

"He certainly was the Spotlight Kid tonight."

"It seems the more money you make the higher the stress level is. I'd have preferred less money and less stress."

"Didn't you have any fun?"

"No, Cosmo had all the fun. Did you notice all the boobalicious babes at the bar in tonight? If he hadn't been so drunk, he could have had any one of them."

I pulled the business cards out of my pocket and tossed them on the table. There were six in all. "I guess that's what these are all about."

"One woman had him autograph the newspaper article," Aidan said.

"In my day we called them groupies."

"These days we call them whores," Aidan said. "There was a steady stream of them all night."

His cell phone rang again.

"Oh shit, I forgot to call Mom back."

"Here, give it to me." I answered the phone. "Hi Joannie. We're just about done. I'm putting him in a cab. He'll be home in fifteen minutes."

When we finished the beer I walked Aidan down to the street. At the corner, I hailed a cab, slipped the driver a ten dollar bill and told him to take Aidan straight home. Then I walked back into the bar and poured myself a glass of Macallan 18. Back upstairs in the apartment, Cosmo was right where I left him.

With Aidan gone and Cosmo out cold, there was no one to tell stories to except Louis the tortoise, busy munching romaine. The little brown dude, named after my grandfather, was usually a good listener.

I pulled a chair up beside the pen and sat down.

"Hey Louis," I said, rubbing the ridges of his shell. "I'm going to tell you all about my night," I said. And then I began.

When we unlocked the restaurant door at five, one patron was waiting outside. He was a small, dark haired, Indian man in his forties who looked like an accountant. He was no taller than five-foot-four. weighing about a hundred-thirty pounds. He made his way in an unsteady gait into the bistro and was the first person at the bar. He had a hooked nose, thin hair, a weak chin and a nervous demeanor. Since Cosmo had yet to arrive I walked behind the bar and greeted him.

"Good evening, sir. What can I pour you?"

"I didn't come here to drink. I just wanted to see Cosmo Della Rocca."

"Well, I'm afraid he's just a little late for work but…"

Just then Cosmo burst through the door. He walked behind the bar, grabbed his apron and stood in front of me.

"Don't say it, I already know, I'm such an asshole. Damn, of all nights to be late. But I just kept having these amazing dreams and I couldn't wake up. Sorry, Joe. It won't happen again."

"This gentleman came in to see you," I said.

Cosmo wasn't sure what to expect. He squared his shoulders, reached out and shook his hand.

"Hello, I'm Cosmo."

"I just want to say that you shouldn't ever feel guilty about shooting those kids," the man said, still holding Cosmo's hand.

"What's your name?' asked Cosmo asked after a long pause.

"Depok."

"What makes you say that, Depok?"

"Those were the same criminals that held me up at gunpoint six years ago. I recognized their picture in the newspaper. I was with my wife and they grabbed at her. They beat me with their gun and kicked me when I fell down. They stole my watch, my wallet and rings. Because of the blow to my head, I still haven't regained my sense of smell.

"You know on TV when somebody gets hit on the head, they wake up the next day and everything is fine," he continued. "But I was on disability for two years. I'm still afraid of Black people and my wife is ashamed of me. I know a lot of people are going to talk badly about you. But you should know not everybody feels that way. So I came to tell you how much satisfaction I gained from reading about your return here in this morning's paper."

"Can I buy you a drink, Depok?"

"No, thank you. I don't drink. I said what I came to say and now I'll be going."

That little exchange was probably one of two-dozen meaningful exchanges Cosmo had that evening. But because it was the first, I'd guess it was the most meaningful.

Ironically, two hours later, when the place was packed, two of the Black toughs who provoked the drama strutted through the door. They were the ones in charge of watching Thomas's back while he confronted Cosmo at the bar.

There was something brazen about the way they walked in. They were dressed in the same suits and ties as before. But because it was so crowded no one took much notice, except me and Cosmo.

I couldn't blame them for returning. Like me, they had been the supporting cast in this drama. I suppose they just wanted to bask in the spotlight they helped create.

They found two stools at the bar and sat down. Kennedy the cop stood at the kitchen door flirting with Anya and didn't see them come in. But despite the crowded bar, Cosmo noticed them immediately and slapped two shot glasses down in front of them.

"Gentlemen, nice to see you back. My name is Cosmo Della Rocca. What's yours?"

"Quincy."

"Tesell," said the other.

He shook their hands.

"I know you guys probably prefer Hennessey and Coke, but since it's nearly the anniversary of the day I shot Gaston Thomas, and Dominique Matthews, I think we should celebrate. You know, that Gaston was a bad motherfucker. He had the look, know what I'm saying, that look of hate in his eyes. It could turn your blood into ice water. When I confronted him that night on the street my hands were shaking. Yeah, that Gaston was a bad motherfucker."

Quincy and Tesell, sat stone faced. Cosmo reached up to the top shelf and grabbed a half full crystal bottle.

"An occasion like this calls for the good stuff. Check it out. It's French brandy, Louis the XIII. It's a hundred years old. I'm sure you guys have had it before. When they made this stuff, Woodrow Wilson was President of the United States and the flag was missing a lot of stars. But what the hell. We only live once, right? Let's drink it."

Cosmo poured out a glassful for each of them and one for himself.

Buying a shot of hundred-year-old brandy was not what Quincy and Tesell intended. They glanced down the bar at Kennedy in his uniform. I put myself in their shoes and guessed what they were thinking: Is Cosmo playing us? What if we drink the liquor and cannot can't pay? Will the cop arrest us?

But Cosmo exhibited such high energy, was so emotionally present they were just perplexed.

"Fellows, let's drink a toast to Gaston," Cosmo said. He cast his eyes to the ceiling as if the dead man's ghost was looking down at them. He held up his glass. "God damn it, Gaston, I'm glad you're dead."

Quincy and Tesell reluctantly held up theirs. They all clinked and Cosmo took a long swig. The two Black kids held their drinks midair, not knowing what to do.

"Damn, that's some good shit, fellows." Cosmo said, taking another big sip.

"Did you know Gaston Thomas? He was a little older than you guys."

Quincy spoke. "I never met the nigga'. But my brother used to roll with him in high school. He was into some bad shit."

Cosmo scrunched up his face. "Did I forget to tell you guys that those drinks were on me?"

They cracked a small smile and took a long sip.

"Damn, that is some good shit," Quincy said.

Kennedy now recognized the two of them and walked over. Though sitting on bar stools they towered over the diminutive cop.

"Damn fellows," Cosmo said. "It's Saturday night. How about one more for the road? Kennedy, you're off the clock. Have a shot with us."

"Breaking out the good stuff, huh Cosmo? Don't mind if I do," he said.

Kennedy took a seat next to Tesell. "What are we drinking to?"

"Gaston Thomas," said Cosmo.

"To Gaston," said Kennedy.

They all sipped at it. This time slowly.

"Fellows, I got to go," Cosmo said to the two of them. "I got thirsty people here. Come back again when we can talk."

Sitting at the bar beside a uniformed D.C. cop made Quincy and Tesell visibly uncomfortable. I smelt the scent of marijuana when I passed by them. So they finished their brandy and politely walked out the door.

Once they were gone I walked behind the bar.

"Did you recognize those guys?" Cosmo asked.

"Yeah, those guys played back-up to Tyrone Thomas and Reverend Battle's son last night. Are you okay?"

"Whew. I'm glad that's over," Cosmo said.

"How did it go?"

"Very well," he said. Then he handed me the bar bill and said, "Do me a favor, Joe. Comp this one for me."

My jaw dropped when I looked at the receipt. It was for seven shots of Louis XIII, which with tax totaled $770.00.

He put his hand on my shoulder. "Thanks, man. You're a lifesaver."

Rose came up to me. "Mom called. She needs a table for two in 30 minutes."

"On Saturday night at eight. Is she nuts or something?"

"No, Daddy, she's not nuts. She is a professional lobbyist. Her job is to get people to do for her what they really don't want to do at all."

"Is she bringing Senator Copley in again?"

"She didn't say who she was coming with."

"Tell Stella to figure something out."

"I'll take care of it," Rose said.

As Rose headed back to the front, two of Cosmo's old regulars walked through the door. It was Eli Holbrook, a sixty-year-old lobbyist with liberal ties, and his wife Jane. Eli ran a K Street lobbying firm and was a former associate of Joannie's.

He was a handsome old dog from Kentucky who parted his thick gray hair on the left side and sported a gray goatee. His wife was a thin, raven haired beauty in the old days. But currently, her pallor had the taint of cigarette smoke. When Stella saw Eli and Jane Holbrook at the door, she nudged me. "Joe, look who's here. It's Mrs. Drunk-Drunk. Aren't you lucky? You have a date for the evening."

"Behave yourself."

"Eli, haven't seen you in a long time. How's business?"

"Business is good. We just landed two trade association contracts. You'll be seeing a lot more of me now."

"Good, the twins are going to college this fall and I need your money. You already said hello to Rose. Aidan's behind the bar. Make sure you say hello to him too."

"I saw him last week. Joannie had a little barbecue at the house. He was there with this hot little blonde named Amanda." He paused and raised his eyebrows. "We should do so well."

"Maybe in our next lives."

Eli winked. "Loved the story in the Post today. I didn't know Cosmo was out. How's he doing?"

"He's trying to move on."

"Can't wait to see him."

"Don't let me stop you."

The sight of Eli walking into the bar got Cosmo a little misty. He walked around the bar so he could get a good hug.

Eli ordered a bottle of Don Perignon and popped the cork himself. Then with a small crowd gathered around him, he clinked a spoon against his champagne glass until he owned the crowd's attention. When the chatter died down and all eyes were on him, he offered a toast to Cosmo, which ended with, "Here's to a fresh start and a long, happy and healthy life."

The crowd applauded and Eli poured champagne for his wife, a little more for himself, one for Cosmo and a few others standing nearby.

Joannie walked in. To my surprise her Saturday night date was Jack. She had a black skirt and a tight white cotton top that showed off her seven thousand dollar bosoms. Her long hair was tied up in a ponytail behind her head. Her mother's gold emerald necklace hung around her neck. She looked good. Jack, per usual, had his baseball cap turned backwards.

"Me and Jack were bored and since everyone else was here, we wanted to come too."

"Go say hi to Cosmo," I said. "Eli Holbrook is here too. I'll hang out with Jack until you're done."

"Thanks," said Joannie, "I'll only be a couple of minutes."

Stella led us to a table. I sat down with Jack.

"It's Saturday night. Why aren't you out with your buddies?"

"Mom was bored and she talked me into going to a movie."

"What did you see?"

"I don't even remember, some love story. Dad, you've got to talk to her. With Rose and Aidan out and about all the time she's focusing all her attention on me. I can't take it anymore."

"What did she do this time?"

"I was showing Ted and Harry my new BB gun. I don't know what happened. The gun must have accidentally gone off. A BB ricocheted off the floor, bounced off her bedroom door and hit her right in the butt. She ran into my room with a rolled up newspaper in her hands and started hitting me."

"Did she hurt you?"

"No, but Dad, she was butt naked and she didn't even stop when she realized my friends were there watching. It was really embarrassing."

"Well, remember she grew up in a big family where there was no such thing as privacy."

"You've got to talk to her."

"I can't. You'll just get yourself in more trouble for hanging out the dirty laundry."

"I don't care. It's now a big joke at school now. Phillip Langford came up to me the other day in the lunch room. In front of all my friends, he peeks inside his shirt pocket and starts goofing me. 'Hey Jack, got any nude pictures of your mother?'

"'No!' I shouted. So then he looks at me and says, 'Wanna buy some?' Dad, everybody laughed at me."

"I don't know what to tell you, Jack. Let me think about it. In the meantime ask Aidan to kick Langford's ass."

"Kick whose ass?" asked Joannie, returning to the table with a glass of champagne.

"Nobody you know," I said. "I got to go back to work."

"Eli just ordered another bottle of champagne," Joannie said.

"It's good to see him again. Rose will be done in about twenty minutes. When you order dinner, get something for her and Louisa too."

"What about Aidan?"

"He's working. I'll feed him later."

I gave Jack a wink and excused myself.

At about 10 o'clock, two boys entered the restaurant looking for Rose and Louisa. They were well-groomed white kids, wearing Abercrombie and Fitch.

Rose and Louisa were eating at the table with Joannie and Jack. They didn't see them come in. But Stella recognized them immediately. I was busy in the kitchen, so I sent Kennedy over to check their driver's licenses. At my request he also gave them a breathalyzer. They passed.

When Rose and Louisa noticed Kennedy harassing their dates, they rushed to the door, grabbed their belongings at the host stand and ran out the door before Joannie and I had a chance to introduce ourselves.

As kitchens around town started closing for the night, waiters and waitresses from a half dozen other places came in.

There were three employees from the Old Ebbit Grill, four from Runyon's and two from the Palm. They all demanded that Cosmo do a round of kamikaze shooters with them just like in the old days.

Three times I saw Cosmo line up about a dozen shot glasses on the bar and dole them full from a big silver shaker. He even called me over to do one with them. I thought it was a great gesture until he made the formal announcement that I had volunteered to pay for the round, resulting in the loudest moment of the evening.

Louis the tortoise listened stoically to my entire play by play. But he cut me short. He'd had enough romaine and grew bored with my story. He slowly ambled back underneath the big electric blanket for the evening.

"Well, thanks for listening, Louis," I. said. "I guess it's time for me to retire too."

I put the juice glasses in the dishwasher and tossed the beer bottle. I found a blanket and threw it on top of Cosmo.

Picking up the business cards from the coffee table, I thought to put them back in Cosmo's shirt pocket. But I was curious so I started looking through them.

One was from Theresa Pritchert, who worked for Bell and Coy, a local public relations firm. Another was from Beverly Dean, an editor at the National Review. Mary Rizzo worked at the Department of Housing and Urban Development, another was from Elizabeth Garvin, a computer engineer with Microsoft. On her card, with a felt marker, she had written "the cute one with the short red hair and the purple v-neck sweater".

I recognized the last one. It was Joannie's.

Chapter 7

"You can't break that date." Rose said. Her tone was firm but she wasn't looking at me. Her eyes were on the skillet of eggs, salmon and onions on the stove in my Mintwood Place kitchen. A plate of bacon, on top of paper towels, lay beside her on the counter. Cosmo, Louisa and I sat at the butcher-block countertop in the middle of the kitchen sipping coffee and watching Rose cook breakfast.

When not verbalizing her protest, she banged plates and pans against hard surfaces.

"Daddy, you have no idea how important this is."

"Since when are you in charge of my love life?" I said.

"Somebody has to be in charge since you don't seem to be taking any initiative."

"Says who?"

"Says me."

"Why the sudden concern?"

"Who's going to take care of you and Jack next year when I go off to college? Who?"

"You are not my mother, you're my daughter. Why do you keep forgetting that?"

"You have no idea how much work I do around here, do you? Just wait until I'm gone and you're all going to find out."

"I never take you for granted, Rose. But sometimes it would be nice if you were gracious about it."

"Why is it too much to ask that one of my parents be in a normal relationship? What kind of role models are you offering your children?"

"Who'd want to be in a relationship with a guy with such a pushy daughter?" Cosmo asked.

"Sally Jones. And you stay out of this, Cosmo."

"How do you know?" I asked Rose.

"I know."

"Have you been talking to her about me?"

"Maybe."

"That makes me nervous. What exactly have you told her?"

"Nothing bad. Just the kind of stuff that girls want to know."

"Like what?"

"Like none of your business."

"If it's about me it is my business."

"Listen, you're always saying that America's fight against Kim Jong un and Vladimir Putin is a waste of time because the only battle worth fighting in life is the battle of the sexes." Rose stirred the scramble violently. "I was trying to give her an idea of what she was up against."

"You told her that?"

"Absolutely."

"You can just forget about any date with her now. This all seems like manipulation."

Cosmo sat beside Louisa nursing his hangover. Every time Rose clanked something on the counter, he winced.

"Rose, will you please stop doing that?"

"Cosmo, it's not my fault you can't hold your load. I hope you learned your lesson last night, Mr. Big Shot."

"Hey, Cosmo. She's right," I said. "We have over a hundred reservations tonight. That's rare for a Sunday. You better get your shit together. We're in for another big night and it's all because of you."

"I got to do it again?" Cosmo asked.

"Yes. We're going to ride this horse till it drops."

"Daddy, don't go to work. Your staff can handle it."

"I like being at the restaurant on busy nights."

"You might like Sally too if you gave her a chance."

Rose snarled, her spatula pointing at Cosmo. "This is all your fault."

Louisa turned her attention to Cosmo. "You look like you could use some more coffee."

"Thanks, Louisa. You're a doll."

"And what am I, chopped liver?" Rose shouted.

Cosmo turned to Rose and shouted back. "Right now you're a petulant little teenager who could use a good…"

"A good what, Cosmo? Daddy, are you going to let him talk to me like that?"

I gave Cosmo a look that was unmistakable: Don't poke the bear!

When Rose set her mind to something she pushed her agenda relentlessly. Then she pushed some more. Then, just when you thought you'd seen it all, there'd be a few sneaky little pushes for good measure when you let your guard down. Only then did she stop, usually within seconds of me screaming. That's the way it was with her.

When Joannie and I split up Rose took responsibility for me, her mother and her brothers. Friends told me that it was unfair to place that burden on her. After all, she was only nine years old. But that's what happened.

With her parents consumed by divorce anger, Rose became the only normal parent. And that's why I tolerated her sharp tongue. Her diligence to matters of family gave her the right.

"Nobody appreciates me around here. How am I supposed to go away to college knowing that the fate of my little brother Jack is in the hands of nincompoops? Maybe I should just go to the University of Maryland or George Washington University."

"Don't even think about it," I said. "You're going away to college and that's final. You need to get away from your parents to find out just who you are all by yourself. And don't try to convince your mother to stay in town either because if you do, I'm not paying."

"You don't take anything I say seriously, do you?"

I decided to throw Rose a bone, a minor concession, otherwise brunch was ruined. So this is what I said.

"Okay, here's what I'm going to do. Instead of going to Sally's for dinner, I'll call her up, tell her how busy the bistro is and invite her in for a late dinner when everything settles down. But listen to me. Here is what I am not going to do. I am not going to go out on a date and leave my place of business on a busy night just to appease you."

"Fine."

"Don't say fine to me unless it really is fine."

"Fine."

She walked to the phone and dialed Sally's number. How did she know it? When the ringing started she handed it to me. With Cosmo, Rose and Louisa staring, I found myself tongue-tied.

"Hold on, Sally," I said. I put my hand over the receiver. I whispered, "I think I'll take this call in the living room."

Convincing Sally to come down to the bistro was easy. We agreed on 8:30. The kitchen closed at nine on Sunday and we'd soon have the place to ourselves.

Sunday nights at the Bistro proceed at a slower pace than Saturdays. People are more circumspect about food and wine since they work Monday mornings. And while the reservations weren't as numerous as Saturday night, the increase stemming from the newspaper article was an unexpected boon. In business, there's nothing better than good cash flow.

I only recognized a few customers. One was Dave Paulus, ace reporter, who made a habit of taking his Sunday dinners at the bar.

"What are you doing here, Joe?" Paulus asked. "You don't usually work Sundays."

"Just watching Cosmo's back. Plus, I have a date coming in."

"Anybody I know?"

"Doubt it. By the way, that article was great. I always knew you could write well, but it's a little different when you're a part of the story."

"In the past two days I got more e-mails about it than I could read. It even made the Post's on-line edition."

"I'm booked solid for the next five nights. Thank you."

"Even Monday night?"

"Absolutely. Monday is one of my best nights. Everybody's back in town and they're looking for a good meal and a little action."

"Sounds like you hit the cash register."

"That's exactly what Stella said. I only hope that Cosmo can stand up to the stress."

"He doesn't seem to be having too much trouble right now," said Paulus, raising his eyebrows. It was a subtle reference to the three women who came into the bar individually to check him out.

"Oh, God. Look who just walked in… Mata Hari." Paulus chuckled. "Cosmo's drawing the femme fatale from all over town."

I laughed and eagerly turned to the door to see whom he was referring to. I didn't recognize her at first. Her hair was down and she wasn't wearing glasses.

"Her?"

"Oh, yes," Paulus nodded.

"That's my date."

He drew in a breath and blushed a little. "It's late, Joe. I've got to go."

"Wait a minute. Where do you get off making a crack like that and running away?"

"Forget it. You know what a misogynist I am."

He looked down the bar and called out. "Cosmo. I'll take the check."

"It's on me," I said.

"Thanks."

Paulus finished his drink, left a ten dollar tip on the bar, then reached for the blazer that was hanging on the back of his bar stool. Calling a quick goodbye to Cosmo, he walked out the door. I watched carefully as he passed by Sally. They exchanged glances but no recognition.

Mata Hari? I couldn't remember who that was.

"Hey Cosmo?" He walked over. "Who was Mata Hari?"

"I think she was a Paris stripper accused of spying for the Germans during World War One."

"Are you sure?" I asked.

"It's either that or a fish from the Pacific Ocean."

"No, that's mahi mahi."

"Want me to go look it up on my cell phone?"

"I'll do it later."

I saw Sally standing beside Stella and Rose at the door.

Sally wore a long brown raincoat but it wasn't raining. God, I hoped she wasn't some Sunday school prude. After all, she came from the Missouri Bible Belt. I walked up to the door and greeted them.

"And don't let him con you into thinking that he's some sort of tough guy, either," Rose said. "If you want to see how tough he really is, watch a Disney movie with him. He always cries at the end."

I ignored Rose and turning to Sally said, "Hi, Sally. Wasn't sure you'd show."

"I spent the day at the office."

"Let me take your coat."

"Thank you."

She unzipped her raincoat, revealing a loose fitting black skirt extending beneath her knees and a long purple cardigan sweater made of thick wool in a loosely knitted weave which clung to her body. The five black buttons on her black blouse were all buttoned up. Despite her great rack, there was no cleavage showing and I was grateful.

Cleavage was a big joke at the bistro. On summer nights there were so many partially exposed breasts hanging out of the décolletage of expensive dresses that it had become a running gag.

Women showcasing their breasts were more apt to foment ridicule from my staff than awe. Of course, as men we loved to joke about it with lines like, "Look at that babe. She's got a balcony you could recite Shakespeare from." Or, "Check out table 38," which was not a reference to a specific table but to prestigious bosoms.

So I was happy that Sally didn't embarrass me like that in front of my staff, since the last thing I wanted to hear was Shameem or Cosmo surreptitiously mentioning table 38 with a straight face while I was sitting having dinner with Sally.

I sat her at table 7 located at the window. It afforded a view of 18th Street, now lit up with street lights, while also offering a full view of the bar crowd which was thinning out.

I brought a bottle of merlot to the table. It was from the winery of Francis Ford Coppola, director of "Apocalypse Now," and "The Godfather." I pulled out the cork and poured her a glass. She noticed the label.

"I can remember the time Coppola got up to accept the Academy Award for best director," Sally said. "He rambled on in front of the camera with some idiotic nonsense. He was so high on pot or cocaine or Quaaludes that he actually embarrassed himself at his finest moment."

"Fortunately, he's better at making wine than holding his drugs," I said.

She turned her head to scope out the crowd. And in that time I took the opportunity to look at her closely. It looked as if she had used curlers earlier in the day because there was a shape and dimension to her hair I had not seen before. She had a strong chin; a button for a nose. I once saw big green eyes like hers on a Siamese cat.

"Well, this is certainly a beautiful place," she said. "I can't believe that during all our previous conversations you've never mentioned it before. Most men would have bragged about it at the first opportunity. Why did you hold back?"

I shrugged. "It just never came up."

Looking behind the bar at Cosmo, she said, "Is that the man of the hour?"

"Yes, that's Cosmo."

"Good looking young man. No wonder so many single woman are sitting in front of him. He can have his pick of any one of them."

"Think so?"

"My God, yes. The men in this town are not exactly known for their virility. Half of them are bookworms. The rest are egomaniacs. But here you have a man who stared evil in the face, fought back and paid the price for his actions with prison. That's a sexy story."

"I never thought about it like that."

"I apologize if I seem too romantic. Must be all of those cheap novels I buy at your bookstore."

"I liked your comment about D.C. men."

"Why?"

"About two weeks ago one of the Undersecretaries of the Navy was at the bar by himself. I had to cut him off because he got drunk and stupid. Right before I put him in a cab he turned to me, and slurring his words, said, 'I'm really an asshole. But I always hoped that if I achieved power nobody would notice.'"

"The stress of his job was probably tearing at him," she said. "I've seen it many times."

"What exactly do you do?"

"I work on Capitol Hill."

"Dave Paulus, the reporter who wrote that article about Cosmo, recognized you when you came in."

"Was that Dave Paulus?"

I paused for a moment. "You know it was."

"What did he say?"

"He called you Mata Hari."

"Mata Hari? Why, I don't even dance."

"Is there something you're not telling me?"

"Now, Joe. Come on. You can't expect a girl to reveal all her secrets on the first date, can you?"

"I own a bar, Sally. I'm used to getting played. But I get a little prickly when my children are involved."

"Oh, I forgot, you don't trust women. Rose told me."

That line really made me mad, but Rose was still at the door so I said nothing.

"Do you think I'm out to get you, Joe?"

"Are you?"

"You might give me the benefit of the doubt."

"And just what is that doubt?" I asked.

"I'm here to protect you?"

"From what?"

"Facts."

"What facts?"

"Such as the reason Cosmo shot that second kid in the back was to retrieve the documents the kid stole from him which would have gotten the two of you in a lot of trouble. That a convicted Arab terrorist, Ali Bin Hassan, was Cosmo's cell mate and that you met with him regularly."

"I lent him books," I said.

"Ali has been in and out of Afghanistan six times."

"Anything else?"

"There are suggestions that criminals launder money through your two businesses, that you're going to host a dinner in your Potomac Room next week for representatives of governments unfriendly to the United States, that you have several undocumented workers in your kitchen and that your ex-wife is a former associate of a lobbyist convicted of fraud."

"Is this what you did at work today?" I asked.

"Yes."

"Are you recording this conversation?" I asked.

"Why would I do that?"

"None of this is true, Sally. You're wasting your time."

"Am I? Joe, they let Cosmo out early on purpose. He's enjoyed all sorts of freedom in the last month, freedoms that he cherishes. Don't you see? You fucked yourself. You were so good to him. He loves his new found freedom so much that he's never going back behind bars. What do you think he'd do if we found a reason to send him back in jail? Do you think he'd remain silent? I think the anguish of being locked up again would be too much. Perhaps he might say, I took the fall the first time. Now it's Joe Green's turn."

'I'll take my chances with Cosmo."

She stared at me for several seconds and then let out a soft, condescending laugh. In her mind I was the guy she had by the short hairs.

"Let me tell you about my people," she said. "We like to be the smartest guys in the room. When we're not the smartest guys in the room it tends to embarrass us. We don't like to be embarrassed. You know stuff that we don't. Stuff that would make us smarter."

"Like what?"

"People, contacts, supply chains and a host of other secrets. And you are going to tell us or we'll make your life miserable."

"I think you've got me confused with someone else."

"Look at it from our point of view. Next week, you, Cosmo and Ali Bin Hassan, three vulnerable guys, are all going to be together. We're going to be here too. Somebody is going to talk. Maybe all three of you are going to talk. That would be best. But understand this, you're all going to be squeezed."

Now I wanted her out of my restaurant, but I didn't want to make a scene. so I stood up and bowed in her direction.

"It was very nice of you to come down, tonight. Rose will get your coat."

I turned and headed to the back of the bistro. I didn't look back.

Upstairs in my apartment, the Washington Nationals were playing the Los Angeles Dodgers on ESPN. I watched an inning and a half.

When Ruthie the Tortoise came out from underneath the electric blanket, I stared into her eyes and had a well-balanced temper tantrum. I call it well-balanced because it was angry enough to vent but not so violent as to scare the Russian reptile back into her shell.

"You know, Ruthie, it's bad enough that politics intrudes into family life with Joannie's job stress, but now I'm getting it from my dates. Can you believe the cheek of that bitch? She comes into both my places of business, manipulates my daughter and thinks she knows me. What a bunch of bullshit. Women in this town suck. Fuck Washington and fuck that head tripper, Sally Jones."

I walked back downstairs to the bistro. Rose sat at table 7 with Sally, who didn't look ready to leave.

Stella joined me at the host stand. She wore a big smile and pointed herself in Sally's direction. "Gee, Joe, I never figured you for a chubby-chaser."

"What do you mean chubby chaser?"

"Take a look."

"You think she's chubby?"

"She's three steps away from a BBW," Stella said.

"Don't make fun of her."

"Okay."

"After all," I said, "it ain't the meat, it's the motion."

"I'm Cuban. I think I know that better than you."

I sent Stella home early. A few chores commanded my attention but I did return to table 7.

"Hey, thanks for baby-sitting Sally for me, Rose."

"You're welcome."

"Is Cosmo gone?"

"Yes." Rose said.

"Honey, it's late and you have school tomorrow."

"Okay, Daddy."

She stood, kissed me on the cheek, shook hands with Sally and walked out the door as if she were the most obedient daughter in the world.

"I'm famished. Is it too late to eat?" Sally asked.

"The chef is gone. We'll have to cook for ourselves. Come on."

We walked through the kitchen door. I grabbed a few sea scallops from the walk-in cooler, dredged them in Japanese breadcrumbs and threw them on the griddle with a little oil. At the same time I dry-fried a rib eye steak. In a smaller pan, I reheated a little demi-glaze. I sent Sally to the pantry to make us a salad. I was happy not to talk to her.

She returned with one bowl of salad to share.

"How do you like your steak?"

"Medium rare," she said.

"At least you got that going for you."

"What do you mean?" She asked.

"My staff doesn't trust people who order their steak well done."

"Why?"

"The conventional wisdom is that if a guy doesn't know how to order a steak he probably doesn't know how to tip either."

"Is that true?"

"It's true around here. On parties of six or more, we give waiters the opportunity to add a twenty percent tip. If the host of the party orders a steak rare or medium rare they'll leave the gratuity off the check in hope of a bigger tip. But if he orders his steak medium well or well done, the twenty percent goes right on the bill."

"My God, I never thought my waiter was judging me by the way I eat my steak."

"When you've been dealing with the public for as long as we have, you learn little telltales like that."

The food was ready so we carried our plates back to the table, ate the dinner and sipped the wine in silence. Only when we finished did she speak.

"Joe," she said, "can I apologize? When I agreed to this date, I didn't know about the restaurant, Cosmo, any of the things mentioned in that newspaper article or about anything I mentioned earlier. My head is swimming from all of it and I'm sure I came on way too strong."

"Whom do you work for exactly?"

"The Senate Intelligence Committee. I'm the committee administrator and you're on our radar screen."

"Would you like some more wine?"

"Not to sound ungrateful, but I don't really like wine. Have you got any tequila?"

"Come to think of it I'd rather have a Scotch."

I stood, grabbed the empty plates and walked behind the bar throwing them in a bus tub. I poured us both a drink and handed it to her from the bartender's side of the bar. She sat down on a stool and smiled.

"What's the matter?"

"Your daughter thinks she knows all about your shadow. She really doesn't know the half of it, does she?"

"She's usually a better sentinel. I'm surprised you got by her."

"Don't worry, Joe. I'm used to keeping secrets."

"We had an interesting exchange a little while ago, me and you, about how the rigors of a D.C. job can eat a man up. Does that also pertain to women?"

"Why do you ask?"

"Because you're not married, you have no children and it seems that your whole life revolves around your work, which you're reluctant to discuss."

"It's not my work that kept me from family life, it's my heart."

"Don't be a drama queen."

She sat very still for a moment. Then she let go of her tequila and unbuttoned the top two buttons of her sweater. A four-inch surgical scar hid deep in her cleavage appeared.

"I meant to say that I have a heart condition which limits my physical ability," she said. "I had heart surgery at the age of twenty-four. Doctors were afraid that a pregnancy would kill me so they tied my tubes at the same time. I had a stint put in my heart a year ago January. I was hospitalized several days last month because my doctors decided to change my medication and were worried about the consequences. They hooked me up to a monitor for two days."

"When men find out the extent of my problems they usually run away," she said. "No one wants to get stuck with an invalid. I can't blame them. Men want to be with active, robust women who can keep up."

"What do you mean keep up?"

"I can't hike or jog or walk long distances. Any activity that causes me to be vertical for long periods of time is difficult."

"How about horizontal activity?"

"It's never been a problem."

A dreamy little smile creased her lips. "You really don't trust me, do you?"

"My grandfather was from the old-country. He used to tell this joke: Know how you say fuck you in Yiddish?"

"How?"

"Trust me."

"I'm not actually looking for your trust," she said.

"What are you looking for?"

"To be totally honest, I'm lonely and very horny. My steady date has been out of the country for the past two months and I'm pre-menstrual."

"I have a small apartment upstairs," I said.

Chapter 8

What I remember most is the contempt I felt for Sally Jones as I led her upstairs. She framed my life so all my secrets seemed sinister. She shared confidences with Rose that excluded me and even alleged that her U.S. Senate committee wielded enough power to ruin me.

When she arrived I expected all the plot points of a Harlequin Romance, her alleged genre of choice. But I soon found myself entangled in the tension-filled plot of a thriller. It seemed like a reckoning.

Over the years I've taken responsibility for my anger issues so they would not be inflicted upon my children, employees or customers.

Their origins stem from a white lower middle class Jersey neighborhood, which subscribed to a culture that was more about heat than light, where histrionics were held in higher regard than rationalism, where men defined themselves by their self-hate, and women were the enemy.

It took me years to rise above that nonsense. But just provoke me and it all comes back. Want to talk about the battle of the sexes? That's just what this was.

I did not rant or rave at Sally's provocations. Instead, I brought her upstairs for rough sex. How hard could I get and how much could she take. Let's see how frail your heart really is, bitch. That's the thought that ran through me.

About that heart surgery scar, it was unseen in the dark. Remember that lament about her precarious health? I didn't believe it. She acted more like a cougar than an invalid. So I fucked her in anger and I didn't give a damn about the consequences.

I'll skip the lurid details. But her sexual style wasn't about porn star action. It was about power and domination, which she commanded at the bistro table and submissively gave away in bed.

I was on top, inside her, my mouth on her mouth when she pulled her lips away from mine. A strange look came upon her face. "This isn't what you want," she declared. "What do you really want?"

It was the libidinal green light to bully her. And I did. If her heart gave out and she croaked in the sexual act no coroner could blame me since it was the work of two consenting adults. Perhaps then she'd be out of my hair.

Afterwards, we spooned, naked, laying on our sides with my hand cupping her breast, my chest pressed against her back, the front of my thighs against the back of her thighs. The down blanket at our waist was unnecessary. When she rolled over on her back I awoke.

Well, at least she's still breathing, I thought. The only death that occurred was what the French call the "petite morte," the little death.

The sun was up and memories of last night returned. I realized how recklessly I exposed myself to all the potential externalities that result when two people open their second chakra, the sexual chakra, to each other, including my careless decision to forgo a condom.

But then I remembered how perfectly my penis fit inside her, how well matched our bodies felt, and how, when I was on top, her eyes looked directly into mine, her mouth was right there at mine, how soft and wet were her kisses.

As she slept, the back of her left hand was dramatically upon her forehead with her palm open. That's when I noticed her bruised lip, which did not come from a kiss and the bite marks on her body, which would take a week to heal.

The roar of city bus engines through downtown blocks was punctuated by the application of airbrakes and the squeaking doors opening and closing for passengers. If you listened attentively you could also hear bird songs.

But those sounds seemed insignificant compared to the soft snoring of Sally Jones. Actually, it sounded more like purring, yet replete with all the implications of a Siren's call.

As a man of 50, I've got history with bad girls like Sally. They come along and as dangerous and as unsettling as they are, deep down, you fuck them anyway if only to catch a deeper glimpse of your own manhood.

While I did not trust her, I had this vague hope that as someone working on Capitol Hill for the government of the United States of America, she at least obeyed the law. But of course I couldn't be sure.

But while all these things went through my mind, I inhaled deeply and fell back to sleep.

A cell phone rang. I gently slipped away and began searching through the pile of clothes on the floor. I found it in the pocket of my pants, which lay underneath Sally's skirt, her sweater and her bra because my pants came off first.

I saw that the call was from Joannie. I debated whether or not to answer it. Perhaps I should just let her flow into voice mail but I clicked it just before the last ring.

"Joe, don't forget the kids have parent-teacher conferences this morning at eleven," Joannie said.

"Forget? When did you tell me?"

"I told you last week."

"No, you didn't."

"Of course I told you. It's today for Rose and Aidan at eleven."

"No, you didn't. I hate it when you pull this crap on me."

"You could take some responsibility and keep tabs on this stuff too."

"Fine, have the school send all the paperwork to me from now on."

"What's the matter? Can't you make it? Since they're in the same class I thought you could do both at the same time. Jack's at four o'clock. I can make it to Jack's this afternoon but I have a meeting at ten and I'm not going to make it for the twins' conference."

"Okay, I'll be there. But I saw Rose last night and she didn't mention they had the day off from school."

"Well, they do. Rose slept over at Louisa's house last night and Aidan slept at Tim's."

"What about Jack?"

"He stayed home with me last night."

"What's he doing today?"

"Isn't he at your house? He took the dog for a walk on his skateboard."

"I slept at the bistro last night."

"When he finds you're not home he'll probably come down to see you there."

"Yeah, probably."

"Will you be there for Jack's conference too?" Joannie asked.

"Yes, I'll see you there."

Sally awoke during the conversation. Jack might be on his way and I didn't want him catching me with my pants down. Suddenly the emotional and legal gray areas of our tryst dimmed before the moral obligations of parenthood.

"We better get dressed, Sally."

"Yeah, I don't want him to catch us like this."

We gathered up our clothes. That's when I noticed the rug burn on her tailbone.

"It's funny," she said, "as a young woman I hid my sexuality from my parents. Now I feel compelled to hide it from children."

"Sex is something young people and Hollywood movie stars enjoy, not me, or their mother."

"Most kids never quite get it into their heads that reckless abandon, usually spiked with alcohol, were component parts of their conception."

"Speaking of that, I better hide the liquor."

"Ohhhhh," she groaned, putting her hand to her forehead. Then she paused. "Wow, I'm a little hung over."

"Your lip's bruised too. You can probably cover it up with lipstick."

She laughed and showed me a goofy smile.

"You've studied the Kama Sutra haven't you?"

"Yes."

"I can always tell."

"Was it too much?"

"No."

When I heard Shortstop's paws climbing up the back stairs from the alley I knew Jack was seconds behind. Sally ran into the bathroom to fix her hair while I refolded the bed back into the couch and reordered the cushions.

Shortstop scratched at the door and barked enthusiastically. Sally slipped out of the bathroom as I reached for the doorknob and let my boy and his dog enter.

"Hi, Jack. I just found out you have the day off from school."

"Yeah, it's for parent-teacher conferences."

"That's what your mom said."

"Dad, I have to explain a few things to you before you go to school."

"You're not in any trouble, are you?"

"I think I am."

"Does your mother know?"

"Not yet."

His eyes turned to my guest on the couch.

"You remember Sally from the bookstore, don't you?"

"Sure. Hi, Sally. What are you doing here?"

"Sally just stopped by to pick up a book I ordered for her," I said. I reached for the first book on my desk and handed it to her in front of him. It was Richard Wilhelm's translation of the I Ching.

"Can we have breakfast?" Jack asked.

"Sure," I said. "Let's walk down to Clements."

"Can Sally come?"

"Sally probably has to get to work, Jack."

"Actually, I would love to come," she said.

"Alright," I said. "Let's go."

Then the phone rang again. Jack looked at the caller I.D.

"It's Rose," he said.

"Well, answer it."

"Hi, Rose. We're going to Clement's for breakfast. Want to come?"

Jack listened to Rose talk for a moment. Then he handed the phone to me.

"How'd do it go last night?" Rose asked.

"It went okay," I said.

Sally, suspecting that Rose inquired about our date, gave me the look of one who's been damned with faint praise.

"You buying breakfast?"

I tried to figure out a way to discourage Rose from coming along because Sally was still here. But I couldn't.

"Yes, meet us there."

Sally's cell phone rang a minute later. She whispered that she needed some privacy and retired to the bathroom. I didn't think anything of it until I heard impassioned back and forth from behind the bathroom door. The confident look on her face when she re-entered the room unsettled me. I suddenly suspected that she was an accomplished actress and I should beware. We left the dog at the apartment while the three of us walked to the bakery.

After a block, I grabbed Jack's shoulder and slowed his pace. When Sally turned I said, "Walk up ahead of us, me and Jack need to talk."

Sally gave us ten yards.

"What's going on in school?"

"I punched Phillip Langford in the mouth and got suspended for three days."

"Why did you hit him?"

"That joke about the nude pictures of mom spread all over school and other kids started teasing me about it," Jack said, and as he spoke he teared up. "Langford walked into the lunch room and I just belted him."

"Was there blood?"

"I split his lip."

"Oh shit."

"Sorry, Dad."

"You know, I come from New Jersey and when I was your age New Jersey morality consisted of just two things: no mother jokes, no sister jokes. Everything else was fair game. Something's got to be sacred and in the Garden State that was it. Sounds like Langford violated New Jersey morality."

"I'm probably going to have to fight him again."

"You think so?"

"Yeah, he's really mad," Jack said.

"Can you take him?"

"I'm not sure."

"If he squares off and puts up his hands, throw the first punch and don't stop swinging until someone breaks it up."

His step stuttered as if his knee temporarily gave way. "Okay."

"Toughen up, boy. Your reputation is on the line and you got to fight."

"But what do I do about Mom?"

"You worry about Langford. I'll deal with your mother."

"How?"

"I don't know yet, but I'll think of something."

"Thanks," he said.

When we reached the bakery Sally was at the front door and held it open for us.

Clement's bakery featured a long display case filled with fresh baked goods. It did a good take-out business. It had black leather booths. Sally winced when she sat down. While we sipped hot coffee and ate croissants, Jack had a donut and a hot chocolate.

Rose walked in. She hesitated momentarily when she saw Sally sitting with us, offered her a big smile and said hello.

She was wearing a T-shirt tucked tightly into her jeans and she looked like she'd just rolled out of bed because her curly hair was up in a bun.

We weren't there for more than five minutes when I noticed something about Rose. When Jack got up to get a second donut I could no longer stay silent.

"Rose, this may be a strange question for a father to ask his daughter, but are your breasts getting bigger?"

She pulled back her shoulders with a smile full of feminine pride and said, "God, I hope so."

"Are you taking birth control pills?"

Her shoulder clapped into Sally's, drawn together as if by magnets.

"Yes."

"Are you having sex with that college kid?"

"Yes."

The look on Sally's face made me realize she already knew.

"Is that more information than you really wanted to know, Daddy?"

"Yes."

"Sorry."

"Does your mother know?"

"Not yet."

"I want you to tell her this week."

"Okay."

"What's his name?"

"James Boyer."

"Have James Boyer visit me at the bistro."

"Why? So you can yell at him?"

"Rose, when you have daughters, all men are pigs."

"But Dad…"

"You didn't sleep at Louisa's last night, did you?"

Sally came to Rose's defense. "Joe…"

"Stay out of it, Sally."

Then turning back to Rose, staring until she made eye contact again, I said, "Have Boyer be at the bistro on Monday night."

Sally looked at her watch. "My, it's getting late. I should be going."

"I'll walk you to the Metro," I said. "Rose, take Jack back to the bistro when you've finished and wait for me there."

Sally and I walked out the door to the Metro's red line subway stop three blocks away. Nothing was said the first block. I didn't know where to start.

I could see the tension on Sally's face, and I got the impression when we reached the second block in silence, she hoped to get to the subway without having to talk at all.

Finally I just blurted it out.

"You knew about Rose being sexually active, didn't you?"

"Yes. Rose asked me for advice. She's is in love with James Boyer and doesn't want to leave Washington for college next year."

"Oh really, is that all?"

"And she wants a tattoo."

"Why is she telling you?"

"She trusts me."

"She has a mother, Sally. That's Joannie's job."

"She's afraid to talk about it with both of you."

"I've been divorced a long time and have always been careful not to allow any other woman into my life that might compete with Joannie, who despite her faults is Rose's mother."

"I know that."

"How is it that you worked your way into my family so easily?"

"Just luck, I guess," she answered.

"Lucky for who?"

"Lucky for me, Joe. I like Rose."

"And what about all that crap about my undocumented workers, my secret meetings in the Potomac Room, Joannie's association with convicted lobbyists and Ali Bin Hassan? What's that all about?"

"Ali Bin Hassan gets out of prison in two weeks. He was a good friend of Cosmo's while he was incarcerated and we think he may come here when he gets out."

"What's so great about him?"

"He has ties to the Muslim brotherhood and the Egyptian army here in D.C. We want all the intelligence he has to offer."

"Is that what this is all about?"

"And we want him to work for us."

"You're an idiot."

"Well, I expected more of a patriotic response than that."

"How did I get on your radar screen?"

"A group of Arab diplomats were seen leaving your restaurant last month by some low level munchkin at the White House. He reported it to the President's National Security advisor and you've been under investigation for two months. Your association with Cosmo also peaked our interest."

"I know the law, Sally. And you can't prove I broke it."

"Doesn't matter. They'd come after you just for sport. The attorney fees required to defend yourself would cost you plenty. Then, of course, there would be an I.R.S. audit."

"Are you working freelance or is last night just part of your job description?"

"What do you mean?"

"Don't make me repeat it. You know exactly what I mean."

"Both."

We arrived at the subway stop. The date was over. She stopped at the escalator and faced me.

I must be an idiot. I reached for her.

A look of fear came to her face and her body stiffened. She took a step backwards gave me a wide-eyed stare, as if maybe her husband was watching. But she didn't have a husband.

"No, not now, not here," she said.

I think my jaw dropped. Suddenly, I was looking over my shoulder, first to the left, then to the right. And I didn't even know what I was looking for. Seeing nothing, I turned and walked away.

Chapter 9

When I was a teenager my Uncle Harry told me this joke: "Why do men have pet names for their penises?" he asked.

"I don't know."

"They don't like strangers making all their decisions."

When Sally Jones refused my advances at the Metro station, that joke came to mind as if Harry himself whispered it in my ear.

Okay, so what? I lost my mind. It wasn't the first time that sexual abandon clouded my judgment. I was blameworthy, but not remorseful.

"How did she manage to transcend so many boundaries and insinuate her way into my life?" I muttered that out loud while walking down the block and several heads abruptly turned in my direction.

Sally hailed from the Show-Me State and thus far she was doing a lot of showing but not enough telling. Getting played by a disguised Midwest yokel hurt my Jersey pride.

She knew everything: the kids, the bistro, the bookstore, the divorce and most likely had access to past legal issues and my tax returns too. But what she wanted most she would never get: those detailed stories that Cosmo and I kept secret and he went to jail to protect.

Back in the day, when Black men standing on D.C. street corners teased their friends about how their women controlled their lives, they used lines like, "That bitch got your nostrils wide open."

Back then I wasn't even sure what it meant. Today I only feared that someone might legitimately hurl it at me. That's because I let Sally's soft aroma roll all over me. I inhaled that manipulative, bad-girl, Ozark Mountain, Capitol Hill-billy musk and I was stoned. I finally understood that street corner taunt. She had my nostrils wide open.

But here's something else. At fifty, when you find a partner who can get you as libidinally stoked as Sally Jones got me, you think twice about dumping her. She had moves I'd never seen before.

A half dozen such sexpots just like her have come to me. From my experience I discovered one common fact between them. Each had been sexually violated at a very young age. Their sexual chakra was opened early on, when they were just girls and once opened, there's no closing it back up. Most took too much responsibility for what a wayward uncle, cousin or neighbor did to them.

Their facial expressions were identical. In the heat of passion a lost innocence, bordering on fear, gripped them and they submitted to anything you wanted. And God help you if you held back, didn't rise to the occasion, didn't take control, didn't go hard, didn't go strong. You'd lose their respect.

There was only one way to assuage them. Fuck harder than their assailants. Impress upon them a deeper experience than the one that wounded them. Make that traumatic incident seem jejune compared to the new sexual standard the two of you embark upon. I think they all understood that unconsciously because they invited sexual creativity in order to quench us both.

My cell phone rang. It was Cosmo.

"Sorry I missed you last night." I said.

"Did you ditch your date?"

"No, she slept over."

"Nice work."

"Let me guess what happened to you," I said. "A sweet young thing sat at your bar, you got her loaded and took her home. She never mentioned the newspaper article and swooned over your inimitable Italian charm."

"How did you know?"

"What was her name?"

"Vera," Cosmo said.

"Think we both got played last night."

There was a pause on the other end of the phone.

"You and I are on somebody's radar screen, Cosmo."

"That fucking newspaper story."

"Exactly. That fucking newspaper story," I repeated.

"And you think they sent women to seduce us?"

"Either that or I'm paranoid."

"Total paranoia is total awareness."

"I think their latest interest has something to do with Ali getting out of prison this month."

"Joe, over the phone?" Cosmo whispered.

"Cosmo, we're not doing anything wrong."

"What do they want to know?"

"Sally wasn't specific."

"You still okay with Ali coming here?"

"Tell him I might be able to give him a job while he fights his extradition. But he's got to come clean with everybody. He's going to have to meet with a lot of interested parties. If he cooperates with the feds he might get to stay in America."

"Ali can't go home, Joe."

"It's not up to us. I'll arrange the meetings. Let's see if he can cut a deal."

"He's going to get screwed, I know it."

"Then you might want to stand clear of him." I said.

"Take care of this, Joe. I trust you to do the right thing."

"What is the right thing?"

"I don't know. You figure it out."

"Are you sure?"

"Yes," said Cosmo.

"Alright, I'm on it."

I climbed the stairs to my apartment. Shortstop barked loudly as I ascended. Rose and Jack were inside watching cartoons. I took off my jacket and threw it over the arm of the couch.

I grabbed some orange juice from the refrigerator, poured each of us a glass and sat in the recliner. They sat on the couch.

"We have a lot to talk about, kids," I said.

"Why don't you go first?" Rose said. "The way your jaw is clenched you obviously got something on your mind. Did we do something wrong?"

"It's not always about you."

"Who's it about then?" Jack asked.

"Sally Jones. Where does she get off coming into our lives so brazenly?"

"I like Sally, Daddy," Rose said.

"So do I," said Jack.

"I'm not so sure," I replied.

"Afraid she'll hold your feet to the fire?" Rose said.

"What fire is that?"

"Mom says that your recklessness..." Then Rose, realizing that bringing Joannie's opinion into the conversation was bad form, caught herself and pressed her lips together.

I was ready to pounce on that remark until I looked at the table beside the couch. A pair of long silver earrings, which Sally removed last night because they kept getting tangled up in her hair, lay in plain sight.

Chapter 10

My cell phone rang at three fifty-four. I flipped it open. It was Joannie.

"Are you coming to Jack's parent-teacher conference?"

"I'll be there in five minutes."

"The conference started at three forty-five," she said.

"Then why did you tell me that it started at four?"

"I told you three forty-five."

"No, Joannie, when we spoke this morning on the phone you told me you couldn't make it to the twins conference but you would be at Jack's conference at four."

Her voice took on a slower, impatient tone. "I said three forty-five."

"If you told me three forty-five, I would have been there at three forty-five."

"Well, Miss Ginanne has conferences every thirty minutes until eight o'clock tonight and since you're late we've started without you."

She hung up.

While our relationship was no longer as confrontational as it had been, situations like this still prevailed. The passive-aggressive stuff was still maddening because Joannie could be manipulative and pretend nothing was amiss. My term for it was "head tripping."

Friends coached me that the correct response was to rise above it all. Be the better man, Joe. You're making yourself ridiculous over this divorce. I tried that for about one day. It didn't work.

We were involved in a fight for the hearts and minds of our children and there was no getting around it. Opting out of this pissing contest was tantamount to parental negligence. I was in the game, like it or not, and her manipulation, like purposely telling me the wrong time of Jack's parent-teacher conference, was part of it all. And it was my own fault for trusting her instead of contacting the school and finding out the conference time myself.

This competition was more than just a parental power struggle. It was a microcosmic metaphor indicative of something broader, as if the drama we were playing out in our personal lives was a drama that was also working itself out in the world.

People hail multi-culturalism as progressive but rarely focus on the emotional struggle accompanying the effort of opening your heart and mind to values at variance with your own.

That was our story. I was an urban Jersey Jew, she was a rural, Ohio Catholic. Our kids were Cashews. That was the joke they used to describe themselves: half Catholic and half Jewish. Though we kept the actual religions out of their upbringing, we secretly hoped that they would aspire to the best that both traditions offered and expand their consciousness to one broader than the culture their parents grew up with.

But following our divorce, defending the faith became the ruling passion. Neither of us could let go of the religious values that had molded us individually. When our marriage contract became null and void, we both fell backwards into the Old World prejudices of our grandparents.

There was this nefarious double-dealing between us lest the Cashews become too Jewish or too Catholic. For my part I refused to let them experience the brutality of Catholic culture promulgated by pedophile priests and the bloodless brides of Jesus. There would be no recovering Catholics among my brood. And Joannie was equally virulent lest her children become marginalized, neurotic Jews.

As the Sidwell Friends School came into view I felt the muscles tightening in my neck. I knew that telltale. It always preceded a confrontation with Joannie, as if it were some sort of cosmic signal warning me to gird my loins.

My brisk walk ended and I entered room 205 precisely at four o'clock to find Joannie looking at page three of a book report Jack wrote.

Miss Ginnane, Jack's advisor, was pointing out book report defects resulting from Jack's writing style and they went on about his work for several seconds before acknowledging me. When Miss Ginnane faced me it was with an expression she reserved for deadbeats.

Jane Ginnane was a thin, buxomless, forty-year-old spinster who had devoted her life to the children of Sidwell Friends School. She possessed an excellent chiseled face that strangers passing by admired. She had shoulder length black hair, green eyes and broad shoulders.

But she also had a remote, New England Blue-blood, ice-queen, do-not-touch-me kind of countenance that cautioned men to be appropriate in both speech and behavior lest they provoke her disemboweling scowl.

Her rigorous academic standards were legendary at the school, as was the parental concern for their crestfallen children who hated themselves for not living up to them.

"Mr. Green," Miss Ginnane said through a frightening grin, "I'm glad you could make it. I've been explaining my concerns about Jack. He is forgetful and his daydreaming in class has become an issue with several of his teachers. I've seen a lot of kids with this problem and I fear that he may be suffering from Attention Deficit Disorder. It is my recommendation that he be tested and if the tests pan out that you consider Ritalin to redress this problem."

Joannie sat with a passive look on her face. I knew that look. It was the look of complicity.

"Miss Ginnane, we have known each other since Jack's older brother and sister began school here and I'm concerned that Jack is being judged by the standards of Rose and Aidan, who compete against each other relentlessly. He's not as aggressive as they are, but he has other qualities that surpass them."

"I assure you that Jack is being judged by the standards of his classmates and not the dynamics of his older siblings."

"If the semester ended right now what would his grades be?" I asked.

"She looked through his tests scores and homework assignments and calmly replied, "One B, four C's and a D in algebra."

"So what you're telling me is that you want to put my son on a prescription drug because he's is just an average student at Sidwell Friends?"

"It's more than that. I have observed Jack at length and though he is trying his best, he is dealing with issues that are challenging his ability to achieve mastery."

Joannie let Miss Ginnane do the talking. But now I could see she had something to say. My back straightened up.

"Joe, you gave me your word that we would do whatever it took to see that Jack succeeds here. And let me just say that I never thought you'd be the kind of father who lacked the moral courage to help his son see things through to the end."

"There is nothing wrong with Jack," I said.

"If he's unable to attain the academic standards we set for our students here, perhaps you should consider sending him to school elsewhere," said Miss Ginnane.

"If he withdraws, we won't' get a refund," said Joannie rubbing her hands against her knees. "I am not going to let him fail."

"Why is this about you, Joannie? Why can't it be about Jack?"

"If you would only listen, you would see that it is about Jack," Miss Ginnane interjected. "There is an objective battery of tests administered by an educational psychologist that I'd like Jack to take. We've scheduled an appointment for him on Wednesday at two. The results will be evaluated by a psychiatrist, Dr. Marasca."

"That's a little fast, isn't it?"

"This guy is a specialist," Joannie said. "There's a two month waiting list to see him."

"So what you're telling me is that you've known about this for a while and are only now letting me in on it?"

"Miss Ginnane and I have been discussing this. We wanted to be certain about our concerns before we broached the topic with you."

"Maybe ADD isn't the issue." I asked.

"What are you suggesting?" Miss Ginnane asked.

"Joannie, why is there so much anger in your house?" My voice rose and my neck twitched. I said it loud too. "Could it be that the anger in your home is distracting him? And you, Miss Ginnane, I saw you at the school's Christmas party, which was held at my restaurant. After two drinks you got into a shouting match with one of your colleagues."

"What's your point?" Ginnane shot back.

"My point is that you are both so overwhelmed by your emotional issues that it's easier to put my son on medication than it is to deal with him in a responsible manner."

"Oh, and this is coming from Joe Green," Joannie said. "The responsible guy who made a fortune in the 1980s growing marijuana in Sonoma County, California? Let me get this straight. You're fine with growing and distributing an illegal drug but you resent putting your son on a legal, doctor prescribed drug that might save his academic career?"

Miss Ginnane's face pinched to a disgusted frown. Joannie's face bore the smile of satisfaction, because she found the winning rhetoric. My face was all about rage.

"I'm going to go now before I make a scene."

I stood up and walked out of the classroom. Joannie, followed me.

"Damn it. Why do you have to be so confrontational? It puts our children at such a disadvantage."

"Go to hell, Joannie." I spoke a little too loud and the heads of parents and teachers in the hallway turned.

"This is about Jack. It's not about you and me."

"I'm fed up with your manipulation."

"I meant to talk to you about it, really. But I knew that you would fight it so I waited to have Miss Ginnane around for moral support."

"It's speed, Joannie. Is that what you want for your son, to turn him into a speed freak?"

We were too loud, just like the old days. I saw the headmaster walking down the hall towards us and I didn't like him either.

"Joe, agree to the testing. Let's just find out what's what and then we'll make the decision together. What harm can that bring?"

Mr. Tellwigger now stood beside us, and he was looking for an explanation.

"Hello, Rick." I nodded.

"When you're finished with Miss Ginnane, there's a little matter I'd like to talk to you about regarding Jack," Tellwigger said.

"I'm out of here."

"Wait, you can't go," Joannie called. "Jack's been suspended from school and we need to know why."

Before I made it to the door I turned and shouted down the hall. "When you quit showing your tits to his friends, he'll stop fighting!"

Fuck. How is it that we always ended up in that angry place? God, it's terrible. That bitch makes me crazy and I don't know how to stop it.

It was downhill all the way back to the bookstore. The further I walked the angrier I got. What the fuck? Why I am walking away in a huff? Those two termagants should be storming off in exasperation, not me, damn it. Next time will be different.

But now I had to get back to the bookstore in order to relieve Cosmo. The bookstore was open until eight. but Cosmo tended the Bistro bar on Mondays and I didn't want him to be late for his shift. I should have taken a cab but I was pissed and needed to blow off steam. I took the long way back.

When I arrived at the bookstore I was fifteen minutes late. Jack was sitting behind the counter subbing for Cosmo. His dog "Shortstop," tied up beside him, wagged his tail when he saw me.

"Cosmo was afraid he'd be late for work so he called and asked me to watch the store until you got here."

"Thanks for covering me."

"You look mad. Am I in trouble?"

"I'm just a little annoyed about the teacher conference."

"I'm not doing so good."

"That's what they said."

"Sorry."

"They want you to take a series of tests."

"What kind of tests?"

"They want to make sure that there isn't a problem with the way your brain processes information."

"ADD?" He asked.

"Yes."

"They tested Danny Ellsworth last winter."

"What happened?"

"They put him on Ritalin."

"Did it help?"

"He says when he takes it he can sit down and play video games for six hours straight and only has to stop to use the bathroom."

"Six hours, huh?"

"He sells them for two dollars a piece."

"Ever buy one?"

"No, but I've thought about it. I'd rather spend my money on the chocolate chip cookies they sell in the lunch room."

"The stale kind or the soft kind?"

"Stale kind," he said.

"Those are my favorite too." I reached into my pocket and gave him a couple of singles. "If you think of it, bring me home a couple of them tomorrow."

"I can't. I'm suspended until Thursday."

"Sorry, I forgot."

"That's okay."

"You know, Cosmo's really a math whiz. I'm going to talk to him about helping you with your algebra."

"Do you think it'll do any good?"

"It's worth a try."

"Listen, Jack. There's nothing wrong with you."

"I hope so."

"It's Monday, you're at your mom's for dinner. You better get going."

"See you tomorrow," he said. He untied his dog and the two of them set off down the block to Joannie's house.

I searched through the bookstore stacks to see if I had any books on ADD. But all I could find was a tome about Prozac. When I returned to my chair behind the counter, I saw Jack had forgotten his backpack.

***

Sally Jones walked through the door. She had a big paper bag in her arms and I thought perhaps she was back to sell me more books. But when she put the bag on the counter I heard the rattle of bottles and my guess was that it contained a bottle of Tequila and a bottle of Scotch.

"Hello, Joe."

I did not answer her greeting. Somehow she was the last person I wanted to see. I never did have a poker face. There was this, "fuck off, all women are devils," look about me.

She had never seen that on my face before. Instead of being threatened by it she grew concerned and after a second she spoke. "It's about the kids, isn't it?"

I didn't respond. She grabbed the bag from the counter and put it on the floor.

"Bad news at the teacher conference?"

"Jack's been forgetful and Joannie and his advisor suggested that he get tested to see if Ritalin would help."

"Maybe Jack's so busy thinking his own thoughts that he's not interested in those of his teachers."

"This is going to be a big fight."

"You looked worried."

"I am."

"You scared me when I walked in here. I'm just glad it wasn't about me. That would have hurt. Especially since there were so many memorable moments for me last night."

"Yeah, like what?"

"Well," she said and then paused, "like when you finished inside me and rolled over and giggled."

I forgot about Ritalin, Ginnane and Joannie and I started to laugh.

"Why are you laughing?"

"Because I haven't been that good in bed in a very long time."

"What was good about it?"

"You want me to say the words?"

"Yes, you own a bookstore. You know words."

"Okay, I'll tell you. I liked the way we were a perfect fit." I said.

"That was the second time. The first time you nearly drowned me."

"Sorry, that was premature."

"I didn't mind," she said.

I reached into my pocket and pulled out her earrings. She looked into my palm and studied them for a second as if to make sure all the pieces were there.

"Thanks," she said, taking them from my hand.

Then I remembered the awkward scene at the subway stop this morning when she pulled away. Suddenly, I felt this cramp in the pit of my stomach. Getting played by women twice in one afternoon was the last thing I needed.

Now, if I had any balls at all I would have asked that nagging question: Is your interest in me personal or does it have to do with my business relationships?

But I equivocated and that emboldened her. Truth is, I didn't really give a damn. I just wanted her again. She leaned in closer, and focused her gaze to my eyes. "Is there something you want to ask me?"

No way, I thought. I'm not ready to have this conversation. So I made something up. "Why does such a well-endowed woman like yourself wear a padded bra?"

She didn't expect that. Her eyebrows moved and she leaned back.

"It's my nipples. They're big."

"I've noticed."

"Sometimes they pop out. Men on Capitol Hill notice them when I walk by and it's embarrassing. I don't want to be known for my nipples. I wanted to be known for my professionalism. So I wear a padded bra to hide them."

I looked her up and down. It made sense.

"You look like you could use a drink," she said. "I don't live far from here. Would you like to come over? I could feed you supper too."

It was a tempting offer. She wore a naughty grin and the bag was full of liquor. But Cosmo was visiting Ali in prison tomorrow. Waiting for Cosmo's report seemed best.

"Thanks, maybe another time," I said.

"Oh, come on. It will be fun."

I thought about it for a few seconds. It did sound fun.

"I have some chores to do after I lock up. What's your address?"

Chapter 11

It was a long walk to Sally's place, which was a renovated apartment building from the 1920s located on Wisconsin Avenue. It now housed condominiums with a doorman and a circular driveway. I announced myself. The doorman had been told of my coming and escorted me to the elevator.

Sally lived on the seventh floor and I was in front of her door ringing her bell. She answered the door and stepped forward, offering a soft kiss on my lips. Touching me on the elbow, she ushered me in.

She wore a low cut red top, revealing not only her cleavage, but also her surgery scar. Between the time she left my bookstore and I rang her doorbell she had done her hair and applied make-up.

The first thing I noticed was the picture window in her living room. Its height was above the tree line and had an incredible view of the National Cathedral.

I was drawn to it immediately. The Cathedral was lit up in the dark. I didn't know what she paid for this space, but the opportunity to view that one sight every day seemed worth it all.

She stood beside me as I admired the tall church spires, our shoulders touching. We stood like that in silence for several seconds.

"I see this every day and sometimes I take it for granted," Sally said. "It's not until someone new comes here that I realize what a fabulous view it is."

"It's better than television."

"I don't own a television," she answered. "Can I mix you a drink?"

"Sure, if you have it, I'd like a..."

"I know what you like," she said.

She walked to the kitchen to mix it.

I took my eyes away from the window and gazed around her home. The art on her walls was original and expensive, as was the furniture.

Three large oak bookcases covered an entire wall of her living room, their contents organized by size and color as if they were like an army platoon standing at attention. I went to examine them. There was not one Harlequin Romance.

She re-entered with my drink in one hand and a large shot of tequila for herself in the other.

"Let me guess. You're a closet Harlequin Romance reader."

"True." She led me to a nearby closet and opened it up. Pushing apart a rack of winter coats, she revealed a shelf containing a long row of Harlequin Romances, many of which still had the receipts from my bookstore sticking up out of their pages, suggesting they had never been read.

"You're not really from the Ozarks, are you?"

"I'm from St. Louis."

"And you don't love romance novels, do you?"

"Actually, I was a classics major at Brown University. Later got my master's at Cornell after four years working for the State Department in Germany and China."

"So why the trailer trash act?"

"I didn't want you to take me seriously," she said.

"Why not?"

"I wanted to stay off your radar screen. If I told you my master's thesis was on the patience of Penelope you'd have been all over me."

"How do you know?"

"Your bookstore has the best selection of epic literature in town."

As I said, I never did have a poker face. I'm not even sure what expression I was wearing, but it was probably one of mortification because she smiled when she saw it and gave me a look which in New Jersey could easily have been interpreted as "in your face, sucker."

We retired to the couch and laid our drinks on an Asian coffee table that stood before it.

"Let's talk," she said.

"Are we being recorded?" I asked.

"No," she said as if protesting such an allegation.

"Let's pretend we are," I said. I took a hand held tape recorder out of my pocket, laid it on the table and turned it on. "This way both our butts are covered."

She walked to the kitchen and a second later returned to her place on the couch.

"I think it's best this way," I said. "You go first."

"An interesting set of coincidences occurred. Your file came across my desk at work. Later that day I saw you talking to Rose while she was sitting behind the counter at the bookstore. I didn't know she was your daughter. We knew you owned a restaurant but not a bookstore. I took an immediate interest in you, beginning with Rose."

"Is this a fishing expedition or do you have an agenda?"

"The Senate Intelligence Committee is interested in what Ali Bin Hassan knows about Al Qaida and the Muslim Brotherhood. When he gets out of prison next week, the word is you're are going to give him a job."

"If he has a job then he can stay while he appeals his deportation hearings. We've hired Eli Holbrooke to represent him."

"What makes you think we want him to leave?"

"Why would you want him to stay?"

"Because of what he might know. He could be of enormous value to us. Later on he could become a consultant with whom we could run ideas past as the situation arose."

"So let me guess what you have in mind," I said. "He cooperates with you and in return you put him in a witness protection program and he ends up hiding with his wife and daughter in an outlying area of the American heartland for the rest of his life."

"Yes, but he would get to live the American dream."

"Sounds more like a nightmare. The kid's got talent and ability. If he throws in with your team he'll never get to use it."

"In addition there are people back in Egypt who don't want him to return."

"And why is that?" I asked.

"In part because of you," she said. "You supplied both Ali and Cosmo with books in prison. While Cosmo read a lot of spirituality, philosophy and psychology, Ali read just two things."

"Marx and Mohammed."

"Precisely, Marx and Mohammed," she repeated.

"Your information is two years old, Sally. Ali graduated out of Marx and Mohammed. Lately, he's been reading twenty-first century writers like Tom Friedman and Fareed Zakaria, guys who understand globalization and want to integrate everybody."

"Tell me something about him," she said.

"Ali has a vivid imagination and is a very convincing liar. When I first got to know him the whole world was looking for Osama Bin Laden. I think the reward was up to twenty-five million dollars. Everybody believed that Ali had valuable information. That's why he hid out with the Muslims in jail. They watched his back."

"Did he ever talk to you about Bin Laden?"

"Yes."

"What did he say?"

"He claimed Bin Laden committed suicide deep inside a cave in Afghanistan which was then blown up on top of him so his body could never be found."

"Why would he do that?"

"According to Ali, Bin Laden was more valuable to the cause as a legend, than a soldier. By never being found he'd become a mythological hero to inspired Islamic fundamentalists for centuries. I remember his big line too. 'Compared to Bin Laden, Ali Baba is just a pussy.'"

"Well, that was a lie, wasn't it?"

"A very creative lie, at least that's what I thought when he told me that story. Because I believed him."

"Bin Laden should have done what Ali suggested when he had the chance," Sally said. "As it happened, Bin Laden was shot down like a dog and dumped in the ocean so no one could mourn his body."

"Before Ali was convicted I heard him speak once on stage at Busboys and Poets about the emerging Arab political paradigm. He's very smart."

"We know."

"Is that why you set him up on a false weapons charge and sentenced him to three years behind bars?"

She sat stoically and I realized that unlike me, she did have a poker face.

"Ali is only part of our concern."

"What's the other?"

"Cosmo Della Rocca. We might have to squeeze Cosmo to get to you. We know that he shot down those Black kids deliberately, we just don't know why. What did they steal from him that made him chase down Dominique Matthews and shoot him in the back?"

"I don't remember."

"And then of course there's you. You're on our radar screen too and won't be coming off it anytime soon."

"And why is that?"

"Because the intelligence community in this town is egotistical and we tend to dislike competition. We get a little testy when ordinary American citizens know more than we do."

She stared at my drink, which was nearly empty. "Let me refresh your beverage."

I watched as she rose and walked to the kitchen. I liked her confidence. In addition she seemed to have a healthy attitude about life. Too bad she was stinking it all up with a job like committee administrator for the Senate Intelligence Committee, which I considered an oxymoron.

While she was in the kitchen, I looked up at the ceiling and I noticed the red light on the smoke detector flickered when the air conditioner came on. She returned, handed me a full glass and sat back down.

"You're corrupt, Joe, and your only choices are to play ball with us or go down."

"Those are some lousy choices."

"We want to know who you do business with. We'll squeeze you if we have to."

"I have friends too. You'll have to deal with them first. I'm not saying a word until they tell me to."

"We know who they are and we've already begun lobbying them."

"Until then you're not going to hear anything from me. Call it my attorney-client privilege," I said.

"You're not a lawyer."

"Then call it the sanctity of confessional."

"You're not a Catholic priest either."

"Do you want to know why so many bad mother fuckers in this town trust me, Sally?"

"Sure. Tell me."

"Because I'm so vulnerable. I own two businesses and have three children. That ensures my integrity because if I fuck up, all that I cherish can be taken from me in one afternoon. And you bureaucratic boneheads, who are purportedly restricted by American law, have nothing in your tool box as scary as that."

"Joe, we're the good guys."

"Carl Jung said it best. The bigger the group, the lower the I.Q. I have more virtue than all of you and I'll tell you why. I don't have an agenda and I cleave to only one value."

"Really, and what is that value?"

"Conversation, the conversation between discordant factions. And there is no way I'm going to dumb down to the collective mediocrity of the Capitol Hill clowns who only understand divide and conquer. You're a smart girl, Sally. Aren't you tired of working for them?"

"No, not yet."

Our conversation proceeded for over an hour with her pressing me to submit and me dodging her inquiries with half-truths and obfuscation. Then my tape recorder was filled and it automatically clicked off.

"I'm out of tape," I said. "That's enough business for now. Let's get down to pleasure."

"I have some chicken in the fridge. Are you hungry?"

"No," I said, and pulled her closer. "Sally turn off your tape too and let's really talk."

She stood and made a quick trip to the kitchen. She returned.

"Is it really off?" I asked.

"Yes," she said.

"Honey, take off that big padded bra and let me hold those big-nippled breasts again. That image of you naked and on your knees in front of the mirror was fabulous last night. and I can't get it out of my mind. Then when you rolled over on your belly and I went in. My God, it was terrific. I'm not sure which of your holes are tighter. Prostrate yourself before me sexually like that again. You take it harder than any woman I've ever known. You love bad girl sex and..."

"Okay, enough!" She stared at me with a sharp grimace.

She stood and returned to the kitchen. The red light on the smoke detector went off. She sat back down.

"Is it really off now, Sally?"

"Yes, it's really off."

"Good, come here."

Chapter 12

Something vibrated in my pants. Since I wasn't wearing them, it was easy to surmise that it was my cell phone. The pants had been kicked off in the throes of passion and lay on the hardwood floor in the corner of Sally's bedroom. The room was dark except for the blue lights of her digital alarm clock, which read 12:12. I was alone and naked in her bed.

While debating whether or not to answer the phone, it suddenly stopped and all was quiet but for the humming of Sally's bathroom fan. Suddenly, an awful sound poured forth. Despite the fact that the bathroom door was slammed shut, the sound of her vomiting was clear.

When the phone began vibrating again I feared that it was one of the kids in trouble so I jumped out from underneath her thick down comforter and reached for it. Cosmo was calling.

"Hey, I thought you were coming in to close the bistro tonight. Where are you?"

"I'm in Sally's bed," I whispered.

"You're where?"

"I'm in Sally's bed," I said a little louder.

"What are you, stupid? Dude, you're putting all of us at risk." He paused for a moment. Then, as if remembering himself, he added, "She's not listening to this, is she?"

"Relax. She's in the bathroom puking."

"How come?"

"She tried to drink me under the table."

There was a loud laugh on the other end of the line. "Where is she from again… Nebraska?"

"Missouri," I said.

"And she thought she could drink a Jersey boy under the table? That wasn't very intelligent."

"I thought she was better than this."

"Well, I hope you came first."

When no answer was forthcoming, he started laughing.

"Is there a purpose to this call, Cosmo? Or are you just breaking my balls?"

"I got a call from Ali. He's getting out of prison tomorrow. His train gets into Union Station tomorrow night at nine."

"Great, now I'm knee deep with two prodigal sons. One for each leg."

"You were the one who offered to handle this, Joe."

"I haven't forgotten."

"You haven't changed your mind, have you?"

"Not a bit. But we're both working. I'll ask Aidan to pick him up and bring him to the bistro. We'll have Shameem cook the four of us some porterhouses when the place closes down. We've got a lot to talk about."

"What are you going to do about Sally?"

"I'm going to hang up and make sure she doesn't go into cardiac arrest."

"I'll let you get back to your fun. This should make for some very interesting dinner conversation tomorrow."

I walked quietly to the bathroom and grabbed the doorknob. I was relieved to discover that it was not locked. I opened the door slowly to see Sally naked on her knees before the toilet bowl, sweating profusely and breathing hard. She turned her head to look at me but just then she started to heave and threw up more into the bowl. After several seconds she managed to speak.

"Oh, God… Don't worry… I'm okay… I just need a minute," she said.

By now one might have thought that she had emptied the contents of her stomach, but no, there was more. I reached for her and grabbed a strand of her long black hair and pulled it away from her face. But then she looked like she might also pass out and hit her head on the cold tile floor. I put one hand gently on her forehead and the other on the back of her neck for support. I held them there as she shuddered in an uncontrollable spasm and smelly liquid hurled out her mouth.

"Are you done?" I asked.

Both of her hands were squeezing the toilet seat. She ignored my question. Finally she managed to shake her head.

I flushed the toilet and returned to her bedroom, turning on the light beside her chair. I went back to the bathroom and turned off the bathroom light which was too bright for her watery eyes.

Something caught my eye. It was a patch just above her breast. Not sure how I missed it in bed.

"What's that?"

"It's for my angina."

"What is it?"

"It's an opiate patch. I was feeling a little chest pain."

"It doesn't sound like something you should mix with tequila."

"I took a few muscle relaxers too."

"How does your chest feel now?"

"The pain's gone… but I'm sore from throwing up."

I reached down and rubbed my hand across the adhesive patch. It felt like a thick Band-Aid. I rubbed my thumb against the corner of it. A little piece of it lifted away from her skin and I grabbed it with the fingernails of my thumb and index finger and ripped it off. She startled at my action.

"Should I call an ambulance?"

"No… don't do that," she said.

"Can you come back to bed?"

"I can't…I'm going to throw up again."

I grabbed a terry cloth robe from a hanger on the back of the door and threw it over her shoulders.

"Do you have anything in the refrigerator to settle your stomach?"

"A Coke."

"I'll be right back."

I found a can of Coke in the refrigerator. I opened the can, threw its contents into a saucepan, and lit a fire under it. The heat took care of the bubbles quickly and the steam reduced the water content. After a few minutes I removed it from the stove and put it in a glass. I opened the freezer door and stuck it inside to cool. I returned to the bathroom to check on Sally. The terry cloth robe had fallen to the floor but she didn't seem to notice.

The chill of the tiles brought goose bumps on her arms. She was barely holding onto the toilet and I thought she might just drop to the floor at any minute. We were like that in silence for several minutes in the dim light. Then I fetched the Coke from the freezer and put it to her lips.

"Go slow," I said.

She took a mouthful and swallowed it and fortunately it didn't come right up again.

"Take a minute and then we'll give you another sip."

I sat on the floor beside her. I reached for the robe and threw it over her shoulders again. She rested her head on my shoulders in silence.

"Pick up your head," I commanded.

And when she did I fed her a little bit more of the Coke. She drank about a third of it. Christ, this was the second time I'd dealt with a vomiter this week. Another retch sent her head above the bowl again. But it was only the dry heaves. However, in the middle of it, she farted out loud. She gave me a look of humiliation. I laughed.

Oh God, I know I shouldn't have, but the whole situation was so ridiculous. It was the only a natural response. At first I thought she was going to laugh along with me but she got angry instead and snapped.

"You won't be laughing so hard when you get subpoenaed on Wednesday."

"Subpoenaed by whom?"

"The committee."

"Whose bright idea is that?"

"Senator Lancaster."

"That fuck."

"I tried to stall him… honest Joe. But he's adamant."

"How long have you known about this?"

"About a week."

"Which judge is he taking it to?"

"Judge Salem."

"Well that's lucky."

"Why is that lucky?" she asked.

"None of your business," I said. "Here have some more of this Coke."

She sipped some more of it and I hoped that at long last she was done vomiting.

"Sally, tequila, muscle relaxers and opiate patches are probably not a good combination."

"Jesus, just because I work for the senate doesn't make me a girl scout."

"True, but it's risky behavior."

"What am I saving myself for?" At the sound of her own words, she started to tear up. "A government pension? I won't make it to sixty-five. The best I can do is to make hay while the sun shines."

"This relationship seems to be getting more complicated every day."

"I know," she said.

She reached for toilet paper and wiped her mouth and her eyes. She threw the paper into the toilet and flushed it.

"I think I should go back to bed."

When we stood up she caught sight of the mirror and gazed intently at her silhouette in the dim light. Her sweat-filled hair was plastered to the side of her face and the muscles in her face were limp. The sight of herself brought the corners of her mouth down to form a mournful expression. She pulled herself together though and slipped back into bed without my help.

I pulled the covers up to her shoulders as she rolled on her side. I sat down in the chair next to the bed and watched as she drifted to sleep.

Okay, I thought, so what? She's a little bit of a phony in the way she hid behind the mantle of her Capitol Hill persona and the trappings of power. Still, I liked her.

Then I slowly and silently began to dress but as I slipped on my pants, the change in my pocket gave me away. I saw her hand reach for me. Realizing I wasn't beside her, she called out my name.

"I'm right here, Sally."

"I ruined our evening."

"Are you better now?"

"Yes, I think so. Are you coming back to bed?"

I thought about it for a moment.

"Don't leave."

I removed my pants and slid into bed next to her.

"Thanks. I'll make it up to you."

"So is this the real you at last?"

"I wanted to be dangerous and mysterious," she said softly. "All I am is a middle aged bureaucrat with a disability and a short shelf life."

Somehow, shorn of her persona I felt compassion for her. I don't know why but it moved me. Perhaps because it revealed a soft side, a vulnerable side that Joannie never acknowledged.

I must have dozed off because I had this brief but vivid dream. I unzipped the skin of Sally's back and it revealed a body filled with light. I crawled inside her to get closer and then I reached over my shoulder and pulled up the zipper behind me so that I was actually inside her skin.

When I awoke a moment later I startled. Lifting my head from the pillow I found her asleep.

Morning came. The sound of Sally's voice in the living room woke me. It was eight o'clock. She was calling her office and telling them she was sick and would not be in today. She came right back to bed and lay close against me. We both fell back to sleep.

At 9:30 I jumped out. I had to open the bookstore at ten. She got out of bed too. But she could barely speak. The tequila and then the tequila mixed with stomach acid had singed her uvula and her voice was raw.

"Come on, I'll buy you some juice and a cup of coffee," I said.

"Just let me shower. I'll be right with you."

At eleven, I opened the bookstore and sat behind the desk with Sally beside me. We sipped coffee while Ibiza Sonica played on the bookstore stereo.

"It was good last night, before I got sick, wasn't it?"

"Before you got sick? Yes, it was good. What happened? Did you get scared and fuck it up on purpose?"

She didn't expect that kind of indictment. Though initially defensive, she considered my question.

"Maybe."

I began writing out some checks for the store's utility bills. Sally picked up a book from the classics section. She had abandoned the pretense of reading Harlequin Romances and instead held a copy of J.A.K. Thompson's book "Irony," a handsome hardback from the 1920s. But she was still not feeling well. She could not concentrate on the text for more than a few minutes at a time.

At 11:30 Cosmo showed up at the store. He wore his Jersey Devils hockey cap, which I had given him. He was all smiles until he saw Sally. They both startled.

"Cosmo, I think I introduced you to Sally the other night."

"Sure. Nice to see you again, Sally."

"Nice to see you too," she said with her raw voice.

Cosmo and I had matters to discuss which we could not do with Sally present so I stood and said, "Cosmo and I have to talk business. Stay here and mind the store."

She looked surprised by my request. Since she could not think of an excuse, she nodded her head in agreement. Cosmo and I walked down the street to the coffee shop where we might have some privacy.

"What did you do to her throat?" he asked.

"Take your mind out of the gutter."

"Hey, you're the one who said Sally takes it harder than any woman you've ever had."

"Can we talk about something else?"

"No, I don't like this relationship. I feel like you're sleeping with the enemy and putting both of us at risk."

"Are you really afraid that I'll sell you and Ali out to a bunch of brown-shoed squares?"

"Isn't that what your relationship with Sally is about?"

"You asked me to help with Ali. Are you changing your mind?"

"No, not a bit."

"Then let me work my magic."

Chapter 13

I was on my way to the bistro but decided to stop off at the bookstore and get Cosmo. The sky was gray. A spring shower looked likely so I brought an extra umbrella for him. We marched down 18th Street. A small bouquet of flowers tied together by string sat atop of a City Papers newspaper box.

Cosmo grabbed them as we went by. "What are these—violets?" he asked.

"Yes," I said. "Seems a little early in the season for them. They're probably from a greenhouse."

"What's your guess? They were left there by some jilted guy whose girlfriend refused him?"

"Maybe."

"They're pretty," he said. "Here, take them—give them to Sally."

"Not sure when I'm going to see her again," I said. "You keep 'em. Give them to your new lover."

"No thanks. That might send the wrong message."

"What message is that?"

"That I want to move things further along," he said.

"You don't?"

"No, I really don't. Joe, Washington women aren't very feminine. They're dedicated to their careers. They demand equal opportunity and equal pay, which I understand. But in doing so, they take on all the shadowy aspects of men. They're not even fun to be around. Back in Jersey, women are primarily interested in love and sex. Here they only seem interested in money and power."

"Tell me about it! I'm chained to Joannie. Her career is everything. It makes her crazy, which trickles down and makes me crazy too."

"Maybe I'll just put them in a vase behind the bar," Cosmo said.

Along the way, we stopped off at a dirty-water hot dog stand. We bought two hot dogs with mustard and sauerkraut for $1.75 each from an Iranian guy named Mo, who's been selling kosher hot dogs at that corner for years. We've eaten dozens.

Cosmo handed Mo the violets and offered a deal. "I'll trade you these flowers for a bag of salt and vinegar potato chips."

Mo examined them closely. He touched them to measure their freshness. Then he sniffed them. He gave them their due. But he handed them back to Cosmo. "Not interested," he said.

Cosmo laid the violets upon Mo's soft drink cooler while we finished our hot dogs. Then we continued down the sidewalk.

After a few steps I said, "Wait a minute. Don't forget your flowers." He took ten steps back and retrieved them.

At the bistro a half-dozen Black women were waiting for the place to open. Homemade signs were on the ground beside them. One was visible. It read: "Murderer. Get out of our neighborhood." Reverend Battle's son, Chris, was there too. The restaurant was about to be picketed.

"What should we do?" Cosmo asked.

"Nothing we can do. The city owns the sidewalk. It's their First Amendment right to demonstrate."

"That's just great. Now walking into the bistro is going to be like crossing a union picket line," Cosmo said.

"Reverend Battle threatened me with demonstrators last week. Didn't think he'd follow through so quickly."

"Stay here, Joe, it's me they want. Let me handle it."

Cosmo walked right up to them. An angry, heavy-set Black woman came forth. The crowd moved with her. "There you are, killer. Do you know who I am?"

"No," said Cosmo.

"I'm Violet Matthews, Dominique's mother. You remember who Dominique Matthews is, don't you?"

"Yes," said Cosmo. "I shot him dead."

"That's right, you back-shooting piece of shit."

Looking at the flowers in his hand, Cosmo offered them to her. "Guess these are for you."

She wasn't falling for his tricks. "I'm not taking anything from you," she shouted.

"I see Dominique all the time," Cosmo said. "He's in my dreams. His ghost follows me around. He's here with us right now."

Violet took a step closer. Her grimace was all contempt. The crowd surrounded Cosmo. "You are the devil," she shouted. "Stop with your lies."

"I'm not lying."

"Yes, you are."

"Why's Dominique going like *this*?" Cosmo did a pantomime by grabbing the small finger on his right hand with two fingers from his left. He made a motion as if he were turning a ring around a pinkie. "It's about a ring, isn't it?" Cosmo looked at Violet's hand. "He wants to know why you took it off?"

Violet Matthews looked hypnotized. She suddenly stuttered, "Because he…" She caught herself, realizing she was surrounded by zealots.

"Take it out of your closet or wherever you're hiding it. It's a symbol of the love your son still holds for you," Cosmo said.

"It was an emerald. He gave it to me for my birthday. After he passed, I felt so bad. I figured he stole it or paid for it with drug money. I was ashamed to wear it."

"He wants you to put it back on," Cosmo said. "Please."

"I wish I could hold my boy right now."

"He wants you to know he's okay and he'll see you again."

She took the flowers from Cosmo's hand and they both started to cry. "I'm so sorry, ma'am."

"I got to get to church. That's right, I got to get to church, right now," Violet said, half crying, half laughing. She led the procession away.

Cosmo stood dumbfounded as he watched the women walk down the block. The last one to go was Chris Battle. Before he turned away, he gave Cosmo the middle finger.

They forgot the signs.

"How did you do that?" I asked.

"I didn't do anything," Cosmo answered. "Dominique did."

Chapter 14

Thursdays at the bistro are best. Unlike many restaurants which cash in on Saturday evenings, the fourth night of the week is when my place glows. And it's because all the politicos leave Washington and go home on Fridays and are looking for a little action the night before.

Tonight a dinner party of twelve made up of lobbyists, politicos, corporate executives, and several military men out of uniform were in the Potomac Room. Two U.S. Senators representing states from the Deep South, showed up late and made an entrance. They were all celebrating the Senate passage of a defense appropriation bill, which included their little piece of the pie: a nine hundred million dollar contract for radar equipment from Aero-Tech Specialties, a Jacksonville, Florida firm, which was picking up tonight's tab.

Grimaldi brought them in. He called me to reserve the Potomac Room because a companion bill had already passed the House and its signature by the President was greased. His entourage arrived at seven p.m.

Grimaldi celebrated with an eight-pound lobster appetizers, shelled at the table, Silver Oak Cabernet, Porterhouse steaks and Grams twenty-year-old Port.

Blowing a big wad in the Potomac Room was a ritual with him following his victories. Every waiter clamored to get that party because he also tipped thirty percent.

I liked doing business with Grimaldi, a swarthy Jersey Italian with style and substance, because he paid attention to detail. Each participant arrived in a black limousine and departed in a black limousine. I appreciated that since I didn't have to worry about over-serving them. Dram shop law stated that I could be held responsible should they crash their cars. Cutting Grimaldi's clients off at the bar was a delicate pain in the ass so he took care of the problem himself.

When Grimaldi was hosting, a man's inability to hold his liquor, puking in the bathroom, slurring words, falling asleep at the table, were sins. Individuals lost face, lost contracts, even lost jobs for such weakness. In my mind it was an epic underpinning of New Jersey culture: hold your load or you're a piece of shit. As a former Jersey tough he believed in it.

In showboating his big wins, Grimaldi sought to impress Stella. His offer to set her up in her own apartment with a monthly stipend if she'd be his mistress, was unconditional. Stella was the reason he chose my place for his soirees. He even knew her schedule. And he only ever made reservations following a big win on night's she was working. That made me a little jealous because in comparison Stella saw me in good times, and bad times when I acted like a gigantic asshole.

The deal he was offering was certainly a better one than I could offer her and he repeated that offer every time he hosted a celebration in the Potomac Room, which lately seemed monthly.

Men are inspired by feminine beauty. It breathes life into us. Thus Grimaldi's longing for Stella was an effort to stay young, strong and on top. She was manna to both of us.

"Joe, you're holding Stella back. Let go of her, she's got bigger fish to fry than restaurant hostess."

"Don't lobby me Grimaldi, lobby her," I replied.

"One day Stella is going to come to me," he said. Stella was quite aware of the rivalry between the two of us, which she enjoyed immensely. I hoped she'd resist the well-kept mistress on a pedestal role. But Grimaldi didn't give up and I feared that one day I'd have to take her for my own mistress or lose her to him.

I tried not to act jealous or possessive. He was unrelenting because winning was all he respected. Sometimes I padded his bill. It was my way of saying fuck you. He knew it too. Part of me hoped that he might take his business down the street to "The Palm" or some other trendy place. But what the hell, as I said, he wasn't paying, his clients were. And the Palm didn't have Stella.

When Grimaldi walked out the door at ten, rock steady in his gait, accompanied by his minions less adept at holding their load, I sighed in relief. I touched Stella lightly on the arm, thanked her for a job well done and left her alone to man the front door.

Then I went to Cosmo. "Tomorrow I want you to call Little Brucie Ackerman, our beloved Newark stockbroker. Tell him about the soiree Aero-tech Specialties had in the Potomac Room tonight. Ask him for some advice."

"Got it," Cosmo said.

Dave Paulus was sitting at the bar and I sat down next to him. Soon he'd be too drunk to talk. So I caught him early.

As I sat down a blonde got up to leave. Cosmo was saying goodbye.

"Merry Christmas," she said with a wink to Cosmo. "Call me."

"Maybe."

As she made her way to the door, she wiggled her butt in a life affirming gesture that we all found compelling.

"Merry Christmas? What's that all about?" Paulus asked.

"I brought her home to my place the other night," Cosmo said. "She wanted to shave her legs and in the process I talked her into letting me go a little further up. Christmas Tree designs are kind of my trademark. But you know I ran into this problem with her when…"

I held up my hand like a traffic cop. Cosmo got it right away and offered a quiet apology.

Paulus, always impressed by Cosmo's luck with women, looked at me and said, "God, I love a good fuck story. Why did you make him stop?"

"Save it for later," I said.

"How does he do it?"

"Mostly, he doesn't drink and they do," I answered.

"Cosmo mixed me up an Arnold Palmer."

"That's kind of a panty-waist drink for a guy like you, isn't it, Joe?"

"It's only ten, much too early to start drinking."

Cosmo looked at his watch and said, "Where are they? You don't suppose something happened, do you?"

"Relax, I called Aidan on his cell phone. The train was late. They'll be here soon."

"Your mother coming to town?" Asked Paulus.

"No," I said.

"Christ, I'm as nervous as a cat," Cosmo said.

"What do you have to be nervous about?" I asked.

"I just want this to go well."

"OK," said Paulus, "quit playing me fellows and tell me who you guys are talking about?"

"Ever hear of Ali Bin Hassan?" Cosmo asked.

The Post columnist scrunched up his nose and forehead a little bit. "Wasn't he the low level munchkin at the Egyptian embassy who started ranting all over town against his own government?"

"You got it," Cosmo said.

"My buddy, Jim McGregor, was the reporter who interviewed Ali," Paulus said. "Ali's comments were certainly ill-advised, but I know Jim and it's not beneath him to take some journalistic license with what was said at the interview."

"That's what got Ali fired," Cosmo said.

"He tried to hide behind his diplomatic status when he was arrested with all those guns in his trunk," Paulus said. "Since the embassy fired him and he was in the country illegally, he had no immunity."

"Did you also know he was Cosmo's cell mate?" I chimed.

"No, I didn't," he said.

"All I remember from the article was that Ali ran around D.C. for six months carousing with rich Arab boys and in the process succumbed to the modern American seductions of sex, drugs, rock and roll and violence," I said. "The media loved that irony."

"What prejudiced him in the court I think is that he is related to Osama Bin Laden," Paulus said.

"He was framed," Cosmo said.

"He was lucky," Paulus said. "If he'd returned to Egypt God knows what would have become of him. American justice is certainly preferable to Egyptian justice."

"I remember when the verdict came out, " I said. "The Post put it on the front page because he was one of the first individuals convicted under the Patriot Act."

"He's been released from jail and Aidan went to pick him up at Union Station. He should be here any minute."

"You sent Aidan to pick him up?" Paulus said.

"The boy volunteered," I said. "He's dying to find out about the seventy virgins that await you in heaven when you are martyred for Islam."

"I'd rather have two prostitutes from Atlantic City," Cosmo said.

The two of us middle aged men considered that choice and nodded our heads in agreement.

"I tell you Paulus, I see something in this Ali," I said. "You're a quick study. Give him the once over and let me know what you think. He's almost thirty but he's got this spark that you don't see very often these days."

"He came across as just another hot-headed Muslim who'd rather be violent than thoughtful," Paulus said. "It will be interesting to see what prison has done to him."

"He wouldn't be the first to come out and hold a grudge against society," Cosmo said, and I knew he spoke from experience. "He's applying for political asylum."

"Here's another thing. With what's going on in Egypt he is going to be hounded by everyone," I said. "The feds are going to harass him for information about what he knows about Al Qaida and the Muslim Brotherhood, and the Egyptian military."

"They tried that in prison," Cosmo said. "It got them nowhere."

"I'd be more concerned about the bounty hunters and groups like the Muslim Brotherhood who will try and make sure he doesn't talk," Paulus said. "But he's been in a Maryland prison for several years. What could he know?"

I shrugged my shoulders.

"As a reporter I'd be more interested in a personality profile of him. Where does he stand politically?"

"I don't know?" said Cosmo.

"What was he like in jail," Paulus asked.

"In his first two years he hung out with devout Muslims," Cosmo said. "They protected him. He prayed with them and read the Koran and worked to steel his soul against the secular society, which he claims framed him. Later, it was suggested that his own government set him up. He came from an influential family and the executive branch in Cairo didn't want him returning to stir up trouble.

"One day on the yard someone told him it was his own father who set him up for his own protection," Cosmo confided. "It was a blow. He got all confused and stopped talking all together. After Bin Laden was killed, he went his own way."

"Jail does strange things to men," I said. "My own Uncle Harry spent time in Leavenworth on a racketeering charge when he worked for Bugsy Siegel's mob in the 1950s. After his release, the Nevada Gaming Commission wouldn't let him work anywhere in the state. He harbored an incredible grudge over those lost prison years. On the outside he was a rake and reprobate but on the inside he was resentful and distrustful of government authority."

"Joe, you're a bookman. You ever see Arnold Toynbee's "A Study In History?" Paulus asked.

"Sure it comes through my bookstore all the time."

"Who is he?" asked Cosmo."

"A historian who wrote this book about how civilizations rise and fall," said Paulus. "He interpreted history through something like Jungian archetypes that are consistent through history instead of following it in a linear way. There's this essay called "Withdraw and Return". He postulated that very often great men are forced into exile, in Ali's case prison, which releases them from work and other responsibilities so they can deal with their own issues and societies at the same time.

"I can list examples," he continued. "Moses going up Mount Sinai and coming down with the Ten Commandments, Lenin's long exile in Switzerland before returning to Russia to take power."

"How about Mohammed's own Hegira," I said. "His exile from Mecca to Medina to escape religious persecution is an example Ali would understand. Part of me expects Ali, fed on a diet of my books, would come out of prison an inspired prophet ready to bring his Arab people into the twenty-first century, but maybe not."

"Ali is going to be Ali," said Cosmo, a bit irritated. "Don't try and fit him onto some old man's Procrustean bed."

Cosmo had just finished his sentence when Aidan strolled through the front door smiling and carrying the convict's suitcase. Ali walked three steps behind him and stopped when he entered the bistro to gingerly take in the sights and smells.

And of course the first thing he saw was Stella Diaz. Forget the plush carpet and photographs, the loud laughter and conversation. Even from across the room you could tell he was smitten.

Stella greeted him with her usual aplomb having no idea of who he was or where he came from. No one could tell by the way he was dressed. The cut of his suit was top shelf.

Standing tall and straight made him look taller than his five-foot-eleven frame. His coco colored complexion was accentuated by a thin dark goatee and from the track lighting above him you could tell he had gel in his hair. The diamond pinky ring and gold watch suggested that he was the son of a rich Arab sheik instead of a recently released inmate.

Aidan gave Stella a high five when he saw her and immediately introduced Ali to the hostess who treated him to her big smile.

But it had been a long time since he had an unsupervised moment with a beautiful woman. That something so natural as an exchange with someone like Stella had been denied him for so long made him realize, not in anger, not in defiance, but in a deep sadness, what he had lost. I could sense it all from across the room.

Upon his introduction, he took her hand and kissed it. If Grimaldi tried that crap on Stella I'd have moaned in disgust but somehow Ali pulled it off. Instead of being some cliché, it seemed like an act of gallantry. Ali hadn't had the opportunity for gallantry in a long, long time and he reveled in it.

"Are you Arabic?" he asked with a boyish enthusiasm.

"No, Cuban," she answered.

There was the beginning of small talk. But when two customers arrived, Stella excused herself and attended them. Yet he remained transfixed by her as she led the couple to their table.

Cosmo called out a greeting to his old friend but Ali's attention was firmly on Stella. Finally, his patience expended, Cosmo shouted out, "Hey you!"

Shaken from his dream Ali marched into the bar and faced Cosmo. Clutching each other by the biceps, they stared at each other from a foot apart. Ali broke the ice. He uttered a single word, "Brother."

Their kinship renewed, Cosmo reached for him and gave him a hug that lifted his feet from the ground.

Aidan came up to me and Paulus, after he checked Ali's suitcase in the cloakroom and said, "There he is."

"Nice job, boy," I said. "Did he tell you about the seventy virgins?"

"Do you think it's really true?" Aidan asked.

"Maybe for Muslims. Unfortunately, you're a Cashew."

"I could convert."

"I don't think your mother would approve of you changing religion for group sex."

"Let it go, Aidan," said Paulus. "Seventy women at once is a lot of work."

I think Cosmo was a little hurt that Ali seemed more interested in Stella than in him. While they spoke in an animated fashion, Ali positioned himself so one eye remained upon the hostess stand. Finally he could no longer contain himself and excused himself from Cosmo. Ali walked right up to Stella.

"Do you date?"

"You have to ask my master," she said laughing and pointing to me.

He turned his head and recognizing me for the first time marched over and extended his hand.

"Welcome back, kid," I said.

"Rabbi," he said, "thank you for your kindness."

"Ali, let me introduce you to Dave Paulus."

"I read your column, sir."

"And I've read all about you," Paulus said with just a hint of sarcasm.

What happened next surprised me. Ali eyeballed Paulus up and down and instead of continuing his graciousness, he became sullen and distrustful of the reporter. Perhaps it was because Paulus had been drinking.

"Why is it some men rise to the top and others wallow in the dirt?" Ali asked Paulus.

"I haven't got a clue," he answered.

The fact that such an unimpressive specimen like Dave Paulus should have such power and influence, a man who drinks like a fish and had none of Ali's passion, pain or integrity struck him as an injustice.

Ali longed for all Paulus had. His lack of it revealed a shadowy side of his personality that I had not seen before. And it was only out of politeness and breeding that Ali restrained his contempt.

If Stella was Ali's first reality check, meeting Dave Paulus was the second. The tension remained until Ali excused himself and made his way to the men's room.

"Cosmo and Ali are an odd friendship," Paulus said. "Together they might cause a lot of trouble for each other."

Chapter 15

In my dining room the power table is referred to as Minnie's table. It's a half moon black leather booth whose bench is two feet higher than the dining room floor. Its height allows diners to rise above the masses. While feasting at it, one can easily pretend to be cock of the walk.

The two booths that flank it are not as grand. When sitting at it nobody comes in or leaves without you noticing. The opposite is also true. Nobody enters or leaves the room without them noticing you.

Accommodating as many as six people, it's suited for small groups of big shots. There isn't enough room for their flunkies. When the occasion warrants conspicuous consumption it's the requested spot. I'm picky about who I let sit there.

Tonight, the reserved sign never came off. I wasn't sharing it with anybody except me, Aidan, Cosmo and Ali.

On the wall behind it is a life size portrait of Minerva Battle framed in black with a glass shield. My Uncle Harry's ex-lover is stretched out on a black couch with a small orange scarf covering her hip. She was African-American, middle aged and voluptuous.

"Who reserved Minnie tonight?" It's one of the first questions my staff often asked when beginning their shifts. On the seating chart it's also listed as table 31.

I don't know much about Minerva except that she died in a car crash in 1972. Harry felt responsible because she was on her way over to see him when it happened. His guilt remained and he pined for her the rest of his life. Later he commissioned Francis Chioffi, a local portrait artist, to recreate his favorite photo of her in oil on canvas.

To me, the painting looked good right from the start. But Harry rejected it four times, a fact that exasperated Chioffi, who wasn't getting paid by the hour.

The first time Harry saw it he told Chioffi to redo Minnie's face. "Where's the love and hate that took turns in her? It's missing!" he shouted. "You've made her look way too passive. Fix it."

When Chioffi returned it, Minnie wore an expression of intense sexual desire, which worked for Harry. But the breasts Chioffi painted, while alluring, were just too small. "Those are not the breasts of a Black woman," Harry carped.

The artist returned to his studio to make them larger. Quickly rectified, Chioffi returned the painting, this time with bigger breasts.

"They're still not big enough," Harry shouted. "And that's not how they looked when she leaned forward."

Chioffi went back to his studio and made the breasts bigger. He came back three days later.

"Finally, the right size," Harry said. "Now take it back to your studio. Make them shiny."

Chioffi finally understood what Harry was looking for and a week later the portrait was hanging above table 31.

Minnie's reputation is that of a talisman. It always struck me as ironic that such deference should be ascribed to her since in this town Realpolitik holds sway. But she was the guardian of good intentions, the Goddess Fortuna.

Can you remember those scenes in the Odyssey when Athena confers great good fortune in order to save Odysseus? Though just a painting, Minnie had that kind of magic. And anyone wanting a share of her good earth-mother energy was expected to shell out big bucks for the privilege since spiritually they were paying for her blessing.

When arguments arose, when somebody broke bad news, when people overindulged to the point of making themselves sick beneath Minnie's visage, my staff always attributed it as a sign of Minnie's disapproval and were never surprised by a bad tip.

As superstitious as it sounds, we were wary of people who fared poorly at 31. They were suspected of a character flaw. On the other hand no waiters ever received a good tip without giving Minnie a wink of thanks. It was part of the restaurant's culture.

The Minnie saga had one wrinkle. She was Reverend Battle's aunt. That his aunt was a former prostitute, then lover, then consort of my uncle, Harry Green, pissed him off. He claimed his family's honor was besmirched by the public display of Minnie Battle.

Perhaps I should have taken the painting down and appeased the Baptist. But deep down I knew that much of the restaurant's good fortune resided in her pagan portrait. I couldn't bring myself to do it.

I considered this dinner with Ali significant enough to reserve the big medicine table. He had come into my life through Cosmo, and Dave Paulus hit the nail on the head when he compared Ali's story to that Toynbee metaphor, "Withdraw and Return."

His prison sentence complete, now was the time for Ali's return, just like Cosmo. And the return was everything. For some men finding their true path takes a long time. Ali was such a man and I thought it incumbent upon myself to do the good dad thing and see him through.

In addition, I thought Ali's drama might somehow be representative of the plight of his own Arab people and I was hoping for some sort of insight that might hasten his transition to a productive life. So I enlisted Minnie's juju.

When the four of us sat down, the dining room had emptied out and all that remained was a two top lingering over dessert.

The wait staff was finishing up so we waited on Ali ourselves. Cosmo took care of the drinks. He and I drank beer. Ali and Aiden drank Pepsi. On a big tray, I delivered two forty-eight-ounce Porterhouse steaks, cooked medium rare, accompanied with horseradish mashed potatoes and crème spinach in smaller dishes from the kitchen. Aidan grabbed four Caesar salads garnished with crostinis covered with black olive pâté from the pantry.

I thought to open a good bottle of Cabernet but Aidan was underage, Cosmo hated wine and Ali decided that he shouldn't drink his first day out of jail since even he admitted that he was lousy at holding his liquor.

It was funny to see Ali turning the big sharp steak knife around in his hand. He hadn't held anything so sharp in a long time. Before he cut into the steak he considered its weight and ran his thumb across its sharp edge. Then, with the precision of a surgeon, he began cutting the steak up into tiny little pieces.

We hadn't been eating for more than a minute when Rose came in. Before she even greeted us she called out, "Hi, Minnie" to the bistro deity. Then she said, "Is this a sausage party or can a girl join in too?"

"Grab a plate from the kitchen, honey."

Rose turned her attention to Aidan. "Why aren't you answering your cell phone? Mom's been calling you for over an hour. It's a school night. She told me to stop here on my way home and bring you in."

"Christ," Aidan said. "I'm eighteen. Why can't she just back off?"

"Bro', don't forget that I turned eighteen the same exact day as you and I play by the rules. Why can't you?"

"Dad," he implored, "I just started eating. I can't leave now."

"Aidan, I'm not getting busted so you can gorge yourself on red meat," Rose said.

"Since when did you become a vegetarian?" Cosmo asked.

"I'm not." Rose said.

"Where are your manners?" I said. "You didn't even say hello to Ali."

"Oh, Ali, didn't recognize you looking all dressed up like that. When did you get out?"

"Just today," he said.

"I'd watch it if I were you," she said. "Compared to prison this food is way too rich. It might make you sick."

"Rose, I'm not sharing my steak with you," Ali said.

"You can have some of mine," I told her.

"What am I going to tell Mom?"

"Call her on your cell phone, ask her what she's hungry for," I said.

"What Mom needs is not on your menu," Rose said.

"Call her anyway and don't be such a smartass. Tell her you'll be home in a little while with doggy bags."

"How is Shortstop?" Ali asked, only half paying attention.

He was busy chewing each morsel thirty times, a habit Cosmo said he picked up in prison. Nobody responded.

But when Ali, his eyes half closed in a dreamy expression, said, "It tastes like cotton candy." Rose and Aidan burst out laughing.

"What's so funny?" He asked.

Aidan had a hard time explaining the exact reason for laughing. He smiled, shrugged his shoulders and resumed eating.

When Rose returned with a plate I began slicing her pieces of steak.

"Just a bit of the filet," she said. "I'm in the mood for tenderness tonight, not flavor."

Aidan let out a sarcastic moan. No doubt he was disappointed that with Rose there he wasn't going to hear about the sexy blonde stalking Cosmo at the bar. Cosmo seemed disappointed too. He wasn't going to hear the story about Sally puking in the bathroom.

"How's school going, Rose?" Cosmo asked.

"Good, I'm taking a film course this quarter and will be making my own documentary."

"That's funny," Ali said. "Your father is a great bookman and instead you make movies."

"Books are old school, Ali," Rose said. "Movies are so much faster and accessible to people. I read as much as the next girl, but film is a better medium."

"Movies will never replace books," Cosmo said. "It's an inferior way to tell a story. About the only emotion that comes across better in movies is violence, which is probably why there's so much of it in film today."

"The violent nature of America is a big problem in the world," Ali said.

"That sounds pretty funny coming from an Arab," Rose said.

Suddenly her body startled. Her face turned red. "Which one of you guys kicked me? Who was it?"

Nobody admitted it.

"At the Green dinner table you can say fuck you, but you're not allowed to say shut up in any way, shape or form, right, Daddy? So don't try and censor me."

Still no one confessed.

"Daddy!"

"Hey, it wasn't me," I said.

Finally Cosmo confessed. "Alright, it was me. Jesus, Rose, lighten up a little bit. There is such a thing as manners."

"Am I supposed to stifle free speech to protect a grown man's feelings? The truth is the truth."

"It's a horrible problem with my people," Ali confessed. "We have rage. And in prison I kept asking myself, what is to be done? With civil war in Iraq, Syria, Egypt, Afghanistan, it seems as if Arab rage is the only appropriate response to the modern world."

"I'm not buying any of that," Rose said. "The problem with the Arab world is about the way you treat women. If women had a greater role in the decision making process they would neutralize the Arab militants who screw everything up. Plus, if you let them take off their veils and enter the work force, you're families wouldn't live in such poverty."

"You think you know it all, don't you?" Ali said quietly, with a mounting sense of humiliation in his voice. "Is this what they teach you in your fancy private school?"

"No, it's what Louisa's grandmother told me. She's from Beirut and is a Maronite Christian. What she tells us about her experience with Islamic militants is not flattering."

"It's not that simple," Ali said.

"So explain it to me," Rose said.

"That would take hours," he said.

Then Aidan chimed in. "Hey, Ali, my mom thinks the President should send in an army of 30,000 Americans to the Arab World."

"Is your mom crazy?" Ali protested.

"No, she thinks the Arabs are," Aidan said. "The thirty thousand Americans wouldn't be soldiers, they'd be therapists."

"Hey Rose, why don't you do your documentary on Ali?" I asked.

"He certainly has a good story."

Suddenly Rose's confrontational attitude softened. "Ali, I didn't mean to come off like a bitch. Would you let me do my documentary on you?"

"Why should I trust you with my story?"

"Why not? Is anyone else begging for it?"

"No," he sighed.

"Media breeds media, Ali. Even if I do a mediocre job, somebody else might see it and re-film it for a bigger venue."

"Could be worth it," Cosmo said.

"Let me think about it," Ali said.

"Awesome," Rose said. Reaching her hand across the booth, she shook hands with Ali to close the deal.

Then she drew in all our attention as she focused all her energy into a creative trance. "Wait, wait," she said. "I can see it now. Rose Green presents an insider's look into the life of an Arab terrorist."

"Rose!" Cosmo shouted. "That's enough already."

"What? I heard he was a bad motherfucker. Did you go and get soft in prison, Ali?"

"Cosmo's right, honey," I said. "Back off."

"That's just how they portrayed me in the papers. I can't blame her," Ali said.

"I can hardly wait to run this idea by Mrs. Ginnane," Rose said. "Daddy, ever since your parent-teacher conference about Jack she hasn't been very nice to me."

Aidan's cell phone rang. He opened it up and I saw that it was Joannie. He gave me a look as if asking permission to blow her off, but Rose interjected.

"You pick that up, Aidan, or I'll hear about it in twenty seconds on my cell phone."

"Hi, Mom," he said. "I'm at the bistro. We're almost done eating. I'm putting together a doggy bag for you."

"Bark, bark, bark," Ali shouted with a big grin on his face.

Aidan took the phone away from his ear and laid it against his chest. He glared. "Don't goof around, Ali, my mom's on the phone."

Joannie added twenty extra minutes to their curfew. The twins wolfed down their meals. Aidan put part of his steak into a small box and then into a bag with the bistro's name on it for Joannie. Then with a handshake from my boy, and a kiss on the cheek from my girl, they were gone.

"Your girl is precocious," Ali said.

"A ball breaker," said Cosmo.

"She gets that from Joannie," I said. "The guy who marries her is going to need a lot of support."

We went on to finish our dinners.

"Ali, what are your plans now that you're free?" I asked.

"Not sure. I have to figure out a way for me to stay in America first. That won't be easy."

"It's a serious problem," I said. "As a former convict who wasn't born here, you don't have much standing with the Department of Homeland Security."

"But we have a plan, Ali," Cosmo said. "Our attorney friend, Eli Holbrooke, agreed to take your case."

"He's a lobbyist, not an immigration attorney," I said.

"But he's going to meet with someone at the Justice Department to help delay any deportation hearings."

"Good luck with that," Ali said. "Even if the feds say yes, I still have to answer to the Arab factions in town."

"We'll need Joe to grease that for us," Cosmo said.

"I'll have a conversation with Sammy Rasouli and ask his advice."

"Thank you, Joe," Ali said. "Sammy is a reasonable man."

I gave Ali a serious look intended to bring him back to reality.

"The hell he is. He's a butthead lieutenant in a large organization of buttheads. But he's probably the place to start."

Suddenly Stella Diaz stood beside me.

"You are still here, Stella?" Ali asked.

"Oh yes. I'm always one of the last to leave. Part of my closing side work is to chase out the evil spirits."

It was her little joke. Ali didn't get it. She bent over and whispered in my ear. "There's a woman at the front door named Malika. She's looking for you or Cosmo. She says you know where Ali Bin Hassan is. What should I do?"

"It seems like you have company, Ali," I announced.

"Is it Malika?" asked Cosmo.

"You called Malika, without telling me?" Ali protested.

"Dude, she's here to take you home. After all, she's your wife. Go to your family. I got a bachelor pad to maintain."

"You have children too?" Asked Stella with a big grin.

"Two, American born."

"So much for our torrid romance," she sighed.

"Back off, Stella," Cosmo said.

"Is she Egyptian?" I asked.

"She is a Berber, from Algeria. Malika is a naturalized citizen. She is a French teacher at Woodrow Wilson High School."

"Stella, ask Malika to join us," I said.

But Ali, suddenly nervous, put up his palms. "Stay here, please, all of you. This is going to be awkward enough without an audience."

He stood up and walked to the door.

Chapter 16

I turned the last light off in the bistro, then walked upstairs and sat down beside the tortoise pen to unwind.

Tonight, two of my four tortoises were out from underneath the electric blanket and were sunning themselves in the full spectrum light bulb that hung up above them. Ruthie was sunbathing directly beneath it with her eyes closed and her neck reaching upward to the light.

Sometimes we called her "Big Momma." When I got her she was smaller than my fist but since then had grown to nearly a foot in length. The family joke was that she had an eating disorder. Rose would say, "Poor Ruthie, she thinks food is love," especially when she tore into romaine heads like a snow blower pushing down a snowy winter sidewalk.

Beside her stood her consort, Louis, who I'd bought from a small pet shop in Chevy Chase on the same day. He was no larger than a soft ball.

Tonight, Louis was uncharacteristically active. His mating ritual consisted of a grimace on his tortoise face and a menacing dance around Ruthie. Though the pace was ridiculously slow by human standards, Louis was actually busting a move. When Ruthie opened her eyes at the sound of dried up romaine scraps crunching beneath his one-pound girth, he snapped at her face.

I had never seen him display this kind of behavior before and I recognized the fact that my teenage reptiles were becoming sexual.

Despite his lethargic pace Louis looked menacing, and also ridiculous, since he was half of Ruthie's size.

I didn't want to scare him out his sex ceremony so I sat very still. But the stud was so pumped up that he didn't even back off when Cosmo entered the room. Suddenly, Louis mounted her.

"Hey, what's going on?" asked Cosmo.

"We got action in the tortoise pen."

"What the hell is Louis doing to her arm pit?"

"Beats the crap out of me," I said. "I think he's fucking her."

"Is that the way tortoises mate?"

"Not sure."

"Louis, you idiot," Cosmo called down, "take her from behind."

"Shhh, don't scare him."

"Joe, I know you've always had this dream of breeding your own Russian tortoises, but he's never going to knock her up like that."

"I know."

"What an idiot," Cosmo said. "I can see him trying to mount her face, that's male behavior, but the arm pit?"

"If he's smart he'll stay away from her mouth. She might chomp down on him."

Suddenly, Cosmo had a big smile. "Instead of Big Momma, you can start calling her Big Moheil."

"Quit goofing on my tortoises."

Tortoises are not usually expressive, but the dynamic Jersey look upon Louis's face impressed us. Were it not for the fact that he was doing her all wrong, I might have bragged about him at the bar.

"Maybe it's some sort of tortoise Kundilini love dance that gets females hot," Cosmo said. "Maybe he knows exactly what he's doing."

"Should we give him the benefit of the doubt?"

"Maybe, but you never know. I once read this article about how they couldn't get the pandas to mate at the National Zoo. So the zookeeper actually placed several posters of male pandas mounting female pandas around their cage. After about a week the male figured it out and started having sex. It worked for pandas, maybe it would for your tortoises."

"Are you suggesting tortoise porn?"

"Got a better idea?"

"No," I said. "But where am I going to get a picture of two Russian tortoises humping?"

"Does it have to be tortoises? Maybe a picture of pigs doing it would work. They're both round."

"What have I got to lose?"

"Nothing," he said. "And it's not like having those pictures around is going to be inappropriate for the kids."

"Maybe there's something at the bookstore on reptiles. I'll take a look tomorrow."

"Wow, look how far Louis's head is out of his shell," Cosmo said.

"I never knew he had so much neck."

We stared at the muscles straining in his neck. His eyes were bulging too. The creases of his skin looked like war paint. But it didn't seem like he was having much fun. Then I started cleaning my fingernails, knowing that given the tortoise's pace it would be several minutes before anything new happened.

"Say, what did you think of Ali tonight?" I asked.

"He was ridiculous. I don't want to tattle but I bet Aidan got him stoned on the way over to the bistro."

"You think so?"

"For Christ sakes, Joe, he was barking like a dog at the table when Aidan was on the phone with his mom. And mooning over Stella like a lovesick school boy."

"I did think that was strange."

"If he was sharp he'd have engaged Rose in an hour long debate," Cosmo said.

"I was surprised by how easily Rose bullied him, and by how easily you pawned him off on Malika."

"That was a bit of luck," Cosmo said. "I might have to thank Aidan for that tomorrow."

"Malika might be the only person who can save him from deportation."

"Yeah, I had to call her. My apartment's too small. Living with him again would remind me too much of prison."

"I'll call Sammy Rasouli tomorrow and find out whose ass Ali has to kiss in the Muslim community."

"If they think he has any secrets about Al Qaida and the Muslim Brotherhood they'll want him shipped back home fast."

"Throwing the feds a bone about Al Qaida may be his best trump card," I said.

"He's been in jail for a long time," Cosmo said. "I can't imagine anything he knows is still valuable."

"I get the feeling from Sally that they're not interested in what he knows of the past. It's what he might find out in the future that makes him such an attractive mark. They want to turn him. But if that happens then he'll end up in a witness protection program for the rest of his life. That won't be good. He'll never get to use any of his talent. In the meantime, get him here after work tomorrow night. The three of us need to talk."

"About what?"

"About what Ali is going to do while Holbrook goes to work."

"Yeah, I guess Ali needs a job."

"Precisely."

"I'd like to see him doing twenty hours a week at the bookstore and another twenty hours here," Cosmo said.

"You could try and make him a bartender," I said.

"No way. He's a fish. Can't hold his liquor. Making him a bartender will ruin him."

"Can he cook?"

"I don't think he wants to be around your pork tenderloin."

"Maybe we can make a waiter out of him," I said.

"He may not get along with women and Black people."

"Either Ali takes a job or it's back on Daddy's payroll."

"Daddy's not an option," Cosmo said.

"I can pay him off the books until he gets a green card, but he may have to compromise some of his Muslim virtue."

"You seem to have this grand vision for Ali."

"I do." I said.

"So tell me already."

"I saw him speak once. It was a lecture at Busboys and Poets. He talked about the Arab Spring and he was impressive, impassioned and smart. If he was my son I'd want him to start his own think tank. I'd want him to lead his Muslim folk into the twenty-first century and I'd want to bring him into our business. I think I can coach him into greatness."

"Is that all?"

"Yes, that's all."

"What if he supports jihad and wants to take down Israel and America?" Cosmo asked. "Will you still support him?"

"If it contributes to the dialogue."

"So it comes back to that dialectic thing again, huh?"

"Don't be naïve, Cosmo. It's what we do."

"That's one way of looking at it."

He reached into his pocket and pulled out his cell phone to check the time. "I'm meeting that blonde," he said. "I've got to go."

"Does the blonde have a name?"

"Alicia."

"Good luck."

"If you're looking for company, Stella's still downstairs burning sage in the restaurant."

"I think I'll wait."

"She's become aware of what we do in the Potomac Room and she wants to be a part of it," I said.

"I think she wants to be more than just a part of the Potomac Room," he said, flexing his eyebrows.

"She's only twenty-eight."

"And the problem with that is…?"

"If she finds the skeletons in our closet and the feds subpoena her, I'll have to marry her just to keep her from testifying."

"In your dreams."

"Make sure she leaves when you do."

"What should I tell her?"

"Tell her I'm staring at tortoises."

"She won't believe me."

"It's the truth."

Just before Cosmo turned and walked out the door he hollered down, "Tap her, Louis."

His loud voice frightened the stud, who bolted back into his shell.

I poured myself a Scotch. The phone rang. It was Sally.

"Hello, Joe, what are you doing?"

"Watching porn."

"Are you alone?"

I looked at Louis who had yet to come out of his shell. "Sort of."

"I'm in trouble," she said. "Remember that date I mentioned who was out of the country for a while? He's coming back tomorrow from Afghanistan to take personal charge of Ali Bin Hassan."

"What's the trouble?"

"The marks on my body are still visible. If he finds out it was you who put them there he'll come after you with a vengeance. I won't be able to stop him. He's my boss."

"What are you going to do?"

"I'm not sure, but I'm scared for both of us."

"What's his name?"

"Bill Lyons."

"How many days before the bruises heal?"

"Another three of four."

"Can you blow him off for a few days?"

"I might have to re-enter the hospital with chest pains to keep him at bay."

"Sounds like a difficult situation," I said.

"I also called to thank you for last night," she said. "I'm so embarrassed. I've never been so out of control before. Thanks for staying the night and watching over me."

"You can make it up to me."

"Really. What do you have in mind?"

"It's work related."

There was a pause on the other end of the line.

"Tread carefully, Joe."

"I need a favor."

"What kind of favor?"

"I want you to find out if Stella Diaz is on anybody's payroll besides mine."

"Stella? Is she that pretty hostess who stands beside you at the door?"

"Yes."

"Is there a problem?"

"No. I just want to make sure she's not snooping."

"I'll need her social security number."

"I'll get it to you tomorrow."

"What if I find something?"

"I'll fire her."

"What's in it for me?" Sally asked.

"She propositioned me."

"So I can get rid myself of my competition, and rid you of a spy at the same time?"

"It's a good deal for both of us."

"You're not trying to compromise me, are you?"

"Not yet."

"I might be able to find out something."

"How long will it take?"

"Just a day."

"Good," I said.

"What if she's working for us?"

"Don't say a word and I'll know."

"What if I just can't tell you either way?"

"I'll still know."

"No, you won't."

"Yes, I will."

"Really? How?"

"You'll hold back in bed."

Chapter 17

A strong, sudden gust blew in through the open apartment window. Papers fluttered from my desk to the floor. I awoke from my nap.

I picked my head up from the couch. According to the clock, it was almost four o'clock and time to get ready for work. I picked up the fallen papers, which were financial disclosure forms from several of the colleges where the twins were applying.

The twins wanted to go to college in Chicago. Joannie had family there whom they both liked. But they couldn't agree where to go. Rose wanted the University of Chicago because of its prestige. Aidan wanted Northwestern because of its Big Ten sports.

There was no way they were going to school together. They're too competitive and wanted to break free from the other. I suspect that after high school they'll divorce and go their own ways, just like Joannie and me.

I showered and shaved, put on a black suit with a starched white shirt from the cleaners, threw a blue silk tie over my shoulder and walked downstairs to the bistro.

Saturday nights were kind of slow. The majority of my patrons were suburbanites who dined at the local restaurants in Maryland and Northern Virginia on weekends.

Others were politicos who came to D.C. during the week to conduct the business of government, and on Friday afternoons returned to their homes far beyond the Beltway.

So a sense of ease accompanied the Saturday night shift. We kept the Roosevelt Room dark because unlike Monday through Thursday we didn't need it. There were only about forty reservations on the book, a lean night by most accounts, but since I rarely had more than four servers on the floor it was enough to keep them busy. It had been a beautiful spring day in D.C. The cherry blossoms around the Tidal Basin were in bloom, the harbinger of the Washington spring, and the majority of diners tonight, I suspected, would be eating outside at sidewalk cafes to celebrate the return of spring.

Tonight's reservations were regulars who lived in the neighborhood. The rest were tourists.

There was no sense of urgency when I ambled up to the front door. Stella had everything under control. She wore her little black cocktail dress on Saturday night because, she said, it made her feel festive. The long string of pearls, given to her by her Cuban grandmother, glowed against her smooth Latin skin.

"You look fetching tonight," I said.

"Are you saying that I look like a dog?" She never looked up.

I suddenly found myself defensive when I shouldn't have been.

"There's Internet access in that reservation book. Go to a dictionary and look the word up," I snapped, watching myself tie a double Windsor in the mirror. She did.

"Oh, thanks."

"You seem distracted, are you okay?"

"I feel a migraine is coming on."

"Want me to call Rose and ask her to come in to work for you?"

"No, don't ruin her Saturday night. I'll get through it."

That smile of hers was something I took for granted. I suddenly felt unsettled. My good luck charm was dim.

I walked out the front door to the 18th Street curb and looked at the sky. Though still clear, a thin layer of clouds, like wax paper, was moving in. Inhaling deeply, I felt the breath of a rain shower. I returned to the hostess stand.

"Do you still get headaches when low pressure systems are on their way?"

"Yes, that might be it. The weather's changing."

"Get on the Internet and see what the National Weather Service says."

It only took her a few seconds to get to their website.

"Heavy thunderstorm for Montgomery and Prince George's County and Washington, D.C.," she read.

Cosmo came over from behind the bar.

"There's a storm on the way," I told him, "I think we might get swamped tonight because nobody's going to be able to sit outside."

"We'll probably need extra guys for valet service," he said. "No one wants to look for parking spaces in the rain."

"Get Petey on the phone and see if he can rustle up an extra guy or two. Tell them to bring their rain coats."

"I could call Ali," Cosmo said.

"Does he have a D.C. driver's license?"

"No, not yet."

"Then let's not call. My insurance agent will cancel my policy if he crashes somebody's car."

Just then the phone rang. Stella answered it and took a reservation for four people. No sooner did she hang up the phone that it rang again. As soon as she set down the receiver there was another request for a table. Then four more reservations came up on the computer all by themselves from Open Table. I realized the outdoor cafés weren't doing any business tonight, but maybe I was.

"Stella, see if you can find a server willing to come in at such late notice," I said. "I'll text the twins and ask them to work too."

I pulled out my cell phone and sent a text message to Rose: Need help@bistro.

"Let me call Aidan," Cosmo said. "If you call him he might not pick up. I owe him tip money. He'll answer the phone for me. I'll get him to come in."

Rose called back immediately.

"Honey, I got a feeling we're going to get slammed tonight. Any chance you'll come in and work the door with me and Stella?"

"Daddy, me and Louisa have plans," she complained.

"I'll have you out the door by nine with enough money for three Saturday nights," I promised.

"Are you really going to be busy?"

"That's what my intuition tells me."

"Can Louisa work too?"

"Sure, I'll take you both. You can help Stella at the door and Louisa can do coat check and escort people to their tables."

Rose put her palm over the phone and negotiated with Louisa. A muffled sound came over the phone. "She'll do it, but only if you throw for two orders of shrimp cocktail."

"Tell her one order and I'll give her half price on the second."

Again Rose's hand went on the phone.

"She said okay."

"Thanks, honey. Get here by six."

"Daddy, I think now is a good time to talk about my tattoo."

"Forget about it, Rose. You're not blackmailing me with that tattoo stuff."

"Mom said it was okay," she said.

"Jews don't believe in tattoos. It's a graven image and against one of our Ten Commandments."

"I'm only half Jewish," she scolded, "If you want to claim half my body for the Jews then declare which half because I'm giving the other half to the Catholics. They don't mind tattoos."

"What?"

"Do you want the left side or the right side? You can't have both."

"It doesn't work like that," I protested. "It's top or bottom and I'm claiming the top."

"Daddy, that's not fair."

"When King Solomon was deciding between the two women both claiming to be the baby's mother he didn't propose cutting the child right down the middle, but in the half at the waist, just like I'm proposing. It's all there. You can read it in the Old Testament. And that's my last word on it."

"How high to the top?" she demanded.

"Third chakra."

"Where's that?"

"Everything above your belly button."

"Wait a minute…" she said, trying to interrupt. But I didn't let her cut in.

"Rose, the last thing I want is for you to get something inked on your arm that makes you look like white trash."

"Hate to tell you, Daddy, but white trash is very chic these days."

"Be here in an hour and don't dress like a trollop."

"Fine," she snapped.

"And don't say fine unless it's really fine."

Rose and Louisa, arrived at 5:45 looking very conservative and prim.

"You two look great," I said as they walked through the front door.

"These are Mom's Ferragamo dresses."

"Rose, you can escort guests to the table. Louisa, you check the raincoats and the umbrellas. I'm going to troubleshoot."

Aidan arrived at six o'clock. The sky started pouring down rain seconds after he arrived. Stella stayed busy answering the two phone lines and marking down reservations until we'd booked every table.

Then people started to arrive. The line at the door was pushing up against the hostess stand as diners crowded forward into the small lobby area to get out of the rain. Rose and I escorted people to their seats and chatted amiably while Louisa kept busy in the little cloakroom.

By seven every table was full and still there was a line at the door.

Mary Costigan, my old Irish stalwart, appeared at the hostess stand and said. "Joe, you have to hold the door. I can't keep up with my tables. The kitchen's got thirty-minute ticket times and we have an impatient crowd tonight."

"Mary, go back in that dining room and make love to those people," I said. "I'll take care of it."

I turned to Stella. "Tell anyone who asks that there's a forty minute wait."

As I left the podium I heard some guy with a New York accent call out, "Hey, I'm hungry here."

The cooks were understaffed. The tickets were lined up on the line and all my guys were glued to their tasks. Shameem, my Pakistani sous chef, had a frightful look upon his face.

"Joe, we're just buried."

"Just get through this crunch. We're going to slow it all down. It's raining out so the customers aren't going anywhere. Just make sure what you send out is hot and not undercooked."

They were three people deep at the bar, and all clamoring to get Cosmo's attention with their drink orders. Aidan had the good sense to get behind the bar, pull beers and pour wine. The fancy martinis he left for Cosmo. Though Aidan was good at filling glasses, he was lousy at keeping track of who owed how much money.

"You guys holding up alright?"

"Piece of cake," Cosmo said.

I grabbed some beers and brought them to Shameem's kitchen crew. I pulled the dishwashers from the pit and had them make salads and cold appetizers.

Back at the hostess stand I checked in on Stella.

"Joe, some of these people aren't going to be seated for an hour. I think I should tell them to make sure they want to stay."

"It's a captive audience, relax."

"Some of them are getting testy."

"Honey, flirt a little."

"You're no help."

"Okay, here's something. Gather up the nasty ones and tell them you'll have their table very soon."

"Really? Who's going to wait on them?"

"I am. And don't give me anybody we know. I won't have time to schmooze."

I removed my jacket and handed it to Louisa in the cloakroom. There was an apron on the top shelf with a crummer and a corkscrew.

"You're going to be a waiter?" She asked.

"What's the matter, don't think I can cut it?"

"Well, we'll see, won't we," she teased. "Garcon, before you get start-ed, how about bringing me a shrimp cocktail? A girl gets hungry in here."

"Louisa, keep your head in the game."

Back at the hostess stand I gave Stella instructions.

"Seat me three tables. Wait ten minutes and bring in two more and after another fifteen minutes, bring another two more. That should help."

And so I went to work. It had been almost a year since I'd put on an apron and carried a tray. Though semi-retired, I loved the job, since at my age it was as close to being a professional athlete as I could come.

Around the restaurant with cork tray in hand I was all confidence and grace since there was nobody to come down on me should I screw up. It's good to be king.

Now, Derek Jeter of the New York Yankees hits .320 and is considered great. Tom Brady completes sixty percent of his passes. Both are future Hall of Famers. The flip side of that is that Jeter makes an out sixty-eight percent of the time and Brady fails 40 percent.

In the restaurant business we're allowed no such luxury, especially when customers are paying fifty bucks for a rib eye. We have to bat a thousand or we suck. Because the prospect of not living up to our customer's expectations was now nearly a certainty, a sense of urgency presided.

I instructed Stella not to seat friends in my section because ninety seconds of conversation was deadly. In that time I could pour coffee, drop off a guest's check, take a drink order and refill water glasses in my entire station.

"God is motion." Sometimes it's paraphrased, "God is movement."

Those lines have been repeated by George Wilhelm Hegel, Aristotle, Carl Jung, as well as in Hindu mythology.

For me that was one virtue of the waiter. You enter your body, focus your attention, and get in motion at high velocity, graciously feeding the masses.

While Mary stood beside me at the soup station, I poured out three cups.

"Well, look at you," she said. "Just like the old days, hey kid?"

"How you doing out there?" I asked.

"Jesus, it's like a flash flood," she said.

"Come on, Mary. Show me some of that tough Irish."

"They're grumpy, Joe."

"Hang in there. It will be over soon."

Just as I spoke I let go of the ladle too high above the soup. It splashed all over the left side of my shirt.

Mary burst out laughing as she marched through the swinging doors to the dining room.

Louisa busied herself running plates of food to the tables. Rose went to the kitchen to help with desserts. Stella refilled water glasses and helped the busboys clear and reset tables and soon we were keeping pace with the demand.

In my station, I had three people from Brazil, a grandma, a grandpa and their granddaughter. We discussed how multi-cultural our two nations were. Whites, Blacks and Hispanics all lived side by side.

"One major difference is that we have no Muslims, thank goodness," the old man said.

At another table I had a single woman from Toronto, Canada, sightseeing the nation's capital. She was a college English teacher here all by herself. I recommended a few of the city's better bookstores and a few small museums worth seeing, like the Renwick. I almost offered to chaperone her around the city myself. She was attractive and a good conversationalist. But I had no spare time in the coming days and let the opportunity pass.

Stella intercepted me on my way to the bar. "Joe, Joannie is at the door with seven guests. She claims that she has a reservation, but I don't know anything about it."

I delivered a round of cocktails and went right up to the door.

"What's up, Joannie?"

She grabbed me by the sleeve and walked me to the coat check.

"You're incompetence and disregard for me is what's up. I had an 8:30 reservation with some of my best clients and your bozos can't find it. Damn it, Joe. Are you trying to humiliate me?"

I should have been focusing on Joannie but the look on Louisa's face, who was forced to witness this embarrassed me.

"I walked through the whole place and there's not a Goddamn

table open," said Joannie. "What the hell am I supposed to do? Take them to Burger King?"

Now the old Joe would have shouted right back, but I was trying to transcend all that. So I took a breath.

"Take your group to the bar. Let Cosmo buy you all a drink and I'll figure something out."

"I knew I should have taken them to The Palm."

Back at the hostess stand, I asked Stella, "Do you have any record of Joannie's reservation?"

"No. Did she tell you and maybe you forgot?"

"Are you kidding? I remember every word she says. Failure to do so results in having to eat shit. This time I'm innocent."

"We won't have a table that big for a while."

"Great, the last thing I need is to have her stinking up the place," I said.

"We could open the Potomac room and seat them in there."

"Okay, let's put them in there."

I walked into the kitchen to find Rose at the dessert window. She wore Shameem's white chef coat over her dress garnishing the dessert plates with artistic lines.

"When you catch up here, take off the coat and sit with your mom in the bar. She's with her clients. Play the dutiful daughter and buy me some time."

Rose's face went white as a ghost. "Mom's here?"

"Be charming and get me off the hook."

Twenty minutes later I caught up on my tables and was at last ready to talk to Joannie. She wore a sarcastic look.

"We're going to seat you in the Potomac Room. You'll have the whole room to yourself. I'll even wait on you."

"Your shirt's dirty," she said, "and no, you will not be waiting on me. I didn't come here to have my privacy violated so you can tell our children nasty stories about what goes on between me and my friends."

"You can have Mary wait on you, but it's going to be another ten minutes."

She stared at the soup stain and said in her most defiant voice, "Fine."

"Have another drink." I turned and walked away while she explained the predicament to her friends.

I found Mary, who was filling a pitcher of water in the server's station.

"How are you holding up, Mary?"

"I'm flummoxed, Joe. In the old days I could have handled this, but the old gray mare ain't what she used to be."

"Don't sell yourself short, Honey. You're still my ace."

"Well, thanks for saying so."

"I need you to take a party of eight in the Potomac Room. I wouldn't ask except it's Joannie and she made it clear that she doesn't want me anywhere near her."

She looked around at her station, six tables full. "Most of them are nearly done," she said. "I can do it."

Stella gathered up Joannie's party and walked them, menus in hand to the Potomac Room.

I began restocking water glasses and silverware fresh from the dishwasher. I also took a minute to drink some water. I was dehydrated from the day's walk and the night's work.

Later, I pulled Mary aside and asked how things were going.

"Well, Joannie's a little steamed," Mary said. "By the time she was seated all the big appetizer lobsters were gone, as was the Beef Wellington. They ended up ordering rib eyes and Jack London Cabernet Sauvignon wine from the Captain's list."

"What's their bill?"

"Well, over a grand," she said.

Finally, after holding it for two hours, I had to piss. At the urinal, a customer stood beside me, surprised to find a waiter there.

"Are you with Joannie's party?"

"Yes," he answered. "She represents our trade association."

"How was dinner?"

"The potatoes that came with my steak were cold and I had to send them back, but all in all it was a good meal."

"Glad to hear that."

"Been working here long?" he asked.

"Yeah, a long time."

"I hear the owner is a real asshole."

"The absolute worst," I said as I zipped up and went to the basin to wash my hands.

I hadn't taken five steps out of the bathroom when I nearly bumped into Joannie as she came around a corner. She had good wine inside her now and had calmed down a bit.

"Next time I bring a group in here, I'll thank you not to treat us like we're a bunch of pork producers from Iowa."

"Okay."

"Christ, you're letting this place go to seed, Joe, and that means only one thing to me. That come next fall I'm going to have to pay for the twins's college tuition all by myself because you won't be able to contribute."

Now I was mad. She never made reservations and she was head tripping me. Her clients weren't around. It was time to step in her shit.

But no harsh words passed my lips. Rose was watching. Seeing the two of us together, and always hopeful that someday we'd reunite, she walked over with a big smile. Then she'd heard our exchange. Crestfallen, she retreated to the kitchen.

Joannie never saw Rose standing behind us and when she rejoined her group in the Potomac Room, I followed Rose into the pantry. She sat on a metal counter top with her head bowed.

"It's my fault," Rose said. "She asked me to make the reservation on Thursday and I forgot."

"You hung me out to dry tonight," I said.

"I'm really sorry."

"Damn it, Rose."

"I said I'm sorry. I'll tell her the truth tonight."

I grabbed a cloth napkin from the table and handed it to her so she could wipe her tears.

"I'm sorry too," I said. "We always seem to put you in the middle of things. Your mom should have called me and asked for the table herself instead of making you responsible. I'll talk to her about that."

"Daddy, we all sucked tonight."

"We were understaffed. These things happen. We'll do better next time."

"I hope so."

I reached into my pocket and pulled out a wad of bills. "Hey, guess what? You're old man can still cut it."

"Really?"

"It was a throw-money-at-Joe night."

"Those are my favorite," she said.

"Me too. After tipping the bar and the busboys I'll walk with $285."

"Not bad for an old guy," she said.

Then I handed her the money.

"There's no way I can ask Shameem to make an employee meal for all of us. Call Mr. Ping at the Panda Inn. Order some Chinese food. Ask him to deliver. Make sure everybody gets an egg roll and tip the driver twenty percent."

She walked off to the phone.

My skin was covered with a thin film of sweat. I was itchy. But the night was over and I was grateful for that. But then I saw Stella cornered by an angry customer in the lobby. He was screaming at her. She backed into a corner.

I recognized the guy. He sat with his wife at table 105. I'd refilled his water once. I swiped my manager card in the computer and re-opened his check for a look. He spent $165, drank several glasses of wine, skipped dessert and stiffed the waiter.

The name on the reservation was Warren Sieben. So I googled him.

"What's the problem here?" I asked, walking up behind him.

"I'll tell you what the problem is. We waited sixty minutes for our damn food and it wasn't worth our time or our money. This was totally unacceptable and I'm never coming back."

"If you're never coming back why should I give a flying fuck about you?"

He looked surprised that I baited him. "Because I'm going to tell all my friends what a rip-off this place is?"

"Are you Sieben from Georgetown University or the Commerce Department?"

"Mr. Sieben to you, Undersecretary of Commerce, and I want to see the manager."

"I'm in charge here tonight."

"You? Then I want to talk to the owner."

"That's me too."

"I'm going to bad mouth this place to everyone I know. And it's going to cost you business."

"Take your moral umbrage and shove it up your ass," I shouted. "I have friends too. Congressman Drinkwater of the House Commerce Committee has been coming here for six years. My bartender's his bookie and he has a crush on Stella here. When I tell him and everyone else how badly you treated her, everyone is going to hate you, I promise."

"Are you threatening me?"

Just then Kennedy the cop walked through the front door. He'd heard the last part of the exchange and got between us.

"This guy giving you trouble, Joe?"

"No, he's just about to leave."

"Damn right I'm leaving. And I'm never coming back."

"Oh, you'll be back. Not to eat or drink, but to apologize to Stella for being such an asshole. Drinkwater is going to insist."

He huffed out the door with his wife trailing three steps behind him.

I walked to the bar. Cosmo gave me a big smile. "Hell of a night, hey?"

"Pour me a scotch."

"Aidan did a good job tonight," Cosmo said.

"Well, that's good."

"I'll make a bartender out of him yet."

"Did I see Ronnie Brown from the Redskins in here tonight?" I asked.

"Yeah, he was here with his brother."

"What did he order?"

A big grin came over Cosmo's face. "Louis the XIII and Coke."

"I thought you were going to have a talk with him about that," I said. "He's making five million a year. Somebody should teach him how to drink."

"Next time, I promise."

When the Chinese food came, the staff gathered in the bar and we gobbled it all down. Everyone was so exhausted that the meal was consumed in relative silence, except for Louisa, who sat apart from the group eating her shrimp cocktail and gabbing on her cell phone.

Restaurant evenings have a beginning, middle and an end. They begin when the doors open and end when the last customer walks out the door. And when the story is over, all's forgiven and forgotten until tomorrow night when it begins anew.

Slowly my employees left one by one. The last ones to leave were Stella, and Cosmo and Aidan. The four of us sat and relived the evening's events like ESPN newscasters on Sports Center.

Then we cleaned up the empty white food boxes, the napkins and forks.

"Come on, Aidan, it's getting late. Your mother's already angry. Let's get you home."

"No worries. She's dead asleep by now," he answered.

"I'm going that way," Cosmo said. "I'll walk him home."

"Make sure he goes home. I don't want him gallivanting all over town until dawn."

I locked up the walk-ins and liquor cabinets while Stella paced the bistro with a stalk of burning sage in her hand to drive out any bad juju.

When she went to the ladies room, I went to the kitchen for some romaine, corn kernels and carrot sticks. They were in my hands when I saw her again.

"How's your migraine?"

"Better," she said.

"Considering how you felt at the beginning of the night I thought you were a real trooper."

"Thanks." She extinguished the sage stalk coals in a glass of water. "Seeing Joannie in action was enlightening. I think I understand now why you don't trust women."

"Joannie is a lot of work."

"You have the best of both worlds, family and freedom."

She looked at the assortment of vegetables in my arms.

"I've worked here a long time now. You've never invited me up to see your tortoises. After tonight, I think I've earned it."

"Don't you have somewhere to be?"

"No."

Chapter 18

"Where are they?" Stella asked as she stood beside the tortoise pen.

"Pick up the blanket," I answered. "The security of their shells isn't enough. They like to hide underneath things as well."

She reached down and lifted the quilt. There they were, all four of them like in a football huddle. She threw the blanket to the side and studied the reptile crew.

"Do they always hang out in a gang like that?"

"It's a recent thing. See the big one, Ruthie? She's the social director. They like being close to her."

"Why is that?" Stella asked.

"I guess it's because she's got so much good energy. They just naturally gravitate to her."

"Can I pick one up?"

"Sure, just make sure you don't drop them."

Stella reached down. When she lifted Louis in the air, he hissed and retreated into his shell.

"That's Louis. He's the alpha male of the group."

"Him?"

"Yeah, him. He's Ruthie's mate. If any of the other tortoises get too close to her when he's horny, he bites."

"Where did he get his name?"

"It's a family name. Both my grandfathers were named Louis. Louis Meckler and Louis Green."

When Louis poked his head out momentarily to see who was holding him, she laughed at him. "He even looks like a Jewish grandfather."

Did that line hurt Louis's feelings? Maybe, because he ducked back into his shell and started pissing. Stella shrieked and held him out and away from her. It was sheer luck that she averted a wet leg.

"Give him to me," I said. "Hold him horizontal like this." Grabbing him firmly by the sides of his shell, I began speaking softly. "Louis, come on out and be social."

It took a few moments but he eventually emerged and let me stroke his head with my finger.

When I put him down, he ambled underneath the blanket. Then I served up the romaine, corn and carrot sticks onto a flat white plate. No one moved to it.

"Now what do we do?" Asked Stella.

"We wait."

"How long?"

"It may take them an hour to make it to the food, you never know."

"They sure do take their time."

"That's their virtue. Slow motion. Watching them move so slowly slows you down too. After a fast night at the restaurant it's remarkably therapeutic."

"How long do you spend watching them?"

"Depends on how stressful my night's been."

We waited on chairs beside the tortoise pen to see if they'd be dining tonight.

"Christ, if our customers ate that slow you'd never turn a table."

I opened a bottle of Syrah and poured her a glass. For myself, Johnny Walker Green with two ice cubes.

"There's one more thing I need to know."

"What's that?"

"Do you really keep boxes of Jujubes in your freezer?"

"What?"

"I overheard one of your bimbos telling her friend about it once in the ladies room."

"Nice to know I'm talked about."

"Well, is it true?"

"Go see for yourself."

A peel of laughter came when she opened the freezer door.

"Bring a box over here," I called.

We sat back down beside each other crunching frozen Jujubes and watching for tortoises, who still did not emerge. After a few minutes she lost interest in the tortoises. She began looking around at my apartment. Walking to the two bookcases standing side by side, she studied the titles.

"These are some beautiful old books," she said.

"There's a certain dignity to the way they made books in the old days."

"You have some interesting titles."

"I've owned a used book store for over twenty-five years."

"What do you collect?"

"Lots of things. At home I have shelves filled with old books about European Jewry before the Holocaust. But here is where I keep my books on philology. They're my favorite."

"I'm not sure what that is."

"Philology is the study of ancient texts."

"You seem to like Catullus, and Propertius."

"They were Roman poets who were prurient as hell. The way they write about sex is sometimes hilarious. It's like listening to Tony the waiter tell stories about the Gay bars in D.C."

"Show me your best book," she said.

I walked to the bookcase. Studying the row at eye level, I picked one out and handed it to her.

"This one is called *Paideia: The Ideals of Greek Culture*. It's a first edition written by a German named Werner Jaeger. He was a German professor who fled Nazi Germany in the 1930s because his wife was a Jew. He came to America and taught at the University of Chicago and later at Harvard. What's fascinating about his book is how it details the high ideals of ancient Greek culture, which in a large measure are the basis of American culture too. Once you read it, it's hard to take the Republican or Democrat view of what constitutes a vibrant society seriously." I opened the book. "Here's why it's my best book. Look at this."

"Richmond Lattimore," she said. It was the nameplate inside the cover. "Did he own it first?"

"Yes. He was a college professor at Bryn Mawr College who went on to write excellent translations of Homer's Iliad and Odyssey."

Walking to another shelf, I pulled out a first edition of Lattimore's "Odyssey." I held it out so she could see it.

"That very book, the one you're holding in your hand, belonged to Lattimore. I once heard him claim in an interview that it was Jaeger's 'Paideia,' that inspired him to translate Homer, which is the book I'm holding in my hand."

"Can I see it?"

I handed her Lattimore's book and she handed me Jaeger's book. She opened it up and sampled his prose.

"How did you get it?" She asked.

"The Bryn Mawr alumni donate books once a year for the Bryn Mawr Book Sale. It's a fundraiser. It's the best annual used book sale in D.C. I attended it about fifteen years ago and found this book by chance. Lattimore's wife must have donated it after he died in 1986. It's one of my prized possessions."

"Mind if we sit down? I'm exhausted," she said.

We returned to the chairs beside the tortoise pen. I grabbed the wine and poured her a second glass.

"I want to hear more stories about Joannie," she said. "How long were you two married?"

"Sixteen years."

"We're you happy?"

"No."

"I could have guessed that," she said.

"Why all the interest?"

"Because I'm twenty-eight and three of my girlfriends are getting married. They're having traditional church weddings with two hundred guests and country club receptions. They're all giddy and gooey and full of bliss about it. I suppose I'm happy for them, but some of the guys are losers and I think that what I saw tonight between you and Joannie is what they're really in for."

"Marriage isn't easy."

"But how does a couple deeply in love get from point A which is marriage to point B which is a relationship like you and Joannie have now?"

"I don't know."

"How can you not know?"

"Well, part of it, I suppose, is that we come from such different backgrounds. We were young and thought we could transcend our differences with love. It didn't work out that way."

"I can't believe that after all these years you still have such a grudge against each other."

"Well, it is what it is," I said. "Joannie's the mother of my children. I chose her for some reason. And she chose me for some reason. Maybe it was only to have children together. I think that's where the real story is. But it's an embarrassing fact that I've spent the majority of my adult life fighting her just like you saw tonight."

"You seem to compete with each other when it comes to your kids too."

"Perhaps, but that's the predicament I'm in and there's no way I can back down or run away from it."

"They say Jewish men never leave their children."

"I don't know how much being Jewish has to do with it. I just know that for the past eighteen years being a parent has been the cornerstone of my life."

"So what are you going to do when Rose and Aidan go off to college in the fall?"

"I suppose I'm going to have to get a life. It's funny, but when your kids are young they're totally dependent on you. But when they get older and forge lives of their own you find that you're dependent on them since you've built your whole life around them."

"There sure is going to be a vacuum in your life."

"Well, I'll still have Jack."

"Jack is low maintenance compared to the twins."

"True, maybe I'll have time for other relationships," I said.

Sidney poked his head out of his shell. He stared at the food piled on the plate and contemplated whether walking three feet was worth the effort. Suddenly, or as sudden as a tortoise moves, Rebecca made for the plate. Having no sense of personal space she basically climbed right over the front part of his shell and if he hadn't slipped back inside, he'd have gotten a tortoise foot in the face. We watched as Rebecca painstakingly walked the thirty-six inches to feed.

A thunderclap startled us. The rain continued outside. When a cool wet breeze blew in from the open window Stella sneezed. I could see the goose bumps on her arm.

"It's cold in here."

"That's because you're practically naked in that dress."

"Do you have some clothes I can borrow?"

I stood up from the chair and pulled a flannel shirt and a pair of sweat pants from my dresser. I turned to her.

She stood before me, untying the strap that held up her black cocktail dress up from behind her neck. The dress fell to her ankles and suddenly she was naked except for a small G-string that barely passed for underwear. I took a step backwards for a better look.

"Well, at last," she said. "I finally have your undivided attention."

Then she turned her head towards the tortoise so I could freely gaze at her. She threw back her shoulders and undid her long black ponytail. Shaking her head, she loosened her hair until it fell onto her shoulders.

Her breasts were like two ripe plums. Her belly button was pierced with a silver loop. I liked the way her thighs curved inward, drawing your attention to her recently waxed pubic hairs. Her body was thin and flawless.

When her eyes met mine it was with a wide-eyed look of submission.

Something told me that she had been in this situation with an older man before. It was the way she lowered her gaze, while spreading her arms and turning up her palms as if awaiting commands.

When she finally spoke it was to say this: "You can do whatever you want to me."

She caught me off guard. The word Mary used to describe to-night's fiasco in the dining room came to me... flummoxed. I walked around her and studied her merchandise.

"Not tonight, you have a headache."

It wasn't the response she'd worked for and I could see the anger rising. "Are you suggesting that I'm throwing myself at you because I have a migraine?"

When I showed no immediate inclination to answer her question, she grabbed the shirt and the sweat pants and walked to the bathroom.

Sitting back down in the chair I focused on Ruthie who had stuck her head out of her shell. We began one of our famous staring con-tests. In the quiet of the apartment I heard Stella's voice from behind the bathroom door.

I hadn't noticed when she grabbed her cell phone. Whoever was on the other end of the line was getting an earful. Fearing that I was part of that conversation, I tiptoed to the closed bathroom door and tried to hear her words. I've already seen her naked, I figured, so what the hell, I pushed open the door. She was standing in front of the mir-ror still in her underwear. No cell phone.

"Ahhh!" she shrieked. "You startled me."

"Put those clothes on and come out here."

I closed the door behind me. She returned wearing the sweat pants and the flannel shirt which she did not button. She grabbed her wine glass and sat down.

"What brought this on?" I asked.

"You playing knight in shining armor."

"When did I do that?"

"When Warren Sieben, Undersecretary of Yuckiness, cornered me at the front door. That was the most unprofessional display I've ever seen from you. It was also really hot. You can't do that for a girl and not expect some sort of response."

"I'd have done that for any one of my employees," I said.

"Not like that."

"Stella," I answered, "I'm afraid that..."

"I know what you're are going to say, that this is just some girlish crush by a twenty-eight-year-old who lost her father at a young age and is looking for a surrogate. It's more than that and you know it."

My back straightened and I raised my index finger in preparation to respond but she cut in again. "Don't you feel the hum when we're together at the front door? When we're side by side and it all goes so well. I hear it. I feel it. It's perfect. It's so obvious to me, how can you not feel it?"

"I feel it."

"I've been standing faithfully by your side at the front door of the bistro and we not only work well together, we look good together. Do you know how many of your customers have told me that? And I'm a great catch. You don't have to worry about me freaking out under restaurant pressure because you know I can take it. I know your kids, I know your ex-wife, all the wounded puppies you've been dating these past six months and all your personal issues which you'd rather not discuss."

"Maybe that's true but…"

"And don't you dare pull that 'I'm your boss' line or that other bullshit about not getting your fucks where you get your bucks, either."

There was silence.

"Joe, take a good look at yourself. You're a middle aged chubby chaser. What kind of example is that for your sons? Aren't you tired of all those wounded women who drink at your bar and do whatever you tell them to do when they make it to your bed?"

"Maybe."

"After work you come up here and read your books or stare at tortoises to collect yourself. But no matter how calming you find their company, tortoises can't talk back or console you when life overwhelms you. But I can."

I listened to her discourse and measured it carefully. I found myself speechless, yet at the same time I couldn't get this old line written by the French novelist Stendhal out of my mind. Perhaps it is taken from his novel "The Red and the Black." I have the Modern Library edition on the third shelf. Anyway, Stendhal wrote, "The town that negotiates, like the woman who listens, is halfway towards surrender."

"You've been so busy competing with Joannie all these years that you've lost sight of what really matters," Stella said.

"Remind me what really matters," I said.

"Love. You're good at giving it to your kids and your employees. That's why your kids pay close attention to you and no one ever quits the bistro. But deep down I suspect you don't really believe that you need love or even deserve it yourself."

"Stella, I'll be eligible for social security in twelve years. I'm too old for you."

"Twelve years? You can't keep a relationship for twelve weeks. Why even mention twelve years?"

"Don't pretend that age is not an issue."

"It shouldn't be."

"It is for me," I said.

"It's not for me."

She reached out and put her hand on my heart. "Since when have you ever cared what people think?"

With the other hand she gulped down her wine and finished it. She poured herself another glass. She also poured me another Scotch since I was down to ice.

"Have you ever considered that despite my problems it is my life and I might be enjoying it?"

"No." She took another long swallow.

"Hey, what gives? I've never seen you drink so much. If what you're saying is so true, why does it require so much booze to express it?"

"My alcohol consumption is not about finding the courage to speak."

"Then what is it about?"

"I've had too many drinks. I can't drive home. I'm sleeping over."

Wow, I thought. Usually, I'm a guy that likes to drive. "I need a time out," I said.

Turning aside, I sought the solace of Ruthie's faithful face, which hadn't moved in eight minutes. I knew I'd do the right thing regarding Stella. That was not the problem. The problem was that at that particular moment, the right thing was up for grabs.

"Are you seeing anyone right now?" I asked.

"No. Guys in this town are too shallow to be of any interest." She sipped more wine.

And then after a minute she spoke up. "Are you?"

"Yes, remember Sally Jones? She was the brunette with the retro glasses who came in about a week ago."

"The one who works on Capitol Hill?"

"Yeah, that's her."

"I don't think she feels very comfortable with all the action at the bistro."

"You don't?"

"I saw her pass the bistro with two of her girlfriends last week. They looked in the window but they didn't come in. What's with the scar on her chest?"

"It's from open heart surgery."

"Is your relationship with her serious?"

"Too early to tell."

"Maybe, she thinks you're going to compromise her job on the Senate Intelligence Committee with what you have planned for Ali Bin Hassan."

"How do you know about that?" I asked.

"Joe, you're as good at keeping secrets as anyone I've ever known, but the people around you are not so tight lipped."

"Was it Cosmo?"

"No. I heard it from Ali himself. He calls me. I don't think he's really interested in his wife or daughter. They're just a cover to help him stay in America."

"And he told you of our plans?"

"Yes, all of it. Look, I realize that English is not his first language, but damn that guy takes a long time to tell a story."

Suddenly, I felt as naked as she had been just minutes ago.

As a middle-aged man who pays strict attention, I know how my life happens to me: sometimes slow and subtly, other times all at once.

Like anyone I have my defense mechanisms. Sometimes I lose myself in the books that constitute my library. Other times I stare at tortoises and drink Scotch.

But at a time like this when I had to confront the very legitimate feelings I had for Stella Diaz and now confront the fact that the secret deal I was trying to forge for Ali Bin Hassan was common gossip, I realized… I realized that I didn't know what to realize.

So I resorted to my last line of defense: sleep like the dead and figure out the details in the morning.

I finished my Scotch and made my way to the couch. I unfolded a blue and white shawl, made by my late Aunt Beck, who I named my tortoise after. "I need sleep, Stella. You take the bed. The sheets are clean."

I fluffed the pillows, lay down, covered myself up with the shawl and closed my eyes.

A moment later Stella pulled up the shawl and sidled in beside me. She pressed her back against my chest and pulled my arm around her.

"Are you okay?" She asked.

"It's a little scary when somebody else thinks they know your life better than you do."

"Don't worry, I got your back."

Chapter 19

When the phone rang at 8:30 my arms were wrapped around Stella. My face, deep in her long black locks, inhaled the smell of herbal shampoo. She reached for the phone, which lay on the coffee table and clicked it on. Instead of saying hello, as I momentarily feared, she handed it to me. I cleared my throat.

"Good morning."

"Hey, Dad." It was Jack. "Mom has tickets to the Nationals game today against the Dodgers. They're first row seats above the home team dugout. I could get everybody's autograph. Can I go?"

"You're supposed to work at the bookstore this afternoon."

"Can you please take my shift? They're all going and I don't want to be left out."

I could hear Joannie coaching him in the background with some good rhetoric lest I said no. But I never say no to my kids. So after a moment of hesitation I agreed.

"Go ahead. I'll work this afternoon. Have fun. Bring your mitt. If you catch a fly ball, try and get it signed."

He immediately hung up the phone before I could change my mind.

When I laid down the phone there was an awkward silence. I couldn't tell if Stella was asleep or wide awake. The little pinch jolted her. She turned to face me.

"Sleep well?" She asked.

"Yes, how about you?"

"Better than in a long time. I hate sleeping alone."

"I guess we should talk about last night."

"Yes, let's."

"We're obviously attracted to each other," I said.

"Obviously."

"But Stella, I'm damaged goods."

"No, you're not."

"I think you'd do better with someone closer to your age."

"I'm not interested in someone my age. I'm interested in you."

"It's not as easy as all that. If this is going to work, you have to respect the other obligations I have like my children, my businesses, my other relationships and my own need for privacy. Plus you're an important reason the bistro works so well. I'm scared to risk that."

"I'd like to try anyway," she said.

"Okay, but let's go slow. And next time your dress falls down I'd like it to be my doing."

"Agreed."

Then there was another awkward moment. We were so close that it only took a few inches to reach her mouth. I kissed her. It was a good, slow, soft, wet kiss that lasted almost a minute and seemed to seal the deal.

Sixty minutes later I unlocked the front door of the bookstore and settled in my chair behind the counter surrounded by reference books, the cash register, a pot of coffee and the radio. It wasn't a bad way to spend a quiet Sunday afternoon. Business was generally good on Sundays, I still had the much-needed time to read and relax.

I was reading "The Brothers Mann," a dual biography about Thomas and Heinrich Mann, two German writers of the twentieth century. Nigel Hamilton wrote it. I'd been reading the novels of these brothers for the past two years. Though both were dead, the stories they told offered insights into what it was like to live in Germany in the first half of the twentieth century. Their narratives focused on the microcosmic aspect of life that history books with their macrocosmic approach, don't explain. For me the fact that neither one was seduced by Hitler gave them credibility.

Heinrich, a socialist intellectual, wrote one of my favorite European novels in 1916, "The Patrioteer," which told the story of the type of man who would later make up the ranks of the Nazi Party twenty years later. Another one of his novels was turned into a movie called, "The Blue Angel" starring Marlene Dietrich. He also ran for president of the Weimar Republic in 1924, gaining twenty-four per-cent of the vote. He was an extrovert and a man of the world.

His younger brother Thomas was an introvert who followed in his older brother's literary footsteps. Though not having the big personal-ity of his older brother it was Thomas who went on to win the Nobel Prize for literature.

This reading followed on the heels of another book I read called, "The Brothers Singer," a dual biography by Clive Sinclair about Israel Joshua Singer and Isaac Bashevis Singer, two Jewish émigré novelists from Warsaw who came to New York City before World War Two. They were contemporaries of the brother's Mann but their stories about pre-Holocaust Europe came from a Jewish perspective.

Like the Mann brothers, the older Singer, Israel, was an extrovert and a man of the world. He wrote for the Jewish Daily Forward, a Yiddish newspaper, and was active in New York City politics. Since he could pass for a gentile he frequently attended Nazi Bund meetings in New York to grasp the rhetoric animating his antagonists. Isaac was an introvert.

Just like the Mann's, it was the younger Singer brother, Isaac, who won the Nobel Prize for literature while the older brother's literary reputation fell into obscurity.

My interest in these pairs went beyond literature and history. To me their relationships, as told by Hamilton, as told by Sinclair, echoed what I might expect from the brothers Green, Aidan and Jack.

Like Heinrich and Israel, Aidan was a dynamic extrovert. Like Thomas and Isaac, Jack was introverted and wise. Thus these history books held a personal interest. Through them I hoped to see the basic nature of my sons in clearer light.

At about 12:15 the door to the bookstore opened and in walked Cosmo. He wore jeans, a Nike T-shirt and a Washington Nationals baseball cap. He jumped up and sat on the counter before me.

"Hey, I heard you were here," he said, handing me notes he'd scribbled on two pages of paper. "I just finished the liquor inventory and this is what we're going to need for the week."

"I'll take care of it."

"Say, I noticed Stella's car was still in Petey's parking lot this morning."

When I blushed, a smirk came across his face.

"Did you sleep with her last night?"

When I hesitated some more, he giggled like a schoolboy.

"Come on, after all these years you're going to start holding out on me?"

"Yes, I slept with her. No, I didn't make love to her."

"I knew it."

"How did you know?

"By the way you stepped in that guy's shit, the one yelling at her at the door. It's no wonder. You don't do that for a woman and not expect it to be taken as a token of affection."

"It's an awkward situation."

"So what are you going to do about her?"

"Not sure yet. Love isn't my number one priority right now."

"Joe, you're a rock star and you don't even know it. You could have any one of a dozen women if you wanted to, and it's not because of your looks."

"Really? Then what is it?"

"This is Washington, D.C., man. What ambitious woman wouldn't want you? You own a restaurant and know how to throw a party. The bistro is one of the best salons in town and that's where all the deals are made. Having you as a lover confers legitimate status on a girl."

"I'm not so sure."

"Joe, I think you're just worried what Joannie might say about a relationship with Stella. For two people who hold each other in such indifference you both walk on eggshells."

"Enough about Stella." I said. "We need to talk about Ali. Do you know he's told Stella everything we've planned with Sally Jones, the Senate Intelligence Committee and Sam Rousulli? Christ, the guy's supposed to be a diplomat. He'd make a better gossip columnist."

"Ali's always been a loose cannon." Cosmo said. "He's one of those guys who believes honesty is the best policy. He says whatever's on his mind but he's usually naïve about the consequences."

"Tell him to shut up." Cosmo turned his head and stared at the woman standing outside the bookstore. "Whoops, isn't that Sally Jones?"

"Oh shit, speak of the devil," I said.

Cosmo slid off the counter and said.

"I'm late. I should be going."

"What are you doing today?"

"I'm going to see the Nationals play the Dodgers."

"Joannie and the kids are going too."

"I know, I'm sitting with them."

"Joannie's bringing you back into the fold?"

He looked a little uneasy with my question. "I suppose she is."

"Have a good time."

"And Cosmo," I said before he was out the door, "please tell Ali to keep his mouth shut."

When he passed Sally he stopped to shake her hand. She did not come into the bookstore, but stood still in the open doorway. I didn't smile when we made eye contact.

"Don't return your phone calls anymore?"

When she didn't respond I went off. "You've blown me off for the past week. I deserve better than that."

"Yes," she said softly, "you do."

Her gait was weak and unsteady and her pallor was ghostly. I'd never seen her like this before.

"I had a tough bout with angina. I've been in the hospital all week."

"You might have called and told me."

"No, I'll never call when I'm like that. I just don't."

I stood up and grabbed her a chair and offered it to her. "How about a cup of coffee?"

"That would be nice," she said. "I can't stay. I'm not feeling very well." The last part of that sentence seemed to wind her. I looked outside and saw the taxi waiting for her.

"Just wanted to say hello and confirm the meeting at the bistro on Wednesday night to take Ali's statement."

"I told him to arrive at ten. He'll enter through the back door so no one sees him."

"That will be fine. A man named Bill Lyons will be in charge. I'm hoping I can be there too but my doctors changed my medication and I'm having some problems with the side effects. I may have to go on disability for a few months."

I tried to focus on her instead of Lyons. "Anything serious?"

"Yes. I'm dizzy all the time. Plus, just look at me. I feel like I've put on ten pounds."

Sally was one of those women who gauged her emotional health by her weight. For her it was an erstwhile barometer. Ironically, I didn't notice any difference.

"What about us?" I asked.

"There can't be an us for a while. I don't have the strength to do what we usually do."

"All right, how about dinner tomorrow? I'll grab some take out and bring it over?"

"No. I'll call you when I'm feeling better."

"I'll be waiting."

"Here's one more thing. I checked up on Stella. She has a police record in Miami for shoplifting when she was nineteen. Other than that, she's fine."

Chapter 20

Twenty minutes before the doors opened for Tuesday's dinner, I walked downstairs and met Stella at the hostess stand.

"A man named Gamal called," she said. "He wants to know if he and his wife were still welcome to come in for dinner."

"Call him back and say yes."

"Is he a contractor you're trading services with? Maybe we could get him to repaint the Potomac Room?"

"No, it's gratis for a favor." I said.

Though possessing a woman's curiosity, Stella was careful never to delve deeply into the under-the-table ploys that took place within the bistro walls. Such information was only shared with Cosmo. But she already knew almost all of Ali's business because he told her so himself.

But I didn't want to put Stella off so I told a small truth about Gamal. "Actually, he's Louisa's grandfather. When he comes in make a fuss over him and seat him at table 106."

When Gamal walked through the door with his wife, Nouri, he was wearing a black suit with a white shirt, a purple tie and a shiny gold watch. Nouri was decked out in a bright blue dress that clung to her broad shoulders. It was low cut enough to be sexy but not enough to appear undignified for a grandmother. Thick eyeliner bordered her brown eyes with curving lines and blue eye shadow matched her dress. The sapphire pendant hanging above her cleavage from a silver chain matched her long silver sapphire earrings. There were rings with big stones on her fingers and a gold bracelet around each wrist.

I led them to their table through the crowded dining room. Gamal, wife on his arm, followed me with a majestic countenance, beaming at Nouri as if she was the Queen of Sheba.

Theirs was the dignity of a couple that weathered the vicissitudes of a long life side-by-side, and who belonged exclusively to each other.

But I can only imagine how dissolute he must have been back in the 1970s when he hung around with my Uncle Harry.

Their presence provoked the room's curiosity as they moved gracefully through it. Was he an Arab oil minister? Was he perhaps an Iraqi politician? Was he an ambassador or a member of the royal house from Saud?

When someone in the bar asked their identity I put my finger to my lips as if it were something I wasn't at liberty to share.

It was common for ordinary folk to enter the bistro and magically transform into Cinderella and Prince Charming. And I'd be the last one to ever let slip that they were an immigrant couple who ran a falafel shop in Mount Pleasant.

We gave them a good people-watching table, a four top against the wall where they could see everyone. And everyone could see them.

They were offered the wine list but they declined, preferring instead a diet coke for her and an iced tea for him.

The next time I noticed them they were both eating the lamb lollypops while a shrimp cocktail sat beside their plates uneaten.

"Mary, why did you fire their entrees before they finished their appetizers?" I asked pointing at the table.

"Don't blame me. That's the way they wanted it."

Then Rose and Louisa walked through the front door.

"Hey, Joe. Are my grandma and grandpa here?" asked Louisa. "We thought we'd join them for a Coke."

"And shrimp cocktail?"

"And shrimp cocktail too," she said shamelessly.

"Hi Daddy, hi Stella, hi Mary," Rose said.

"Hey baby." As she leaned into me I kissed her forehead. "What are your brothers up to?"

"They're both at home. Aidan's doing homework. Jack's playing video games with Teddy."

"Stella, please take the girls to the Farhat's table."

The teenagers were met with hugs, kisses and shrieks of joy. It was a warm family scene that didn't play out very often in my den of epicurean abandon. When they sat down, Mary brought them bread and Cokes. Louisa and Rose shared the shrimp while grandma and grandpa finished their lamb.

"Well, I guess that solves the mystery of the shrimp cocktail," said Mary.

"It figures," I said.

"She sure does love her grandparents," Mary said.

"They've been good to Rose too."

"Let me tell you, if I'd have known how wonderful grand kids were, I'd have started with them instead of my own rotten bunch."

"How many grandchildren do you have?" asked Stella.

"I got three little boys who live in Alexandria. I have them every Friday night while their parents go out on a date. It's great. I get them all jacked up on sugar, then I send them home."

"Hey, check this out," I said, leading Mary and Stella a few feet away. We studied a photo of my Uncle Harry and Gamal taken back in 1974.

"Wow, Gamal was a handsome man," Mary said. "Was he good friends with Harry?"

"Yes, good friends. Stella, do me a favor. When they finish their entrees, grab the Nikon and take their picture. Make sure Rose and Louisa are in it too. Offer them dessert. Then ask Gamal to come see me."

A few minutes later Stella took a shot of the four of them while the rest of the dining room looked on.

Then the two eighteen-year-olds got busy trying on Grandma's jewelry. Rose had the gold bracelet around her wrist while Louisa's fingers were adorned with Grandma's rings. You'd have thought they were hand models with all the posing. When Gamal excused himself they barely noticed.

I walked him through the kitchen door. We stood beside the dishwasher.

"I was hoping to meet with Sam Rousulli," I said.

"He will not come," Gamal said. "He says you're being watched. He sent me instead."

"I trust you more than I trust him."

"Sam is not happy about Ali giving testimony to the Senate Intelligence Committee, but he recognizes the young man's arm is being twisted. Perhaps something can be worked out. They'll meet him Wednesday night at seven. Just tell me where."

Recognizing that the meeting between Ali and Sally's people was at ten, I feared we might be cutting it too close. But I figured that whatever they told Ali, at least their words would be fresh in his mind when he came here later that evening to meet with the feds.

"They understand that they'll get to edit whatever he says, right?" I asked.

"Yes, and they'll rely on you to tape the conversation to make sure he doesn't change his story once he gets behind closed doors," Gamal said.

We couldn't make eye contact. We were lying to each other. Ali was going to say whatever he wanted to say, and Gamal's people were not going to let him get away with it.

"It's a stupid plan," I said, throwing up my hands.

"It is, Joe. Do you know what will happen to him if he co-operates?"

"He'll go into a witness protection program. He and his family will have to hide the rest of his life."

"I'm just sick about this. The young man has talent. People listen to him."

"Let's be honest," I said. "We both know he's kind of a goofball, but he's been in prison for so long that it shouldn't surprise anybody. He needs to go home. How are we going to get him to leave?"

"I have a plan," Gamal said. "But I'll need your help."

"What will they do with Ali if he returns to Egypt?"

"Put him in charge. The Muslim Brotherhood will take him back in a heartbeat."

"I think he's gone way beyond political Islam."

"His father is a big industrialist with ties to the army. Perhaps he might forge a third way?

"Like democracy."

"Stranger things have happened."

"I need assurances from Sam Rousulli that he's going to be safe."

"He will be."

After twenty more minutes of talk I walked him back to the table.

Rose, whose own grandparents lived in Florida, had adopted Gamal and Nouri as surrogates when she became Louisa's best friend. At that moment I thought Gamal a luckier man than me, if only for his larger inventory of love. In 20 years, I wondered, who would be sitting beside me enjoying the company of my grandchildren?

It was a rhetorical question, but it suddenly seized me. Speculation about whether I would be alone or with a loving partner raced through my mind as I was walking to the hostess stand. It was just then that I passed the hallway mirror and saw my own image. I stopped and looked at my own reflection. My hair was gray and my eyes seemed dimmer than the last time I looked. Will anyone be beside me when I hit 70?

By then Sally, if I were to believe her words, would be in the ground. Would it be Joannie? Not a chance. Stella? Probably not. Some partner who had yet to arrive? Maybe. It was one of those ridiculous soliloquies that only seem natural in Shakespeare. But it was an honest inquiry of a middle-aged man who wanted it all: sexual adventure and a devoted partner.

Ten seconds later I realized that people in the restaurant were watching me. So I reached for my tie as if I were straightening the knot. And then I moved on.

At the bar I pulled Cosmo aside.

"Call Ali and tell him to be in the G-Spot tomorrow night at 7 p.m."

"How's he going to get there? We're both working and he's living in Silver Spring with Malika."

"Have him take a cab."

"I think he'd feel safer if Aidan picked him up."

"No, the boy can't get involved. If Ali's short of cash send a cabbie, someone we know."

Cosmo grabbed his cell phone from beside the cash register. He walked out onto the street to make the arrangement while I stood behind the bar filling in for him.

He returned five minutes later.

"It's all set," Cosmo he said. "Glad that's done."

"We've done our job."

Cosmo then perused the dining room and stared at the table with Gamal, Nouri and Louisa and Rose. "Do you trust him?"

"Him I trust, the guys meeting with Ali, I'm not so sure. But Ali's life won't be worth two cents if word gets out that he ratted out his Arab brothers for a green card and he won't be able to stay in America if he doesn't talk to Sally's people. So there it is."

Then Cosmo perused the restaurant and focused in on Stella working the hostess stand. "She looks like she's having a good night, doesn't she?"

I stared at Stella from across the dining room. She was in the cloakroom and retrieving a gentleman's jacket. She held up the coat as he turned his back to her. She helped him slip his arms into the sleeves. Her back was straight, her mouth was open in a smile and even from the here I could see her glow.

At ten we closed the kitchen. Except for a handful of people sitting in the bar and at table 106 with Rose and Louisa and Gamal and Nouri the place was empty.

"Rose, it's getting late. I have a few chores to do that should only take ten minutes then we should go home. Gamal, I trust that you can see to it that Louisa gets home safely?"

"Of course," he said.

I walked right up to Stella and said. "I've got the kids tonight and want to get home before they go to sleep."

"Maybe tomorrow night," she said.

Wednesday evening at 9:30 Bill Lyons introduced himself to me at the bar. There were two others with him, a big guy with a shaved head from the FBI named Rick Niland, and a woman stenographer, Joyce Anderson.

She carried two small bags, which I believed carried whatever equipment they needed for a meeting like this. I led them back to the Potomac Room. The tabletop was clear of dishes, glasses and silverware. I left them to prepare.

At 9:55 I sent in bottled water, some strata bread with tomato relish and olive oil and asked if there was anything else they might like.

"No," Lyons answered, "we're all set."

I walked to the kitchen and waited for Ali to come in through the back door. At ten Cosmo joined me. When Ali didn't appear we searched the alley. At 10:05 we reentered the kitchen without him.

Lyon's was Sally's lover, so I figured she'd opted out of coming. At 10:10 I grew concerned. At 10:20 I had Cosmo call Ali's cell phone. It flipped right into voice mail.

I walked to the Potomac Room, a bit embarrassed that Ali was late. At 10:45 the FBI guy got angry and split. At eleven Lyons sent Joyce home in a cab.

Lyons was gracious though. "Look, I want to give this Ali guy the benefit of the doubt," he said. "I'll wait around for fifteen more minutes. If he doesn't show he'll be subpoenaed tomorrow. If he isn't living at the address where he's supposed to be living at, he'll be in violation of his parole. Then he's really fucked."

"There's no reason we have to wait back here," I said. "Let's go see Cosmo at the bar."

When Bill Lyons and I walked up to the bar, three well-dressed men were finishing up their beers. They paid their tab in cash, said goodbye to Cosmo and walked out the door. Except for the busboys and dishwashers clanging around in the kitchen we had the whole place to ourselves.

I sat down on a bar stool but Lyons preferred to stand. I figured him to be about forty-two years old. He was about six feet tall with short-cropped hair, broad shoulders and no neck. He looked a little like a tree stump. With his foot on the bar rail, his elbow on the bar, his hand in a fist, he leaned forward like a tough guy.

"Bill, meet Cosmo Della Rocca."

"So you're Cosmo, huh?" He gave a small nod of his head. "Nice to meet you." Cosmo nodded. They didn't shake hands.

"What the hell?" Lyons said. "No TV's? I was hoping to catch Sports Center."

"If you want to drink here you got to talk."

"What can I get you?" Cosmo asked.

"Bill's interested in a good single malt Scotch," I said. "Why don't we start with a little Macallan 20? Want that neat or on the rocks, Bill?"

"Neat."

"Make it two, Cosmo."

When the drinks were served we grabbed them at the same time and took our first sip.

"Pretty good stuff," he said.

"Well, it looks like we both got stood up tonight."

"You're referring to Ali and who else?" he said.

"Sally," I said. "I'm as disappointed about her not being here as you are about Ali not coming."

"That heart issue is a serious thing for her," he said. "I'm glad she didn't come all the way down here for nothing."

"It's a shame that someone with such a good heart should have such a weak heart," I said.

"I think there's another reason she didn't show up," he said.

"Yeah, what's that?"

"She didn't want to stand next to your hostess and have you compare the two of them."

"Is that it?" I asked.

"That would be my guess," Lyons said. "She's an honest woman, but a little insecure."

"How long have you known her?" Cosmo asked.

"We've worked together since nine-eleven. I know her really well."

"How well is really well?" Cosmo asked, who always liked to hear stories about women.

"We had an off again/on again affair about four years ago, okay? If I wasn't married..." But he never finished the sentence.

I said, "Do you know about us?"

"Yeah, I know," he said, looking away and taking a large swig of his drink. "I'm not angry about it either. I've been out of the country for several weeks. Sally's got her needs."

"Thanks for that," I said.

Lyons presssed his lips together and steered his close-set eyes to his drink. After a minute he reached for it and drained the glass.

"Cosmo, let's try something else, something maybe Bill's never had. Give him a shot of Glen Spey." And turning to Bill I said, "Have you ever tried it?"

"No, is it expensive?"

"What do you care? You're not paying."

"Cosmo, give us two shots and pour one for yourself."

"No thanks. I'm not drinking today."

He took out two fresh glasses and filled one three-fingers high with Glen Spey. He short poured me after I gave him the wink. I wrapped my hand around my glass so Lyons wouldn't notice.

"So where were we?" I asked.

"You were about to compare notes on Sally," Cosmo said.

"She's quite the cocksucker." Lyons blurted it out and then blushed at the sound of his own words. "I've been in Afghanistan the past ten weeks. I sure did miss her."

Cosmo let out a loud laugh.

Lyons took a long swallow and wiped the corner of his mouth with his sleeve. I recognized that his mind was with Sally, not with us.

I looked at Cosmo. "Not drinking tonight, really?"

"No, not tonight."

"It looks like it's just me and you, Bill. Let's toast to horny women."

"God bless them all," he said.

When he noticed Cosmo's grin he took offense. "Don't get smug with me Guido or you'll regret it."

Cosmo seemed more amused than offended. That comment revealed a lot about Bill Lyons, I thought. Sit a man down at a bar and give him a drink and after ten minutes I'll tell you what kind of man he really is. The environment at my bar, and most bars for that matter was designed to bring out the community among us as men. But some guys, bitter, thwarted, resentful, frustrated in love and their careers, wear it on their sleeves and reveal as much after just a few sips of alcohol. I figured Lyons for one of those guys.

I was reminded of Robert Louis Stevenson's famous novella, "The Strange Case of Dr. Jekyll and Mr. Hyde." It's about an erstwhile doctor who invents a rare formula that transforms him into a monster. But in truth no rare laboratory formula is required. Give some guys alcohol and the same result follows. Thus, while my first impression of Lyons was positive, I now realized he was a dope, especially after he asked, "So, if I walk into your kitchen and yell, 'Immigration,' how many wetbacks will run out the back door?"

"Hey Cosmo, get him," I said, as if Lyons weren't even in the room. "Bureaucrat wants to be a tough guy."

And then I turned to Lyons. I said, "Where are you from, Jacksonville?"

"Houston."

"Houston? Oh, yeah, Houston." I said. "That would make you a Texan, right. That's one of the few states more polluted than New Jersey."

"Fuck you both. Think you're two tough Jersey boys, huh? You guys got no class at all."

"That's part of our charm," I said.

"Charm, my ass." he said.

"Meaning no disrespect, we just think we're cooler than you," said Cosmo.

"Oh yeah? Why's that, wise guy?"

"Because you're lousy at trash talk and you have no sense of humor."

"Oh yeah?" said Lyons.

"Ask Joe," said Cosmo.

"Think you're Mr. Know-It-All, don't you, Green? You may think you know what's going on, but you don't know shit. Does he, Cosmo?"

He turned his head sharply and stared at Cosmo, who was caught off guard.

"Go on, Cosmo, tell him how you came to be cell mates with Ali Bin Hassan," Lyons continued. "And how you snitched on everybody we asked you to snitch on."

Noticing the surprised look on my face, Lyons let out a sharp laugh. "Didn't know that your fair-haired boy was a government informer did you, Green?"

I took a moment to compose myself. I don't know what kind of emotional satisfaction he hoped to get from revealing that fact but he wasn't going to get anything from me.

"Did they pay you?" I asked.

"No, they shortened my sentence," Cosmo answered.

"You should have asked for money too."

"Cosmo Della Rocca, killer and a snitch," Lyons said. "Not a good combination of traits for an employee or a friend."

"Cosmo, pour him another drink so when I tell him what an asshole he is he'll be drunk enough to listen."

"When are you going to break out the good stuff?" Lyons scoffed.

"He's right. Let's move on. How about a little of that hundred-year-old Grand Marnier? And put it in a brandy snifter." I turned to Lyons and said, "I don't think they sell this in Texas."

"I'll drink some of that," Cosmo said.

"How much do you sell it for?" Lyons asked.

Cosmo shook his head. "You don't want to know."

Lyons picked up his snifter and clinked glasses with Cosmo, ignoring me. Then they both shot the sweet orange liquid right down.

And when they slammed their glasses down I refilled them both from the bottle that stood before me on the bar. Cosmo picked up his glass, Lyons picked up his glass and each took a gulp.

I figured between the two big Scotches and his second Grand Marnier, Lyons would be shit-faced in about five more minutes.

"So what do you think of your Italian stallion, now?" Lyons said.

I took a minute to carefully choose my words, and when they were clear in my mind this was my reply.

"When Cosmo was indicted for killing those two men they offered him a deal. Testify about my part in the shootings in return for a lesser sentence. He didn't go for it. He took the entire blame for what happened. As a result he spent time in jail and I got to father my three kids through their teenage years. So if he wants to do whatever the fuck he wants to do, it's fine with me because I'm beholden to him."

"Well, my suspicion is that you're both part of the reason that Ali didn't show tonight."

"Why would Cosmo do that?" I asked.

"I haven't figured that out yet, but if I can prove anything you'll both be in big trouble."

"Bill, I've got to be honest with you. I had Gamal Farhat set up a meeting between Ali and a group of Arabs before his meeting with you tonight. It was in my garage at seven p.m."

"Gamal Farhat, that old stooge for the Muslim Brotherhood? What the hell were you thinking?"

"You fuckers can't keep secrets. I figured once word got out that Ali testified to your committee he was dead meat. So I tried to play both sides against the middle."

"You'd sell out your own country to an Islamic Fundamentalist?"

"Ali's been in prison for years. What could he know?"

"Why don't you ask Cosmo? Did he ever tell you that Ali's passport had five stamps from Afghanistan?"

"It's something Ali told me himself," I said.

"So what did you guys do to him?"

"We didn't do anything," said Cosmo. "We've been here all night."

"Did he forget, have cold feet or is laying in a ditch somewhere beaten to a pulp?"

"That's my biggest fear," said Cosmo.

"So, you think he's been murdered too?" asked Lyons.

"Joe…" started Cosmo. But I threw my hands in the air like a traffic cop and stopped him in mid-sentence.

"Do you really think Gamal Farhat is going to come into my restaurant, eat a beautiful meal on my dime, entertain his wife and granddaughter and my own Rose throughout the evening, get his picture taken and then turn around and fuck me over for doing the right thing? Are you both stupid?"

"If he's not dead then where is he?" asked Lyons.

"I don't know, and all I know is that I don't know."

"If he's still alive, we've got to get to him before anyone else does," Lyons said. He took another long swig of his drink. "The guy's a liar anyway. He peddled a bullshit story for years saying that Bin Laden was injured in a bombing by U.S. jets and elected to commit suicide in a Pakistani cave, which he then blew up upon himself so he'd become a mythological hero to his people like Robin Hood."

"Good story. Certainly a better outcome than the one that actually happened," I said.

"I was in on the interview when he told that story," said Lyons. "We asked him when it happened and he said it was the day that George W. Bush was watching football and nearly choked to death on some pretzels. He said that was Bin Laden's last act on earth before his soul went on to the seventy virgins in heaven."

"Nice use of imagination," I said.

"No, it was just a bunch of bullshit," said Lyons, slurring the last syllable. Then he changed the subject. "I got to piss."

He returned a few minutes later and flopped onto the barstool.

"Jesus, look at him," I said.

"He's done," said Cosmo.

"Call him a cab."

"I don't need a fucking cab," he mumbled.

"Fuck you, you're not getting a DUI and suing me for over-serving you. Give me your keys. We'll take care of your car. Pick it up across the street in Petey's lot in the morning."

We put Lyons in a cab without too much trouble and sent him away. Looking at Cosmo, I said, "Come with me. Let's check out the G-Spot."

We walked to Mintwood Place. Behind my town house we entered the garage. It seemed certain that Gamal's people had shown up. The room smelt of smoke. A cigarette butt was on the floor, a Turkish cigarette, one that neither of Aidan and Rose's friends smoked. But there was no sense of a struggle, no blood on the floor, no overturned furniture and no other clues. Still, the fact remained that Ali Bin Hassan was missing.

Cosmo pulled out his cell phone and called Malika. She said she had not heard from Ali since 6:30 when he got into a cab.

"Let's go inside and see if he left a message on my land line."

We walked in, went straight to the kitchen and I picked up the phone. There was one message.

It was from Stella. "Hey, I just called to say goodnight."

"Was it Ali?' Cosmo asked.

"No, Stella."

"What's up?"

"She called to say goodnight."

"So what's the problem?"

"I'm the problem. I've been so busy competing with Joannie these past years, I don't know if I can handle a healthy relationship. If I go with Stella, I can't be the cynical middle aged bum. I have to let go of my anger issues and try to be real. And if I do that I'm afraid Joannie will walk all over me."

"Stella's pretty on the outside and pretty on the inside," Cosmo said. "She's not soiled by life like we are."

"It's so much easier to be with Sally. She's damaged goods. A night with her is all about spanking, rough sex and biting. She'll suck you four different times. She'll provoke you just because she just wants to be pummeled. And as vulgar and sick as it sounds it is also incredibly exciting. She helps still my rage. I just give her everything I got and when I'm done there's nothing left of me."

"Sounds like you have to decide whether you want to slake your rage, or cure it."

When I didn't respond. Cosmo said, "I'm going home. Maybe Ali will show up there. I'll call you if I hear anything."

"Wait a minute, Cosmo. Are there any other secrets I should know about you? I don't like being shocked by guys like Bill Lyons."

"Yes, there's one more."

"And what is it?"

"I can't tell you yet."

The next day there was still no word about Ali. Perhaps I fucked up by telling Gamal about his interview with Lyons and his ilk.

I did my shift at the bookstore. Rose was a little late relieving me so I was also late getting to the bistro. I found Cosmo and Stella standing at the waiter's station sipping coffee.

"Any word from Ali?" I asked.

"Not one," said Cosmo.

"Stella, any chance Ali might have called you?"

"Maybe—I had a call about 2:30 in the morning."

"Who was it?"

"I don't know, I was asleep." She said. "My phone was recharging on my kitchen counter at the time and the number was blocked."

"Did you get my message?" she asked.

"I think we have a lot to talk about," I said.

"Let's talk soon."

"Why?"

"Do you have any idea how many times I've masturbated in the past few days?" Stella asked.

"More than all your fingers and all your toes?"

"Don't make fun of me. If you don't want to be with me, then have the courage to tell me."

"Honey, allow me to enjoy the chase."

"Joe, there's a phone call for you," Cosmo called from behind the bar.

I turned and took a step towards the bar, but she grabbed hold of my sleeve and pulled me back. Though she didn't speak, the gesture was unmistakable: "How dare you blow me off when I'm standing right here for somebody on the other end of a phone line that you may not even know."

"Who is it?" I said, never talking my eyes off of Stella.

"It's somebody from the Egyptian embassy."

"Take a message," I called.

"He wants you to come to the embassy for a meeting. He says it's important."

"Tell him if he wants to talk to me he has to come here. Tell him I'll be available tonight after 10. Tell him 9:45 if he wants to eat."

"No, not tonight," Stella whispered.

"Yes, tonight.

"Why tonight?"

"Because, it's probably about Ali and I don't want to put it off."

There was a pause and then Cosmo called out. "He can't do it tonight. He says he'd like to come in tomorrow."

"Make it around five," I said.

The idea that I almost blew her off made Stella furious. She reached for a packet in a sugar bowl sitting on a shelf by the waiter's station. She held it up at eye level. It was a brown packet of Sugar in the Raw. Ripping off the top, she reached for the lapel of my suit jacket and pulled it towards her. With her other hand she emptied the packet's brown colored sugar into my shirt pocket. I never realized how many granules were packed into that little envelope. It made a small pile inside my shirt.

She smoothed out my jacket with both hands and buttoned it up so the jacket pressed the sugar pile right against my heart.

She stared me in the face like a brazen Jersey girl waiting for me to scream at her, hug her, slug her, kiss her or do whatever it is one is supposed to do when provoked.

Chapter 21

It's my opinion that one of the great progressions of human consciousness was promulgated by a Californian from Saint Luis Obispo back in the 1960s named Jim Wheeler.

Wheeler along with his cronies at the Ampex Corporation created something important. Like most inventions its real utility did not manifest itself all at once but slowly crept into the hearts and minds of mainstream American society in manifold ways. Its biggest impact came in professional sports. That invention was the instant replay.

It allowed a second look at individual athletic feats, not only to see if referees made the correct call on the field but also to allow audiences to admire expressions of athletic feats by the human body.

I mention Wheeler's work because the concept worms its way into my own mind when returning to specific instances that delight me, and at other times foil me.

The opportunity to return to moments, which have extraordinary meaning, emotionally and visually, is something I've always enjoyed. But as a result of Wheeler's instant replay and the perfection of its method by new technology, I think my mind does it better now too. And yesterday something worth replaying occurred that brings me as much pleasure in the reverie of it all as the original act.

The image that I have been returning to is the glow that became part of Stella's aura. It was so bright a blind man could have seen it. And I could pinpoint the moment it emerged. It was following that little mischief of pouring sugar into my shirt pocket. At that moment her lumen seemed to surge and did not diminish.

It was one of those dramatic moments, significant perhaps only to me but nonetheless meaningful. There was no missing it. Casting my eyes upon her was like a cool, quenching refreshment, the kind a hiker finds from his canteen on a summer march.

In that replay Stella stands in the center of the image and I am not present. Especially since it took me so long to respond to that prank of hers.

When Cosmo called me to the phone I had a legitimate excuse to leave her side. But no, I stood stalwart beside her. And when I finally decided what constituted the proper recourse, I mulled it over for a few more seconds to make sure it was measured.

It wasn't anything dramatic like a slap across her face, a warm embrace or a kiss. I did not pinch her butt, storm off in some impotent rage or tell her to go to hell.

No, I made myself very still and, looking into her big brown eyes, I told the truth. "You look very beautiful tonight."

She started to pout. Perhaps she feared I was patronizing her but after a few more seconds she softened. "Nice of you to notice."

"I hope you're free after work," I said, and taking hold of her hand, gently removed it from my sleeve.

But let me return to that glow one more time. It must have been felt by customers too because after they ate and paid their tab, they congregated at the front door, conducting warm conversations with Stella because they didn't want to leave.

James Britton walked through the door. It was the end of the night and he was dressed like he was on his way home from work. In his hand he held a large white envelope. It was an invitation.

"Alfred Kenessee is coming to America. His return to Nigeria after ten years of exile has been negotiated. The Secretary of State is hosting a reception for him. Considering your work on his behalf, we thought it only right to have you as a guest of honor."

"I can't come. You know that, right?"

He paused for a moment. "I forgot that part of the story. I'm sorry if I compromised you. I meant..."

"It's all good. Thanks for thinking of me."

"You came all this way, can I buy you a drink?"

"Better not, I'm driving. But let's keep in touch."

"You know, I know someone who would really enjoy the opportunity to meet Mr. Kennesse. Mind if I give the invitation to him?"

"That depends who you'd be giving it to."

"Reverend James Battle. He's pastor at the Baptist Church on Mount Pleasant Street. He's running for D.C. City Council."

"I read about your rivalry with Battle in the Post. Why would you throw him a bone?"

I threw up my hands acting like I didn't know why. But I did know and Britton was gracious enough not to make me say it.

"Is that who Cosmo was protecting, Kennesse when...?"

"Yes."

"Everybody thought it was racially motivated but it wasn't, was it?"

"No."

He took a deep breath of the restaurant air. When he exhaled this is what he said.

"Reverend Battle would be very welcome at the reception. In fact I'll mail him the invitation myself and make up some reason why."

"Any chance you might be able to snap a picture of the right reverend and Mr. Kennesse shaking hands?"

A big smile creased his lips. "When will you need that photo?"

"The following morning."

"Where should I have it sent?"

"I'll be at the book store."

"When Battle finds out the truth he's going to feel like a real dope."

"Let's not tell him yet. I want him to get full of himself first."

"You know, I changed my mind. I think I'll take that drink."

"I think I'll join you."

When the last servers had been paid their tips and when the dishwashers had mopped up and were gone out the door, it was just me, Stella and Cosmo.

"I'm feeling a lot of discordant energy in the restaurant tonight," Stella said. "I think I should sage the place."

"That's funny, I thought the night went well."

"It did go very well," she said. "It wasn't until that last couple opened the door to leave that I felt it."

"What did it feel like?"

"It feels yucky, like a cold clammy breeze blew right in through the place," she said.

"Then go ahead and sage it," I answered. "Meet me upstairs when you're done and I'll take you out somewhere for a late dinner."

After I'd showered, combed my hair, and finished dressing, I emerged from my bedroom to find her at my desk. Two candles were burning, one in the kitchen area and one on the desk where she sat reading beneath the Tenser light. My laptop was open and playing music.

"Nice music," I said. "What is it?"

"Just a Pandora station that I put together."

"Nice sound."

"Yeah, very soothing. You can read to it, write to it, make love to it—whatever you want. It flows really well, adds atmosphere and doesn't interfere with what you're doing because most times there are no words to distract you."

"Let's see what you're reading."

She stuck her finger in the page so she wouldn't lose her place and showed me the cover. It was an old volume written by William Finck that she had taken from my bookshelf. The book was entitled, "Romantic Love and Personal Beauty."

"Interesting title," I said. "When was it written?"

"1897."

"When did I read it?"

She opened it to the first page and there was my signature and a date: 8-17-2007.

"Oh, right after the divorce."

"It's a pretty cool book," she said.

"In my early years I made a point to read as many cool books like that as possible."

"How come?"

"I was influenced by a quote I once read from Voltaire: 'To be original one must be eccentric.' I owned the bookstore and had time to read so I made a point to read rare books that were out of the mainstream. That way when I got involved in cocktail party conversation I could make myself seem interesting."

"I like the way the author tries to define what the magnetic attraction between men and women consists of."

"Does he do a good job?"

"In some parts, but it's such an elusive topic. What I find more fascinating is the fact that it's something men thought about back in the 1890s when it was published."

"Love is a timeless theme."

"Here, listen to this passage," she said. "To women, Cupid is kinder. Instead of making them appear ludicrous, love has the power of transforming even a homely feminine face into a vision of loveliness by throwing a halo of tender expression around it."

"Nice quote."

"Yes."

"Now consider the effect that halo evokes on a pretty face like yours."

She didn't answer, but, instead she sat up straighter in the chair.

"Keep the book."

"Thanks," she said.

"Are you ready to go?"

"If you don't mind, I like to stay in tonight."

"You sure? I thought we'd go down to Runyon's. Their kitchen is open until midnight and we could have a few drinks and come back here."

Then I saw the two tuna sandwiches she'd made on the kitchen counter.

"Do you remember the last time we were at Runyon's?" She frowned. "It was me and you and Sacha and Shameem?"

"Yeah, I thought it was a fun night."

"Runyon's wasn't fun for me," she said. "The blonde who runs the place sat down and monopolized your attention for twenty minutes and then had the nerve to suggest that I was your niece. And if that wasn't bad enough, when one of my old English professors from George Washington University stopped by and found out you owned a used bookstore I had to listen to another twenty-minute conversation about a paper he was writing about captivity narratives from pre-revolutionary war America. When you told him you had an old copy of *The Narrative of Cabeza De Vaco*, for sale he almost peed his pants."

"It's a famous book. The author was shipwrecked in Florida and captured by the Indians. He wrote one of the first accounts of what it was like to live among them in the 1500s."

"Great, do you know what Cabeza de Vaco means in Spanish?"

"He's a distinguished author of that time period. I thought it was just a name."

"Joe, you have to let me teach you Spanish. It means head of a cow."

"Really?"

"Trust me. So between the chubby blonde who opened up two shirt buttons of her shirt before she sat down and an English professor who gave me a 'C' in his damn course because I wouldn't date him, I had a boring night. So if it's just the same to you, I'd like it to be just me and you, right here."

"Okay, I'll run down to the bar and get a bottle of wine."

"How about a bottle of rum instead?"

"Are you going to drink that straight?"

"No, a little Diet Coke would be fine."

"Here's an idea. There's a clean towel for you in the bathroom. Why don't you wash off the evening too. I'll get your rum."

"Are you inviting me to sleep over?"

"Yes, there might be some sleeping too."

Chapter 22

The next afternoon I arrived at the bistro early to receive someone from the Egyptian Embassy. I suppose I should have asked for more information when they'd called yesterday since I was certain it was about a missing young Egyptian named Ali Bin Hassan.

At precisely five p.m. a small Arab delegation walked through the front door in single file. The first, second and third men wore angry expressions. Gamal Farhat, brought up the rear. He just looked glum. We gathered at the front door and made introductions.

The first man in the door introduced himself as Mr. Mohammed, an attaché from the Embassy of Egypt. His English was very good. He was a small thin man, with a small thin face and if he had been in Aidan's class I'm sure he'd have been labeled a nerd.

The second man, also Egyptian, was the opposite. He was tall and heavyset, and his face was scarred from childhood acne. His thinning hair was not obvious because he towered in height over all of us. He was not introduced and said nothing. I figured him to be the muscle.

Mr. Mohammed then introduce me to the star of the show. He too was a large man about my age with a fat face that included jowls at the bottom of his cheeks. He had two black skin stains under his deep-set eyes.

"Mr. Green, may I introduce Anwar Bin Hassan who just flew in from Cairo."

He impressed me as a man worn down by his responsibilities, but jet lag, worry and fatigue could have accounted for much of that.

"Is this Ali's dad?" I asked.

I reached out to shake his hand but he waved it away with a flick of his wrist wanting no part of any courtesies.

I led them to the empty dining room and we all sat down at a round table. Upon Mr. Mohammed's cue, Bin Hassan began shouting at me in Arabic. It was a short rant that he stopped after fifteen seconds so Mr. Mohammed could translate.

"He is here to save his son from the outrageous and precarious predicament you helped put him in."

And when the senior Bin Hassan's face flushed and his hands started to shake in rage, I turned to Mr. Mohammed and said, "No need to translate. Let the man speak."

He keened in upon me with the wrath of Moses down from the mountain. He started in a measured controlled tone but once he got going he lost all control of his narrative and realizing that his team outnumbered me, flew off into a vituperative Islamic rage in a language I did not understand.

But no words were necessary. His histrionics were enough. I could see his passion and feel his wrath for my part in sending his son down a precarious path that endangered his life.

Finally he could no longer control himself and he had to stand up to do justice to his passion. His hands were flying so fast in the expression of his rancor that he accidentally batted a wine glass against the wall. It shattered into a dozen pieces. And even that did not slow him.

When he finally vented the speech I imagine he had practiced for ten thousand miles on a jet he turned to Mr. Mohammed and shouted at him. If I were to guess what instructions he gave Mr. Mohammed, it was to translate his words precisely and sugar coat none of it.

A small crowd, Stella, Cosmo, Aidan, Mary and Shameem stood off in the distance watching. Shameem, who understood Arabic, looked like he was translating Bin Hassan's words to the group, which was unsettling since it now appeared that I was the only man in the dark. Though they were reluctant to interfere, I felt sure that should things get out of hand they would come to my defense.

"Does he know where his son is?" I asked Mr. Mohammed.

"Yes," the diplomat said, careful to stay calm. "Ali is on a jet flying back to Cairo and his family."

"That's good. He belongs with his family," I said.

Ali's dad continued his browbeating and I had to wait for Mr. Mohammed to translate. "How could you openly encourage my son to take such a foolish risk as to testify against his own people in a government inquiry?"

I met Bin Hassan's stare. "I was told that it was his only chance to stay in America since his father had paid someone to put guns in the trunk of his car so he wouldn't be sent home and risk Islamic justice."

It took Mohammed a few minutes to translate my response. Then there was some back and forth between Bin Hassan and Mr. Mohammed in Arabic. Then Ali's dad really flipped.

He picked up a steak knife and if his pantomime was correct, he was ready to slit my throat. Despite the fact he waved the knife around in the midst of his rhetorical flight, the blade was pointed down with the sharp side towards his own body.

Now Gamal intervened, standing up and putting both hands on Bin Hassan's shoulder attempting to calm him down.

Mohammed finally translated it saying: "Does setting his son up on a weapons charge in a Christian country sound like something a father would do to his son?"

"No."

Bin Hassan set the knife on the table and finally spoke without translation in broken English. "Then how could you think that I might ever do that to my own son?"

"It was what I'd been told."

Suddenly I couldn't remember who told me. When Bin Hassan threw his hands up in the air as if he were dealing with an idiot it was intended to make me look small and foolish.

Several excuses came to mind. But since I would have to endure the time-consuming problems of translation, I decided to just shut up. When the time seemed appropriate I spoke in simple English.

"Please offer Mr. Bin Hassan my humblest apology. I'm sorry."

He wanted me to grovel.

I thought to stand up and shrink away from the table like a school-boy leaving the principal's office. But fuck them, this was still my place. My own emotional surge deepened when I suddenly realized that it was Ali himself who told everyone the story about his father's complicity in his bust. Suddenly, it felt that Bin Hassan was castigating himself for his failure as father as much as he was castigating me for my complicity in what now appeared to be a kidnapping. The dad came to deliver ransom money himself. He'd traveled half way across the world at great expense in order to save his son's ass. I wonder how much Gamal had charged him for Ali's release.

"I'm done with you," he said, in heavily accented words. "Now, where is Cosmo Della Rocca?"

I walked gravely to my crew and told Cosmo it was his turn.

Cosmo's eyes grew wide at the thought of receiving the same tongue-lashing. But he removed his bar apron from around his waist, handed it to me and walked bravely to the table.

Ali's dad greeted Cosmo with a handshake, a hug and a kiss on each cheek. Motioning to Mohammed to leave his seat, he had Cosmo sit down next to him.

Their conversation lasted fifteen minutes as Bin Hassan, some-times praising Cosmo in his limited English, sometimes asking Mohammed to translate, offered his heartfelt gratitude for the friend-ship and protection he had offered his son while behind American bars.

When the father was done, he stood up and everybody else stood up too. He stood, shook Cosmo's hand again, kissed him again on both cheeks like he was his own son, handed him an envelope and headed for the door.

Mr. Mohammed, the silent muscle man and Bin Hassan all gave me the silent treatment going out. But Gamal took slower steps and I intercepted him.

I grabbed Gamal's arm gently and whispered, "It was the good dad thing we did, wasn't it?" I said. "Ali's home now."

A small nod was all I got.

An awkward silence prevailed in the bistro after the door closed behind them. No one knew for sure what it was all about and an awkward silence prevailed.

Cosmo slapped my back, and thought the whole thing was hilarious. "Well, it's like they always say back in Newark, Joe. You got the feeling, you got the right to express it."

"I have to admit I'm a bit shaken by all this. But ultimately, I'm relieved by the news that Ali's on his way back to Egypt."

"Well, that's the end of that saga."

"What's that in your hand?"

"It's a voucher for a round trip ticket to Cairo. First class. They want me to come visit."

He handed it to me so I might examine it. Then I returned it.

"You asked me to help Ali do the right thing, didn't you?" I asked.

"Yes."

"That's what I did."

Chapter 23

A strange confluence of ideas were swimming around my mind as I walked shoulder to shoulder with Aidan on our way home following a slow night at the bistro. It was about 11:15 under a clear, starlit sky. With the temperature at about sixty-five degrees and a cool breeze blowing, it was a great night to be out.

"Hey Dad, what's going on? You haven't said a word since we left work."

"I'm a bit distracted."

"Be distracted on your own time. You're walking with me now," Aidan said.

"You're right."

"I can guess what you're thinking."

"Am I that transparent?"

"No, I just pay attention," he said.

"Okay, pretend you're a psychic. What's on my mind?"

"You're pissed at yourself because you let those Arabs dis you in your own place tonight."

"That's part of it."

"Ali's dad threatened your life and you didn't even blink."

"That part of the conversation didn't get translated."

"According to Shameem, Mr. Mohammed was sugar coating everything you both said."

"Why did he do that?"

"Maybe so nobody lost their cool."

"I figured Ali's dad was calling me out. But compared to what I knew in Jersey, he didn't seem that menacing."

Aidan stopped in his tracks and let out a laugh. We stood face-to-face in the middle of the sidewalk. "That might have been what saved you."

"What do you mean?"

"You weren't intimidated."

"Yes, I was."

"Well, they felt ridiculous," he said. "They gave you their meanest face and worst bad-ass threats."

"I've experienced deeper intimidation from Muslims selling carpets."

"You didn't even look scared."

"I was."

"From what Shameem translated they threatened to blow up the bistro and cut your throat," Aidan said.

"They did?"

Suddenly our walking started again but at a slowed pace so each aspect of the story would be considered.

"Dad, Ali was kidnapped by some Muslim Brotherhood dudes. His dad had to come all the way here to pay a ransom and only then would they put him on a plane back home, and it was from Baltimore. Did you get that part of the story?"

"No. I missed that."

"Ali's dad thinks you were in on the kidnapping."

"That's baloney."

"He doesn't think so."

"Anwar Bin Hassan raised a fool for a son and he finally had to face that fact. That's really why he's so pissed off."

"You know what's really interesting?"

"Tell me."

"The whole time Anwar was dissin' you, according to Shameem who translated the whole thing for us, he never made one anti-Semitic remark."

"That is interesting."

Then Aidan became very focused as if he was centering himself.

I could tell he had something on his mind by the way he put his head down and clasped his hands behind his back. And I was ready to listen. It was only after another block that he let it spill.

"Rose and I have decided to go to college together."

"That makes me happy," I replied. "It will be good for the two of you to find your friendship together without your parents getting in the way."

"We get that, Dad."

"What changed your mind?"

"We found a school we both like."

"Really? Which one?"

"DePaul University in Chicago."

"DePaul? That's a Jesuit school, isn't it? I thought you were leaning towards Northwestern in Chicago."

"DePaul's campus is cooler. Northwestern might be better academically, but everyone we know who goes there is a nerd. And you said yourself that the social aspect of college is as important as the academic."

I could tell his enthusiasm was real. As he spoke about the plan he'd made with his sister, his brisk pace returned as if he was on his way, walking right there, right now to college in the Lincoln Park neighborhood of Chicago.

"Rose and I know three people who go there and they say it's really fun. If I do my school work and choose my professors carefully it will be just as good as Northwestern."

"I was hoping that if you chose a school with a religious affiliation it would be Brandeis."

"No, Dad, we want to go to DePaul."

"Then DePaul it is."

"Mom's happy because it's close to her sisters, who both live in Chicago and your cousin Ellen lives five miles from campus. Even though we're far away we'll have family there."

Just then his cell phone rang. He flipped it open and saw it was his sister.

"Hey, Rose. I just told dad about DePaul." he said.

He didn't get another word in. It seemed like she wanted to do all the talking. After a few seconds with his head into the receiver he began to respond.

"You did? Where? What color is it?"

He spent another minute listening to his sister. I couldn't hear any words.

"I'll be home in twenty minutes," he said. "Can't wait to see it."

Rose continued talking. Aiden's eyes widened. "What do you mean, don't tell Dad? He's walking right here next to me."

She must have hung up. Aidan closed the phone and stopped in his tracks. I stopped too.

"Are you going to tell me or should I guess?"

"Rose got a tattoo."

"Oh fuck. How bad is it?"

"Hey, don't get me involved," he protested. "This is between the two of you."

We began walking again but with slow, deliberate steps.

"Christ, I hope she didn't tattoo her boyfriend's name on her ass," I said. "What's his name again?"

"I don't remember."

"Neither do I."

After a few steps I said, "Is it some sort of totem animal? I suppose if it was a tortoise I could live with it."

"No, Dad, it's not an animal."

"I hope it's not in a conspicuous place that will prevent her from getting a decent job."

"You're just going to have to wait and see for yourself."

The idea of my little girl staining herself with a tattoo bothered me because it marked her in time and I wanted her to forever be young and fresh. Perhaps it was the trauma of her youth, caused by the all-out war between her parents that wounded her so that she felt the need to visually express it on her body. That might have been it.

We walked up 18th Street and when we eventually got to Mintwood Place we walked past my townhouse and down the block to the one that Joannie and I bought together in 1988 which was now hers alone.

We walked up the steps and through the front door. Aidan ran up to the bathroom while I stood just inside the doorway waiting for permission to enter. Rose appeared from the kitchen with a sheepish look upon her face.

"So, you did it anyway."

"Yes," she said.

"Where's your mom?"

"She's out."

"Where is it?"

"You told me to put it on the bottom half of my body so I did."

"On your legs?"

"No," she said, "the small of my back."

"You got a tramp stamp?"

"Yes, Daddy."

There was a short pause. I didn't know what to say. "Well, I should get home now."

"Don't you even want to see it?"

"No."

"Come on, don't be that way."

"I'm sorry, I was against this from the start."

"I'm eighteen. I should be allowed to make some of my own decisions now."

"How tacky is it?"

"Real tacky."

"In that case I better see it."

She turned her back to me and pulled up the back of her shirt. There it was, written in blue ink. I stared at it and was speechless.

"What do you think?" Rose asked.

"That's Hebrew," I said.

"Yes, Mishpahcha."

And suddenly I was embarrassed because I couldn't remember what the Hebrew word meant when translated in English.

"It means family. Mishpahcha. Family."

I stared at it for almost a minute. Damn, she just marked herself for every Jew baiter in the world, I thought. I was about to say that, but I stopped and thought about it some more. Not only do Jews not get tattoos, they definitely don't get tattoos written in Hebrew. I almost shouted that too. But those words weren't right either. So I stifled myself. Finally, I figured out how I really felt about it out.

"Hey, that's not bad."

"Really?"

"Yeah."

She squealed loudly and turned to give me a hug.

"What does your mom think of it?"

"I think she's upset that I acknowledged my Jewish side and not my Catholic side."

"Well, hell. You are going to DePaul. Tell her you're balancing the two faiths."

"I offered to get another one tattooed on my stomach written in Gaelic for her."

"Really? What would it say?"

"Dysfunctional."

I laughed.

Aidan returned and Rose lifted her shirt a little and seeing his sister's tattoo said, "Damn girl, that's tight."

"You really like it?"

"Yeah, it's bomb as hell."

"Right now it's killing me."

"You're supposed to put some Vaseline or some moisturizer on it to keep it from peeling," I said. "Does your mom have anything like that in the house?"

"I'm not sure," She said.

I walked up to the second floor bathroom and started rummaging around under the sink for something to ease Rose's discomfort. "I don't see anything," I called.

"Maybe it's in Mom's bathroom," Rose said.

Without thinking I walked to Joannie's bathroom whose pale green walls I had painted myself fifteen years ago when it had adjoined our bedchamber.

Reaching for the handle I pulled opened the medicine cabinet and started studying its contents. There were seven different prescription drugs inside. Some were old. Others were current. On the second shelf I spied a jar of Vaseline.

"Eureka," I said out loud.

I grabbed the jar and closed the cabinet. Then I noticed the white shirt hanging on a hook at the back of the door. The sleeves were rolled up just like when Joannie used to wear my shirts as nightgowns. The pocket was monogrammed. It was Cosmo's.

Chapter 24

My first customer at the bookstore was a thin, dark-haired woman of about thirty. She had pale white skin, a high forehead and a pointy nose. She wore jeans and a blue T-shirt. Her hair, colored with soft red highlights, was pulled back in a ponytail. I could tell that it was her first time here because she looked around my aisles as if she were navigating downtown Boston.

"Can I help you find something?"

"I'm looking for a birthday present for my boyfriend," she said. "He's kind of a Civil War buff. Do you have anything?"

"Actually, I've got quite a lot," I said as I led her to the proper shelf. "Where's he from?"

"He's from Mississippi. He's up here working for the Department of the Interior."

"Let's see what we have. Have you ever heard him call it the War of Northern Aggression?"

"As a matter of fact I have."

"Good, at least we know what side he's on."

She let out a soft laugh.

"I have this old biography of General Jeb Stewart. It was published in 1912. Chances are he doesn't have it in his collection because it's a translation authored by a German historian. But it's a beautiful old collector's item and if he wants to read it too the spine is strong enough to stand it."

"How much is it?"

I opened the cover and gazed at the price written in pencil. "It's thirty dollars."

"I'll take it," she said. "Do you have any romance novels?"

"Oh sure, I have everything. They're located against the back wall. I'll wrap this up for you while you look."

Rick Rapson came in too. He was a scholar who worked for a liberal think tank in town and had ordered two books about Walt Whitman's poetry. I found them for him from a friend of mine who had a bookshop in Winchester, Virginia.

Rapson had an interesting intellectual method. He had a Library of Congress library card. During the day he'd comb through their catalogue searching for good reads. When he'd find one, he'd copy down its name and if it was unavailable on Amazon.com or ABA Books, he'd come to me and I'd track it down for him.

The books were wrapped in brown paper and waiting for him at the door.

"Got them for you right here, Rick," I said. "Why the sudden interest in Walt Whitman's poetry?"

"Because he loves America and he loves democracy. Too many conservatives hate it. They want to reserve it exclusively for straight, white Christians, while denying it to everybody else. Whitman is a counter-irritant to that attitude. I get more rhetorical ammunition from Whitman than any source I know."

Just then a familiar face entered the store. It was Nouri Farhat, Louisa's grandmother.

"Hello, Joe. I'm here looking for a graduation present for my Louisa."

"That's funny, I've been thinking about what books I might get the twins for their graduation too."

Just then the young woman came with two hard backs that she liked.

"One minute, Nouri, I'll be right with you. That will be $42.28 with tax."

She paid cash, pulling the exact change from her purse. Then she smiled and made a graceful exit.

I closed the cash register and looked at Nouri's smiling face. The last time I saw her it was at the bistro with her husband and her face was painted with exotic lines of mascara, powder and blue eye shadow. It was less colorful this morning.

"Well, I know Louisa would prefer electronics, clothes, money and gift cards as a graduation present but we send them to that expensive school to learn about books so books must be part of her present too.

"I'd like to give her a nice version of the Koran or the Old Testament or the New Testament but knowing Louisa she'd never read it so I was thinking a nice old volume about of 'The Arabian Nights,' or 'The Tales of Scheherazade.'"

"Look in the back of the store, on the right. If I have anything, that's where it will be."

"What books are you giving to your graduates?"

I turned and went to the glass case behind my desk that housed my rare books.

"I have a first edition set of poetry books by Sarah Teasdale for Rose," I told her.

There were four volumes inside, published individually, from the 1920's, beautiful editions by the MacMillan Company. None had modern day dust jackets, but each of the bindings were blue with gold embossed letters highlighting her titles, "Helen of Troy and Other Poems," "Flame and Shadow," "Rivers To the Sea," and "Love Songs."

I handed them to Nouri for inspection.

"These books had been protected by lock and key for years," I said.

"They are beautiful books, but I've never heard of Teasdale. Who was she?"

"A New England poet from the early part of the twentieth century. She had this mystic vision that seems more New Age than Jazz Age. She won the Pulitzer Prize in 1922, for this volume here," I said, pointing to the book entitled *Love Songs*. "But she also suffered from depression and in 1925 she killed herself."

"Rose has literary aspirations," Nouri said. "These might be good for her. But for Louisa I'm trying to instill in her an appreciation for Old World storytelling and tales about where I and her grandfather come from."

"We're both in for a tough sell," I said. "The advent of new technology makes books seem like old energy."

"There's nothing wrong with old energy," she said. "What about your boy? What do you have in mind for him?"

"Homer. I'm thinking of *The Iliad*, and the *The Odyssey*. But I have my reservations since the poems are written in a difficult meter and might be too hard for him."

"They might only sit on his shelf as decoration," she said.

"They say you can lead a horse to water but you can't make it drink. But I'll give it to him anyway."

"Let me give you some advice," Nouri said. "Back in the old days, Gamal tried to read those same books but could never get it. And it frustrated him because it was said that Yassir Arafat himself used to keep 'The Iliad' on his nightstand and when he lost courage he'd turn to it for inspiration. But my Gamal had no such luck. One night he got frustrated and threw it so hard against the wall that I thought it was a gun shot."

"So this is what I did," she continued. "I went to the library and found it on cassette and made him listen to it on our tape deck. It was a smart idea. The story is from an oral tradition anyway. After listening to the story several times he was finally able to read it."

"I wonder if it's on iTunes? I could even transfer it to his iPod."

"See, there you go. Problem solved." And with that she threw up her hands as if she were effortlessly dispersing clouds.

She walked around the bookshop and when she returned to the counter she held up a newer copy of "The Arabian Nights."

"I'll take this one, Joe." And then she stuck a folded bank check in my breast pocket.

"I trust this check will be enough to cover all we owe you," she said.

I reached into my pocket and stared at the amount. Then I refolded it and put it back inside the pocket. "That will be fine."

"Stop by one morning for coffee and baklava. You know me and Gamal, we're always at Sinbad's."

She strolled out the door.

Later that morning I found a copy of "The Iliad," Homer's story of the Trojan War. The translation was by the English poet Alexander Pope. The edition, published in 1896, still had a strong spine.

It's a book about war, literally and figuratively, and its didactic content—which explored the nature of courage—was something I wanted Aidan to know. But there was one more thing. I deemed Homer's cosmology, specifically the relationship between men and Gods as something more gnostic than the Old and the New Testament.

To go along with Pope's translation, I found a handsome copy of the "Odyssey." It was a grand old Oxford University Press edition from 1932 in perfect condition.

I thought it strange though that the author of the translation did not have his name listed under the title. I had to thumb through the first few pages before I found it: T.E. Shaw.

I figured him for some smug Oxford don who hung out with the likes of Isaiah Berlin and C.M. Bowra, two Oxford contemporaries who wrote history books I enjoyed as a younger man. But then I remembered something. Wasn't T.E. Shaw, a *nom de guerre* for Lawrence of Arabia?

Finding out was easy. In the literature section a few steps away, I grabbed a copy of the "Seven Pillars Of Wisdom," which T.E. Lawrence wrote under his real name. It only took me a minute. There, in the introduction, it was confided that Lawrence sometimes wrote under a pen name: T.E. Shaw.

I grabbed his book and put it under my arm, thinking that in the quiet of the afternoon I might wrap my mind around a pillar or two. But when I reached my hand into the darkness behind the stack, searching for something to replace T.E. Lawrence's book on the shelf, the book's title startled me.

In my hand was an inexpensive paperback lacking any creativity in its cover design. The title was is what stopped me.

And I realized the discovery that I was giving Aidan a copy of *The*

Odyssey written by the World War One hero, who was so dramatically portrayed by Peter O'Toole in the movie "Lawrence of Arabia," was suddenly a minor point.

The paperback book I was staring at was "Sons and Lovers," a novel by D.H. Lawrence. The juxtaposition of those two nouns held my attention while I squeezed the book in my hand.

Initially, I suppose I was struck by how inadvertently revelation finds us. But this little telltale did not surprise me. It's one of those little epiphanies that happen frequently in used bookstores. Truth is, I live for such revelations, especially since the irony of those two conceptions, son and lover, should be so indicative of the feelings that me and Joannie held for Cosmo Della Rocca, respectively, and the important place that he held in my dysfunctional family life. That very title, which I confess I've never read, seemed to sum up a major theme of our whole story.

To me Cosmo was like the brave prodigal son who, when he went to jail, took a hit for me. A Jersey boy with roots from the old country. In conversation Cosmo brought out the worst of my New Jersey accent and along with it the feeling tones indicative of the cultural values I held onto.

But I also realized that he was perhaps the great love of Joannie's life. And it was a sobering revelation that such a role should fall to him and not me.

That reverie did not lift until several customers entered the store at once and shook me out of it. I returned to my desk and carefully gift-wrapped the presents I had chosen for Rose and Aidan.

Looking out the window, I spied Joannie's van as it pulled around the corner in search of a parking space. She came in dressed up, stressed out and in a hurry.

"We have to talk," she called upon entering. "The twins are in their last week of school and I found out from reading their text messages that they are planning a kegger and pot party at the G-Spot, which I have since learned is the code name for what happens in your garage and which I now realize that you not only know about, but also condone."

"What happens at my house is my business," I said.

"It's my business too, especially if they get arrested and embarrass me professionally."

"Why is it always about you?" I calmly asked.

"When is it ever about me? It's always about what you want. I'm just the barking bitch."

"I don't get it, Joannie. We've spent years fighting a civil war and somehow the idea that we've successfully raised two children about to be launched into the world never seems worth talking about."

"Don't act like I wasn't there. I've done the lion's share of parenting."

"That's not the point," I said.

"It's a big point for me since you've always done exactly what you've wanted to do and always left me to do the hard work."

"It's true," she said, before I could respond. "I also know if it wasn't for the temporary success of the bistro you'd have closed this bookstore years ago. Selling used books in an era of high tech is stupid. Come on, Joe. When are you going to get with the program? The smart business decision would have been to rent the building out to Sprint on a long lease when you had the chance and sell your books on-line."

"No," I said, and it was uttered in a deliberate tone void of malice.

So she changed the subject.

"And here's another thing. What right did you have going into my bathroom and rummaging around? Do I need to get a restraining order to protect my privacy?"

"Cat's out of the bag, isn't it?"

"What cat?"

"I found Cosmo's white shirt hanging on the back of your bathroom door."

She put on her poker face. Then I said this.

"That's really what this is really all about, isn't it? A fishing expedition to see how much I know?"

She didn't want this conversation. But she wasn't exiting that door until she talked.

"Cosmo makes me feel safe."

Now she used her bookstore voice. And that small sentence seemed like the first piece of honest oratory she'd uttered in a long time.

"And when they took him away from me and sent him to prison, I hated you. I hated you worse than I've ever hated anybody. I still hate you for it."

She took a deep breath. "Yes, I am having an affair with Cosmo. I've been in love with him for years. And you are going to have to live with it."

"Good, it's no longer a secret."

"Are we done?"

"Yes, Joannie. We're done."

She exhaled a long mouthful of carbon dioxide. Then she grabbed her Coach Purse and turned for the door. She took two steps and stopped. We weren't done.

"DePaul University sent me a bill today," she said. "If we want to secure a place for the twins in a freshman dorm we have to mail them a check by the end of the month. I've already told you what your share is."

I reached into my breast pocket and handed her Nouri's check.

The first thing she stared at was the amount.

Then studying the rest of it she said, "Bank of Geneva?"

"I think they have a branch in Georgetown."

"It's made out to cash."

"They were afraid to spell my name wrong."

She stared at it, narrowing her eyes as if she were handling stolen merchandise. But no, it was just my finder's fee for the opportunity I presented Gamal and his cronies.

"Hey," she started.

"If you don't want it, give it back."

Perhaps she thought a bird in the hand was worth two in the bush. After a moment she spoke.

"Never mind."

She opened up her purse, found her wallet and stuffed the check inside. Then she turned and walked to the door. She threw it open so hard that it crashed against the wall, making the little bell attached at the top fall to the ground.

She marched down the sidewalk in her Ferragamo dress, her five hundred dollar shoes, her tennis bracelet, her rings and diamond earrings, most likely on her way to a fancy downtown restaurant for a three-martini lunch with who knows who.

That's my ex-wife, I thought, the mother of my children, the woman I'm eternally tied to through future generations of Greens.

"If nothing else," I muttered, "the battle between us is a fair fight."

I think she was still pissed about the dubious nature of the check because I saw her look back at the bookstore in disgust, perhaps to deliver one last blast of bad juju before moving on.

When she turned her head forward, she bumped shoulders with another woman passing by on the sidewalk and almost knocked her down. Mortified that she had done so, Joannie's anger stilled. I watched as she touched the woman's arm to take total responsibility for the mishap. Soon, they were exchanging pleasantries.

When Joannie continued down the street I recognized the other woman. It was Sally Jones, who was now walking to my door with a bag in her hand. I opened the door and Sally entered the bookstore.

"Was that Joannie?"

"The one, the only."

"She seems gracious," Sally said.

"Yes."

I pulled up a chair for her and she promptly sat down. "What's in the bag?"

"Two coffees, a cheese Danish for me, and a bagel, lox and cream cheese for you." She laid out napkins and our breakfast.

"Well," I said, "this is a surprise. How are you?"

"Since I retired, I'm learning to take things a little easier."

"Good."

"It's an adjustment, though."

"I called several times."

"I couldn't answer."

"Why not?"

"Bill Lyons is living with me. It seems that the night you and Cosmo got him drunk the cab brought him to me instead of home."

"Is he going to leave his wife?"

"I don't know."

"You know, Sally, I..."

She reached out and took my hand.

"Joe, I need to say something."

"Go ahead," I said.

"I knew I was coming to the end of my career on the Hill. When I discovered your relationship with Cosmo, who was our guy on the inside, I thought maybe I could get to Ali through you and somehow justify my life. I lost my mind. I was overzealous and unethical. I did things that I'm ashamed of."

"You could have gotten Ali killed, too."

"Yes, I know. I'm really sorry."

I took a deep breath and held it in while staring into her big watery eyes. She leaned forward in the chair solicitously as if my response was important.

I wanted that apology to linger for a few seconds. It felt like the comforter you snuggle under on cold nights when you sleep with the window cracked. It was the kind of apology I'll never hear from Joannie's lips.

But, vicariously, this was as close as I may ever get. Joannie apologizes to Sally, Sally apologizes to me, and all within two minutes. There must be a geometry theorem capable of delineating the logic of this. A equals B, B equals C, so A equals C. So I relished what Sally said and let the words echo around my mind a little while longer.

"You don't make things easy, Sally."

"Nothing's easy in Washington, Joe," she said. "It's like you always say—we're hemmed in. And each of us deals with it the best we can."

About the Author

Bob Gilbert was raised in Ocean County, New Jersey but moved to Washington, D.C. to attend American University. He worked several political jobs in the nation's capital before moving to Minnesota in 1984 to manage a congressional campaign in Minnesota's 8th district which includes Duluth and the Iron Range. Instead of returning to Washington he remained in Minnesota where he worked as a waiter and a newspaper reporter. He returned to D.C. in 2011. An avid scholar, he loves the used book stores of Washington and the Twin Cities. He's also a backpacker, who's led over a dozen trips for the Sierra Club to the mountain ranges of the far west. He's also trekked the Himalayas in Nepal three times in the past five years. He can be found on Twitter here: @BobGilbertDC.

www.ingramcontent.com/pod-product-compliance
Lightning Source LLC
Chambersburg PA
CBHW031059020726
47495CB00007B/1958